LIKE THE NIGHT

Her host wasn't wearing a coat or shoes. Also, he wasn't so much standing as squatting on the ledge, a careless hand resting on an iron chain. He looked more than a little bit like the large gargoyles he perched between. As she watched, steam began rising from his body in a cloud, and it swirled about him in a slow, counter-clockwise cyclone.

He was beautiful, as beautiful as any midnight that had ever been. Be he was also very odd, and—at least for Brice—maybe dangerous. As sure as the sun would show up in the east tomorrow morning, Damien Ruthven would be trouble for her if she allowed herself to get any closer.

MELANIE JACKSON

DIVINE FIRE

LOVE SPELL NEW YORK CITY

To my cousin, Richard Magruder.

LOVE SPELL®

February 2005

Published by

Dorchester Publishing Co., Inc.
200 Madison Avenue
New York, NY 10016

ISBN 0-505-52610-7

The name "Love Spell" and its logo are trademarks of Dorchester Publishing Co., Inc.

Printed in the United States of America.

Visit us on the web at www.dorchesterpub.com.

DIVINE FIRE

It was found that his limbs were nearly frozen in place, and his body apparently suffering from rigor mortis, though there had been no time for this to have occurred naturally since the lightning had passed through him. He also suffered from priapism which much disconcerted the ladies who thought him deceased. Their judgment was understandable for I never saw a man who appeared so dead and yet was not. We promptly carried him into the kitchen, and as soon as he had quitted the freezing air his eyes reopened. We restored him to consciousness by a sharp blow to the heart followed by rubbing him with a decoction of coca leaves, and then forcing him to swallow a strong stimulant of coca elixir and brandy. As soon as he showed signs of sturdy heartbeat and respiration, we wrapped him up in blankets, and placed him on a chair in the chimney of the kitchen fireplace where the bricks of the oven might warm him. By slow degrees he recovered his senses. The only marks upon him were a golden scar in the center of his chest and similar ones at his wrists and ankles.

—*From the medical journal of Johann Conrad Dippel*

Prologue

April 19, 1916

Lord Byron, the man who now called himself Adrian Ruthven, stared out into the stormy night. The lightning—power of the gods—would begin soon. He could feel the gathering energy dancing on his skin, calling him again to the purest of matings: the death that led to rebirth. Once there, in the gods' embrace, he would again snatch a bit of that divine fire which kept him alive and his epilepsy at bay. He would continue to live.

But he was not alone that night as he kept vigil. For some reason, the ghosts from that summer at Villa Diodoti had again gathered. They hung about the shadowy corners of the room, smiling or accusing as they chose. Some he felt were still friends. Some were not.

Odd that they should come after all this time. Had his dark thoughts of the war raging in Europe summoned them from their rest? But perhaps it was understandable, even fitting, that they should attend this ritual on this centennial of his death; had they not all been there at the first moment of his new life? And was it not normal that he should on this anniversary contemplate the mortality of mankind and remember all those who were no longer of the earth?

"Hello, my friends. We meet again," he whispered, speaking at last to the shadows.

Atheistic, immoral, subversive—all these words were applied to the people gathered in his memory and now in his parlor. And to a degree, they were all true. For Shelley—brilliant, defiant, ephemeral boy genius— most of all. What was now known as the era that marked the end of medieval obscurantism of thought, and as the birth of modern humanism, had been seen at the time as nothing more than promiscuity and wickedness. To the evangelicals and later Victorians, he—and Shelley especially—were anathema, bringers of chaos and unwanted change. They were the harbingers of the Industrial Revolution, and for that they were shunned, excoriated.

Of course, the greatest master of this new era was missing. Where was Johann Dippel?

"You choose to remain silent even now, do you?" Byron asked the shadows, and when no answer came, he turned again to his window and his thoughts twisted back to the notorious and glorious past where his new life had begun.

In the Year of Our Lord eighteen hundred and sixteen, his actions and speculation about his future plans were always gossip for the peasants at the Swiss lake. In London, too, that long century ago. There had been hypotheses about wild orgies, ghostly hauntings and Satanic rituals—all of which had made Byron laugh because such were so mundane, so much less amazing than the truth.

But the world would never know the truth, for of course an account of what really occurred that fatal night at Villa Diodoti was never to be given by its participants—though it haunted all of them for as long as they lived, and many must have longed for the comfort of confession. It had been a real horror story in which they'd participated.

Many would argue that Lake Geneva was a strange location for a ghost story. Villa Diodoti itself was a fairly pleasant place in good weather; the thriving vineyards around it were certainly handsome and bountiful in the warm season.

But that was in the summer and early fall. Winter was another matter. The snow-covered Alps surrounding the ancient villa, and that infernal blue lake and more infernal winter weather in 1816, made the place seem ever cold and damp, a place in some ring of hell where the sun never shone. And at night, when storms raged and the many candles used for light danced in the wayward drafts that ghosted through the dark rooms, it could seem haunted—by Milton's unhappy shade, if by nothing more sinister.

And it was there, under the great poet's own dead eyes, that history had been made.

"Hello, John," Byron said, and he stared at the shadowy figure of John Polidori whose translucent reflection moved slowly into the window glass.

John's mouth still pouted, drawing a slight sigh from Byron. If one needed a companion loyal and true, the first name to leap to mind was not John Polidori. Certainly, he'd been the one most likely to speak out about the events that night at the lake, for they had parted less

3

than amicably. The physician had hinted at the truth in *The Vampyre* when he made the book's immortal hero so nearly in Byron's image; but though often envious of the fame that came to Byron and Shelley, Polidori had kept his word and never betrayed the secret to which he had been privy.

John didn't speak now, either, and Byron's gaze shifted to the next huddled shade. Poor masochistic Mary. She was present as well, but she did not smile at him as she once had. Her guilt over their actions that fatal night had caused her to write a version of the event in her novel *Frankenstein*. When asked, she claimed to have been inspired by a nightmare. No one had ever guessed that the sad Viktor Frankenstein and his monster were fictional creations born of an experiment conducted by one Johann Conrad Dippel to cure a reluctant and desperate Lord Byron of his violent brain seizures.

Even later, when she hated Byron for his fame—notoriety she claimed he'd torn from a dead Shelley's pale laurels—she'd never told a soul of what was done in Switzerland. She must have wanted to speak out, to renounce Byron as an unholy abomination, but she didn't. Not even after she'd seen his badly autopsied corpse, which had been mutilated about the face and allowed to decompose before being embalmed and then pickled in brine for the journey back to England and his less-than-adoring wife. She must have known from the discrepancy in height that it was not really Byron's body in that coffin, and suspected the truth. Yet she had not spoken.

"Thank you, m'dear. It was generous of you," he said to the dark-haired wraith. "More generous than I probably deserved."

He looked next at Claire Clairmont and Shelley, but

neither his former lover nor his dear friend breathed or blinked or spoke.

"How oddly silent you all are," he said to the blond apparition of the man he'd befriended before Fame had noticed and smiled upon his genius. "You used to be more outspoken, Percy. Had you lived longer, would you have someday told our tale? No, I think not. You, too, would have remained true—though we all seemed cursed from that day onward."

Byron's eyes searched the shadows again, still looking for Johann, but to no avail.

"Where is Dippel?" he asked the room. "You would think that he would wish to attend. I am, after all, one of his great triumphs."

Perhaps Dippel wasn't there because he still lived. People had thought him dead in 1743, but he was alive and well in 1816 when he'd come at Mary's urgent invitation to Villa Diodoti to demonstrate his bizarre research to the ailing Lord Byron.

But surely not. The crowd that had stormed Dippel's castle the following winter had not been forgiving of the blasphemies they found within. Every animal and human construction had been burned, all occupants slaughtered, and the unburied dead returned to the graves Johann had stolen them from.

Byron pushed the horrible memory away.

"This has to be the world's best kept secret," he said to his silent guests. "Truly—governments would envy us, if they knew. And think what it did for the world of literature. No house party before or since has ever been so productive, and it was all because of this one secret event."

Even in his memoirs, where he had been scrupulously honest about every detail of his life, he had not made an accounting of those wild events, or how young Pietro Gamba had helped him fake his death in Greece when it became apparent that he was not aging as a human should.

If Byron's rebirth was the world's greatest secret, then his death was the world's greatest hoax. And he had never regretted his actions—except that they had led to a parting with Teresa Guiccioli. She had deserved better than to be left with the care of his three favorite geese and a storm of gossip about their violently ended love affair. Teresa had not been as obsessive or public about her love as Caroline Lamb, but her affection had been as sincere and as well-known. He had missed her for many years after their parting. He'd had no real loves since. And no real friends either.

The first of the lightning strikes flared in the sky, and the earth beneath his house shuddered from the shock waves. Others in the city wouldn't feel it so keenly, but he had ordered the building constructed of iron girders. The entire structure was a lightning rod designed to attract a peculiar kind of cloud—muscular ones that made up those very special storms, the ones that contained the life-sustaining Saint Elmo's fire.

Adrian turned from the window, letting the heavy curtain fall, and began to undress. He would have to go up to the rooftop soon and bare his body, zigzagged with golden scars, to the wild night and the power that lived in it. If all went well and he survived the pain, then he would return, renewed and marked with fresh disfigurements that he would need to hide from the world.

The ghosts from his past looked on as he moved, approving and disapproving as they chose. Adrian shrugged, as indifferent to their opinions as he always had been, and returned to his earlier reverie about mortality and the decision not to shake off his mortal coil. Not yet.

All that fuss after his death! He had at first been amused and disgusted in almost equal measure to learn that he was posthumously considered alternately a naive saint with an extravagant fondness for animals, or else the devil incarnate who'd spent his life devising the ravishment of women and the corruption of men's souls while dashing off bits of inflammatory poetry in his spare time.

There had been many causes for vexation and worry in the weeks after his death, but his only true moment of anger had been with Hobhouse and Murray for surrendering to Anna's will and burning his memoirs before they could be published. But in the end he'd had to admit that it was probably for the best that his journal had ended on the pyre. He knew that the people of Albion would build their myth about the late Lord Byron, blowing his life out of all proportion—both in goodness and in wickedness—and while they were distracted with expanding the legend, he could go on living as he always had, with no one being the wiser about the renegade poet who still walked and lived among them.

Naked, hair unbound, he stepped over the trunks and other luggage and mounted the iron stairs that led to the roof where the gargoyles and other lightning rods waited. His syringe, loaded with a seven-percent solution of cocaine, was already laid by. The metal was cold on his feet, but that didn't bother him. Soon heat would diffuse every cell of his body. If it did not kill him, then he would come away with internal fires ablaze. He would not know cold for at least another fifty years.

The wall to the east was patterned with flattened bullets grouped to look like flowers. They appeared as imperfectly shaped silver coins when the moonlight hit them. Adrian practiced shooting from time to time, though he no longer soldiered on a regular basis, and was always pleased to discover that his skills as a marksman had not deteriorated. He had learned that Dippel's earlier experiments had not been so coordinated after the lightning passed through their brains and bodies. Of course, Dippel's earlier experiments had mostly started out dead—a fact the doctor had failed to mention before attempting to "cure" him.

In the dark, Byron thought he heard someone whisper: *There he goes, a dead man walking.*

"Not dead," he murmured. "Just possessed of numerous, colorful obituaries."

He'd certainly had a royal send-off that first time. To begin, in Greece there was a thirty-seven-gun salute. Easter was canceled and the country ordered to wear black for three weeks. The fake body had lain in state the whole time, coffin draped in a black cloak and surmounted by a sword, helmet and crown of laurels. Bless the extravagant and loyal Greeks! Their mourning for their hero had been sincere. Their unabashed display of grief had touched him.

His interment in England had been more amusing. So scandalous was his reputation at home—and yet so august his position as the hero of the Greek Revolution—that society had not known how to mourn him. Even his old friends were worried about his widow Anna's reaction. Showing disrespect by boycotting the funeral would enrage her and hurt Byron's sister. Yet expressing any admiration for her late detested husband would also earn them her undying wrath and societal censure.

Finally one man had hit upon the notion of sending his empty carriage, emblazoned with the family crest, to ride in the procession. Thus was respect shown, but in no way could Anna feel that anyone was too worshipful of the notorious lord. Others had quickly followed the example, trying to outdo one another with displays bearing extravagant coats of arms.

Anna, demonstrating no other interest in the affair beyond buying new widow's weeds, had left her husband's sister Augusta to arrange for the hearse. Augusta had chosen one of impressive size that had to be drawn by six black horses to carry her brother's remains to the family vault. The vehicle was necessarily large, to accommodate both the lead-lined coffin and the many urns bearing his organs removed during the autopsy, but Byron was certain his sister had chosen it more for effect than out of any logistical consideration.

The undertaker had seen to it that the numerous vessels were suitably draped in black velvet palls, and that the horses were arrayed in ridiculous black plumes larger than any lady's hat. The procession was enormous, though silent, ghostly even, because most of the carriages were empty. And that was fitting, since the level of mourning among his family was so diminished as to be nonexistent.

All that had been missing from the event were hysterics by Caroline Lamb as she threw herself on his grave and demanded to be buried with him; but she had not heard of his passing in time to attend the services, and so the world was denied the spectacle.

Yes, it had all been very gothic and morbid—and he'd enjoyed it hugely. It was still his favorite funeral.

After, he'd left for America and a new life. He had gone back to his home in England only once during what might be termed his natural lifetime. That was after Mary died. But he'd hated it. Everything he had known and loved was gone and in graves, marked only by cold stone monuments. Even his family estate seemed more like a mausoleum than a mansion—which was fitting, considering that the abbey had seen the burial of hundreds of monks.

His visit to see the aging Claire Clairmont had not been happy either. She did not know him anymore, and had become tiresomely religious. He tried not to judge— would he not have felt the same if the grave had yawned before him and his imagination began tormenting him with visions of hellfire?

Still, he had seen then not just mortal death, but the death of his and his comrades' ideals. He had returned to the States afterward, going south to New Orleans where he'd begun yet another life in a clime warmer and friendlier than the one he had known.

And he was about to do it again. Only this time, he wouldn't die in battle. Like the phoenix, Adrian Ruthven was about to die and George Ruthven would be born from the ashes. In a decade or two, George's "nephew" would come to claim his great-uncle's inheritance.

Until then, these apartments in New York would sit empty—except for the ghosts and the memories. And good riddance. Hadn't he already learned that the past was dead? It should stay decently buried.

Sensing that his last hard thought had chased his friends away, and that he was again alone, Byron turned at the top of the stairs to look back down into the library. There was nothing there but the boisterous fire, and the drapes stirred uneasily with a passing draft. It was as quiet as any tomb he'd ever been in.

Then the eerie peace was broken by a soft sneeze, and his two terriers crept out from under the divan. They began playing with the sofa cushions, worrying them like

10

rats and tossing them back and forth. The ghosts had truly departed. All was normal.

Except, there should be a monkey to supervise the boisterous play. He had always had a monkey for the dogs to befriend. Wolf and Mutz had especially liked the small primates.

Byron smiled sadly. Perhaps, if he lived to see the dawn, he would get another. He'd always loved monkeys. And maybe a monkey would help him forget the war that raged again in Europe. A war that would have to be ended without him. He'd done his part for the cause, had his fill of the holocausts and the man-made hellfire that killed so indiscriminately. He'd done all he could before the epilepsy returned, had wept for the horrible, seemingly endless losses around him—wept scalding tears of rage and helplessness—and he hated that he still had, after all this time, tears in him to give. It made his departure from the field more bitter and left another shadow over his heart.

But that was the price he'd paid—and paid, and paid, and continued to pay—for his long life. There was no point in quibbling. He'd made his bargain long ago.

Your heart needs occupation.
—*Letter from Ninon de Lenclos to Marquis Sévigné*

There is no instinct like that of the heart.
—*Byron*

Chapter One

December 20, 2005

"Good God!" Damien Ruthven began to laugh. It wasn't often that the books he was sent to review provoked this reaction. In fact, none ever had. His personal secretary, Karen Andersen, stuck her head in his door. She looked alarmed.

"It can't be that bad," she said, ready to defend the author. She was always ready to defend the author. Karen was sweet and intelligent, but she'd soon realized that she hadn't chosen well in her career as secretary to a book critic. If she hadn't grown so fond of him, she would have quit only months after starting. Damien knew this and was careful to stay on her good side. "I only just gave you the manuscript," she said.

"I don't know if it's bad. It's certainly long. You do realize that she has written three volumes, each six hundred pages in length? This is only the first installment."

"What? There's more coming?" Even Karen looked taken aback.

Damien chuckled again.

"Apparently, Book Two is devoted to Byron's letters and accounting ledgers. I'm not sure what Book Three is—perhaps his laundry lists." Seeing Karen's consternation, Damien added, "Don't worry. I shall enjoy this. I always enjoy the pompous, long-winded ones."

"Don't be too mean," Karen pleaded. "Obviously, this woman has spent a lot of time researching these books. You might actually learn something about Byron."

"I doubt it," Damien murmured, waving her away with an impatient hand.

What was the author thinking? Eighteen hundred pages! All about one man? Even he didn't find himself *that* fascinating.

Prepared to tear the dry dissertation to shreds, four hours later Damien found himself reluctantly intrigued by the woman's insights into his life and her unusual method of presentation. She had taken a collection of scattered facts and knitted them into a fairly complete portrait. One so complete that it might almost have come from a psychiatrist's couch. It was arranged almost as a stream-of-consciousness story, spinning out the history of Byron's life by theme rather than strictly by chronology. A reader could choose to focus on various aspects of the subject's life—the child, the lover, the poet, the warrior. Within those categories, the author told the story in correct order, but the narrative retained the intimacy of a dinner conversation in which one subject naturally led to another.

The only place she'd erred so far was in some slight details of his love affair with Lady Caroline Lamb, and by misquoting the love poem he'd written to her.

And how he'd died, of course.

Still chuckling, Damien read the last section again.

There were many reasons for Byron's self-imposed exile to Switzerland, Italy and Greece: unpopular politics, his unloving wife, rapacious creditors, and the rumors of an incestuous affair with his half-sister. Yet, the most vexing of his many irritants was Caroline Lamb, the wife of the future prime minister of England. In adultery's hall of fame, there is surely no mistress as annoying—and few so crazed.

Lord Byron wrote first to her, telling her that the affair must end because it made "fools talk, friends grieve, and the wise pity."

When this failed to have any effect on Caroline's outrageous behavior, he wrote next to Lady Melbourne, her mother-in-law, asking for assistance and saying: "I would sooner, much sooner, be with the dead in purgatory than with her—Caroline—upon earth . . . I am already almost a prisoner; she has no shame, no feeling, not one estimable or redeemable quality . . . If there is one human being whom I do utterly detest and abhor it is she, and, all things considered, I feel myself justified in thinking so."

One would think that such a comprehensive excoriation would deter even the most determined of lovers, but the lady apparently could not face rejection. One has to wonder what ever attracted him to her. His usual good sense must have somehow become suspended.

He had been accused of many things during the course of his affairs—wickedness, promiscuity and licentiousness mainly. This was one of the few times anyone had said he was stupid.

Damien flipped ahead to the poem he had dashed off in a moment of anger.

Remember thee! Remember thee!
  Till Lethe quench life's burning streams
Remorse and shame shall cling to thee
  And haunt thee like a feverish dream.

Remember thee! Aye, doubt it not,
  Thy husband too shall think of thee,
By neither shall thee be forgot!
  Thou false to him, thou fiend to me.

Well, the author of this book, one Miss Brice Ashton, was mistaken in a small detail. He'd never sent the verse to Caroline, knowing that though it was deserved, it was too cruel and might unhinge her already rather unstable mind. It had only appeared in print after his *death*. And then it had been printed incorrectly. Though he had written the lines as a question—*Remember thee?*— it had appeared in print in different form, the lines changed to a more emphatic *Remember thee!* Tom Medwin always had been inclined to meddle with other people's work. Editors! They were an annoying breed.

As for why he had been attracted to Caroline—it certainly wasn't her body. She'd been stick-thin, like a dried butterfly. Nor was it her public antics and theatrical fits. Those had been supremely distasteful for all involved. But she had possessed a certain kind of sexuality, one fed by stretched nerves and endless reservoirs of turbulent emotion. For a time it had been intriguing, like being near something elemental. It was only after their affair had begun that he realized that all the deep, unrestrained emotion would eventually drown them both. He'd had one devil of a time fighting free.

Intrigued, Damien broke a rule about reading a book through and skipped ahead, intending to read about his affair with the voluptuous Teresa Guiccioli. However, he got distracted on the way by an account of the deadly battle at Missolonghi in chapter seventeen. His biographer got most of the details right, somehow even managing to describe the delta slime that outsiders had called *mud*—an innocuous name for the unpleasant, malodorous and gritty muck that worked its way inside one's boots and chafed the feet. To this day, the smell of the swamp near his home outside New Orleans reminded him of wading through the shattered bones and blood in the aftermath of that tragic battle.

But though meticulously clear about the details of combat, Miss Ashton skipped over the contributions of Teresa's brother to the cause, and over the boy's efforts to help the Greeks against the Turks. The young man had died in Greece six months after helping Byron disappear. He was a true patriot, a hero. This should also be corrected, credit given where credit was due.

Making an impulsive decision, Damien decided that before writing a formal review, he would contact Brice Ashton about her few errors and give her a chance to correct them. What he had was an advanced reading copy; there might still be time for alterations before the book went to print.

The tomes—three massive and grossly overpriced volumes—wouldn't attract the attention that his autobiography would have done, but somehow it pleased him to think of the record being set straight after all those many years of scholarly regurgitation of the same old Byron myths. It meant breaking one of his hard and fast rules, but he was going to see to it that Brice Ashton knew at least part of the undiscovered truth about her hero.

The fair sex should always be fair, and no man
Till thirty should perceive there's a plain woman.
                                        —*Lord Byron*

Mad, bad, dangerous to know. That beautiful face is my
fate.
                        —*From the journal of Lady Caroline Lamb*

Letter-writing is the only device combining solitude with
good company.
                                        —*Lord Byron*

Chapter Two

Brice Ashton took up her pen in a firm grip and scribbled quickly: *Ninon was born into the era of the bon vivant and embraced it immediately*. Then, just as quickly, she ran a line through the text, grumbling about hating beginnings of books. Brice was a bit of a magpie, gathering up shiny facts about dead people's lives, hoarding them until there was enough to work with. And, like a real magpie, her hoards were inherently disorderly. She never knew quite where to begin her books. And, frankly, she didn't actually enjoy the writing of them all that much. Research was her love, her refuge, the only place where she knew the peace of total absorption. And, even in the vast landscape of history, the only place she'd found complete contentment was with the late Lord Byron. With him, her insights had seemed magical, directed by some form of divinity—probably not a Christian one.

Brice frowned. Her friends had always said she was a bit of a witch. Sometimes, like when she had been interrupted too often, she was also that other -*itch* word, but witches were rarer and more mysterious, so she didn't mind the label as much. It wasn't that she actually practiced any sort of magic—not really. She had a few rituals that helped with her craft—burning gardenia candles and keeping an open pouch of Persian Slipper pipe tobacco on her desk—but all writers did things like that. Still, usually those rites led her to places of insight undiscovered by anyone else and brought fascinating and, too often, controversial results.

Nothing was helping today though. And she had to find a starting place for this biography. Brice turned another page in her notebook and began again:

Freedom was a grand thing for the children, but night was falling. Suddenly a creature of white crossed before them in the gloom of the wood. Young Marsillac was at once dismayed and fell back with a cry, but not Ninon. Armed with her father's rapier, she drew steel on the snarling hound that advanced upon them. Drawing back her sword, Ninon—

The doorbell rang, a klaxon of a bell that her husband Mark had installed many years ago. It shook the walls of her office and made her coffee ripple with tiny waves, but she managed to ignore it.

Ninon called out in a commanding voice—

The bell rang gain, imperiously summoning her from her work.

"Go away," Brice muttered, scribbling even more frantically.

But the bell was not silenced. It whined, it roared, just as it was intended to do. When the strident ringing persisted for a second minute, Brice knew it was the mailman with a special-delivery letter. Aaron Perkins was the quintessential mailman, and he had learned to be relentless with his deliveries here, going so far as to carry them to the door instead of leaving them in the mailbox by the side of the road because he knew she rarely checked it.

Disgusted at the interruption—the third that morning, Brice threw down her pen and stalked to the door. She was going to change that bell, she really was! What had Mark been thinking?

Brice didn't answer that last question, for she knew Mark had been thinking of her and her inclination to get lost in her work. He had constantly scolded her about keeping balance in her life—something she'd been bad about lately.

It took an effort to recall how to be cordial, but Brice forced her mouth into a smile of welcome before she opened the top half of her Dutch door. Hazy and unwelcome light shone in her squinting eyes.

"Here ya go, Miz Ashton. Must be somethin' important, so I didn't want to make ya come down to the post office to get it—not so close to the big day and all. Things are kinda crazy downtown right now." He handed her a large envelope with a gust of cold air.

"Thank you, Aaron. I appreciate it," she lied, wondering what he was talking about. Big day? Had there been another anthrax scare? She really needed to watch the news occasionally.

Then she remembered. It was almost Christmas. The last-minute shoppers would be out in droves trying to get their delayed holiday purchases to parties around the world—a feat not accomplishable at this date unless one booked the Concord, but they would make the attempt anyway.

Brice was further annoyed at being reminded about the season of cheer. She did her best to ignore it. When it caught at the edges of her attention it was quite irritating. And when it really grabbed her notice, every string of lights and every Christmas tree was enough to re-break her heart. This was the season of love and family—but what did that matter when your love was senselessly dead and buried in the cold, wintry ground?

Brice's smile turned bitter and her face began to ache. Her love had died, and she had not. Her family had died, too, but she still lived. That made her lucky, her friends said. But lucky didn't mean happy. Especially not at Christmas.

"Have a good day, ya hear?" Aaron called, retreating down the leaf-choked path, listing to one side because of the seasonal heaviness of his satchel.

"I will, thank you. And you too. Don't let Jack Frost bite you on the . . . *nose*," Brice answered, swapping nouns at the last minute, as she pulled hard on the tab of cardboard envelope she didn't want. She bumped the top half of the door shut with her shoulder and followed that up with a body slam. The door was surly. The wood had warped and needed to be planed. And she would get to it. Soon. Right after the doorbell. In the meantime, she had to be firm about latching the thing or it would spring back open. It was kind of like memory that way.

"I don't believe it," she said a moment later into the propane-heated air. She stared fixedly at the letterhead that topped the expensive stationery, wondering if it was a hoax. Or a mistake. Maybe it was a hallucination brought on by hunger and overwork.

Muttering, Brice began reading the body of the letter, finding her way back to her desk by memory and not by sight. She sat for a while reading and then rereading to the soft hum of the furnace. She always ran the furnace after the first of October. Though the climate here was mild by most standards, she felt any cold deep in her once-broken bones.

"I don't believe it," she said again when she'd perused the letter a second time. But neither her abandoned coffee cup nor her dusty computer answered.

Brice Ashton stared, bemused by the paper in her hands. Normally, she would have been enraged at receiving such a presumptuous missive from a reviewer—especially in her own home. Reviewers were impossible! So many of them thought they knew more about the subjects of her research than she did, and were almost invariably wrong. It couldn't be her agent who had betrayed her. Or her publisher. There was etiquette to these things, after all—but how the hell had he gotten her home address if not from them?

Her building wrath died suddenly. In spite of the invasion of privacy, this note was an entirely exceptional thing. She viewed most critics the way she did dandruff: annoying but easily ignored—at least while at home. But this letter couldn't be disregarded. The tone was one of a scholar speaking respectfully to a peer, albeit in slightly arrogant and archaic prose that might be mistaken for mockery if one weren't reading with a sensitive eye. And the kinds of detail that Damien Ruthven was describing could only be known to someone who had access to the Byron family archive of personal correspondence and who had spent a lot of time sorting through the material.

Or to someone who had a copy of Byron's lost memoirs.

A shot of heat went through her body, a bolt of hope and anticipation thrown at her heart by an overdose of sudden adrenaline.

Could it be? Had this man somehow found a copy of the memoirs? Scholars had always believed that there were only three copies—all burned by Hobhouse and Murray in a misguided effort to whitewash Byron's reputation after his death. But scholars were sometimes wrong. Often wrong, in fact, though she'd never admit it in public. Could the literary find of the century actually be within her reach at last? Was vindication of her beliefs nigh?

Conviction stirred, and the thought was dizzying in a rare but familiar way. Brice had never quite forgotten the first terrifying thrill of actually striking out from conventional wisdom and thinking on her own, of drawing a conclusion that no one else had drawn—and putting it in writing. That day, she had seen the path of her life open up before her and known her true calling. She had always known that she was a writer, but at last she knew just what kind. That day, Brice had put all thoughts of fiction behind her and turned her heart to the task of unveiling the mysterious people of the past.

In the intervening years her heart and hope had somewhat hardened. Investigation was difficult, sometimes nearly impossible. She was often glad that she had met up with Byron and formed her passionate fascination with him before frustration and disillusionment with the veracity of *eyewitnesses* set in. She might never have gone the distance otherwise, never have known him well enough to want to write his biography—and then he wouldn't have been there to save her when her world collapsed and she needed something solid to cling to.

As it was, in the aftermath of her tragedy, all those bits of fertile flotsam that was Byron's life settled by the banks of the stream where her subconscious flowed, and there it had taken root. It remained, blossoming and bearing fruit, waiting to be harvested by the starving woman stranded in an emotional winterland where she had no other meat or drink.

Byron had saved her—if not her life, then her sanity.

Brice brought the letter to her nose and inhaled slowly, drawing in the scent that clung to the fine paper. There was something about the smell of Damien Ruthven's stationery—it called to her in an odd way, whispering blandishments that only certain people would be aware of. Or respond to. It sounded crazy, but she had learned to listen when intuition or other senses spoke to her. A biographer who wrote about the long dead was as much a detective and psychic as anything else, and one learned to trust one's inner guidance systems when questing for the truth. Right now it was saying that she should go to New York.

On the other hand . . .

Brice looked over at the newspaper. It was open to the book section where, in a weird coincidence and against her better judgment, she had been reading one of Damien Ruthven's more scathing reviews with breakfast.

I am old-fashioned. Like most people, I've always thought that a book should be about something—if not a plot, then characters or an idea. I've even been known to settle for coherent sentences that conveyed emotion in some form or other.

But, once again, Torrance P. Broccoli has set out to prove that a book doesn't have to be about anything. Since it isn't about anything, I can't give you a plot summation, and since it has no characters, I can't acquaint you with their names. As it conveys no ideas—well, you catch the drift. Read tea leaves—it will be more rewarding.

Broccoli Stew is part of the small print run, experimental book series being put out by Back Bench Press and therefore is hard to find. Unfortunately, this manuscript found me, and it proves my long-held conviction that Broccoli is great with cheese, but bad with books.

He was an opinionated bastard. Funny, accessible to his readers, but ruthless when he disliked a book—which was often. Rumor had it that he used to do lots of male Hemingway-type activities—mountain climbing, spelunking, sky-diving. Dangerous, stupid things that Brice didn't like even thinking about. And he was a book critic who could attack writers with reviews that served as blunt instruments, bludgeoning them nearly to death with their published missteps. That he was even more brutal with editors' and publishers' errors was beside the point. The writer always got blamed in the end. This wasn't someone she would normally want to know.

She held up the stationery and inhaled again. It still smelled like destiny.

"Damn."

She pushed back from her desk. Normally, she didn't do impulsive things. Not anymore. She had a routine. It made life predictable and controllable, and that was what she liked. Nothing bad could happen if you planned carefully and listened to the voice of common sense. That made what she was thinking of doing doubly insane—unwise, unproductive as well, since she had a deadline to finish this biography of Ninon de Lenclos. But she was going to New York anyway, as soon as she could get a flight. This weird erotic tingling in her brain said she must do it, and right that very minute. She was going to meet with Damien Ruthven, chat with him face-to-face. She wanted to see his expression, to look into his eyes when she asked about the missing memoirs. Only then would she know if he lied about having them.

And what would she do if he did?

"One bridge at a time," she muttered.

Brice reached for the phone and dialed her friend and travel agent. As she waited, she pulled the band from her braid and started unraveling her hair. She needed to get it cut, she really did, but there was never any time. Maybe whoever came to plane the door and rip out the doorbell could saw off her hair at the same time.

"You're nuts," she whispered as she combed out her mane and waited for Susan to pick up.

Of course she was nuts; she was a writer. And therefore it didn't matter if she was insane and pushy—if she got what she wanted. And she wanted. Oh, how she wanted! The longing was almost like an itch, a poison ivy of the brain. She wanted those memoirs.

Brice laughed silently. She had always been more than a little in love with George Gordon, Lord Byron, poet, humanist and hero. He had entertained her when she was young and romantic, and then had saved her reason at a time when grief threatened to drown her and her only anodyne was work. She would do anything for him—for his memory and his words. She'd even face down the world's fiercest critic.

Yes, if this Damien Ruthven knew something more about the great man she had loved all her life, Brice was going to get it out of him or die trying.

Karen stuck her head back in her employer's door and said in a voice of suffering: "Well, you've done it now. I don't know what you wrote to that woman, but Brice Ashton is coming to see you. This afternoon! She didn't even give me a chance to say yes or no, just announced her imminent arrival and hung up."

The secretary had been annoyed and intrigued that Damien had insisted on writing that particular letter himself. He usually avoided his computer, claiming the machine didn't like him—which it undoubtedly didn't since it broke down on him so often. But if Karen had been curious before, now that the Ashton woman had replied she was doubly so.

"Is she?" Damien leaned back in his chair. He smiled slightly. "Well, how wonderfully prompt of her. I thought she might put me off until after the holidays."

Karen pointed a finger at him. "I'm telling you now, if there's blood spilled, you're cleaning it up. I may be old-fashioned enough to fetch coffee, but I don't do windows or bloodbaths."

"My dear Karen! How you do go on. Miss Ashton isn't coming to spill my blood. I think you will find that she is a delightfully polite if rather inquisitive person. Besides, she wants something from me. My hide is sacrosanct at least until then."

"You think?" Karen looked skeptical. "So you weren't planning on going out of town suddenly and leaving me to deal with her?"

"Of course not." Then Damien added, "However, it might be best if you considered taking the day off if you're nervous. I can manage on my own."

Karen snorted.

"Truly. Go home for the holidays."

"Are you kidding? I wouldn't miss this for the world," she said frankly. "Anyway, how will I be able to blackmail you if I don't see where you put the body? Or where she puts yours. Hiding a corpse in Manhattan in winter isn't as easy as it used to be, but I bet you are both resourceful enough to manage."

Damien shook his head, eyes laughing. "Go on and persevere in your lack of faith in my ability to charm scholarly spinsters. But it would perhaps be nice if you arranged for some flowers while you're busy doubting me."

"Flowers?" Karen said the word like she had never heard it before. "You want flowers?"

"Yes, irises, I think. Or orchids. See what they have in rust and gold—it will go well in this room. And make reservations for this evening at Di Serrano's. They're elegant but not too obviously opulent. Make it for seven, please."

"Seven people?"

"No, for two people at seven o'clock. She'll probably prefer to eat early."

"You're taking the author to dinner? Alone? But you don't like authors." Karen stared at him like he'd grown an extra head.

Her boss was a connoisseur of all the best things in life, from exotic tea and vintage wines to the exquisite clothes that adorned his fine physique. He was not a conspicuous consumer, but a steady one who did not stint on himself. Karen had always found it amazing that he did not strive for excellence in women. His infrequent dates were stunning enough by all physical measures of beauty, but he never allowed himself romantic liaisons with anyone who stirred his interest or emotions. He remained determinedly aloof from anyone who evoked mental attraction—including his secretary. And they were never invited to his favorite haunts, like Di Serrano's.

Until today.

"Absolutely. I want flowers, and I want to take her to dinner," he assured Karen. "This lady deserves a fine meal after coming so far to see me."

"Is she pretty?" Karen asked, forgetting for the moment to remain professionally distant. "I mean, insanely beautiful?"

"I haven't a clue," Damien answered. Then he added with a slight smile: "But wouldn't it be brilliant if she were?"

"I've been with you for five years," Karen said, feeling slightly stunned and unable to let the matter go. "Five long years. You've never done anything like this. Are you feeling okay? You haven't slipped into an early midlife crisis, have you? I mean, for the cost of dinner at Di Serrano's you could probably buy a used Ferrari."

"I *haven't* done anything like this before, have I? It's probably high time I did," Damien answered absently. He pulled Brice's manuscript back toward him. "Listen to this! 'The Guiccioli girl is better—and will get well with prudence—our amatory business goes on well and daily. Her doctors insist that she may be cured, if she likes. Will she like? I doubt of her liking anything for very long, except one thing, and I presume that she will soon arrive at varying even that.'"

He dropped the papers. "Where does this woman get her information? I must know. It's like she was sitting in the wardrobe of the bedroom taking notes while it happened. She understands it all—the cause of the affair, and also the spiritual claustrophobia that drove him to seek solace in women's arms."

"Ah. The light dawns," Karen said, coming to sit on the edge of Damien's desk. Her eyes were a little wide.

"She's a sort of mystery to you, then—a puzzle that must be solved at any cost."

"She's certainly a detective. This kind of research borders on true mania! Writers with obsessions interest me."

"And she's ferreted out information about Byron that you didn't know."

"No—not exactly. But she's ferreted out things that no other scholar has. This next bit is from one of Teresa's own journals. She was with Byron when he wrote *Don Juan*," he added, in case Karen didn't know. His secretary admired Byron's poetry, though she liked Shelley's more—but she'd never been much interested in any of the poets' personal lives, in spite of her employer's obsession with the literary giants of that era.

"Listen. 'His pen moved so rapidly over the page that one day I said to him, "One would almost believe that someone is dictating to you!" "Yes," he replied, "a mischievous spirit who sometimes even makes me write what I am not thinking. There now, for instance—I have just been writing something about love!" "Why don't you erase it then?" I asked. "It is written," he replied, smiling. "The stanza would be spoiled." And the stanza remained.'"

"Miss Ashton makes it all come alive, doesn't she? By using letters and journals in the subject's own words instead of paraphrasing," Karen said, watching her employer's face. His expression was rapt. She quashed the tiny tendril of jealousy that dared to reach for her heart. She was genuinely fond of Damien Ruthven, and she nobly hoped that he had finally had enough of intellectually and emotionally lopsided romance. Perhaps he was ready to try something different: an affair with someone who would be his equal, who might love him in spite of

33

his quirks—and whom he might be able to love in return.

"Usually history is bone dry," she said at random, wondering just how old Brice Ashton was. Could she be under fifty? Karen hoped so.

"Yes."

"And the biographies even worse. But this sounds special. Unique even. Something that could even be . . . popular."

There was a slightly asthmatic wheeze from under his desk, and Damien reached down for a moment.

"Yes," he said again, not looking up from the papers in front of him. "Except for Byron's own memoirs, there has been nothing like it."

"I'll go make those reservations," Karen said. She rose decisively. "Hopefully, the florist can scare up gold irises. They've been kind of heavy on the poinsettias the last few weeks."

"No poinsettias," her employer ordered. "They're so common. And please cancel my reservations for this weekend. Skiing can wait until after Miss Ashton's visit."

"Shall I order up a Christmas tree while I'm at it?" Karen asked. She'd wanted to do one in the office for the longest time, but Damien had no interest in the holidays. "It would be a homey touch."

"Don't be ridiculous. I don't do homey. But order some holly if you like. Or ivy. You can put it on your desk—or wear it on your head, if you prefer." Damien took a good-natured swipe at Karen's devotion to the holiday.

"Don't be nasty. What about mistletoe? I think you need some of that too. It's traditional," she added. "It might help you get lucky with your spinster."

"Don't be absurd. And go away," he grumbled. "I'm reading, and Mace is trying to sleep."

There came a second asthmatic wheeze from under the desk, which Karen understood to be agreement. "You males always stick together," she muttered.

"It's for the preservation of our gender identity in the face of feminine wiles," Damien replied.

Karen sniffed but didn't argue.

"I was meaning to ask if you would mind if I left a little early tonight."

"Not at all. Shop to your heart's content."

"It isn't that." Karen hesitated, and after a moment Damien looked up. He raised a brow.

"What's wrong?"

"Probably nothing. I think maybe I've acquired an admirer. Normally I wouldn't mind, but . . ." She trailed off, unable to explain her uneasiness. "Anyhow, I'd like to leave before dark."

"And so you shall. But I'm sending you home in the car."

"That isn't necessary."

"Of course it is," Damien answered, returning his attention to his manuscript.

It is all very well to keep food for another day, but pleasure should be taken as it comes.

—*Ninon de Lenclos*

But Words are things,
And a small drop of ink,
Falling like dew upon a thought,
Produces that which makes thousands,
Perhaps millions, think.

—*Byron*, Don Juan, *canto III*

You should have a softer pillow than my heart.
  —*Byron's supposed words to his wife on their wedding night*

Chapter Three

Brice Ashton climbed out of the cab, taking her small suitcase with her. The snow felt like soft laughter and made her smile in spite of her annoyance at being late for her appointment—if appointment it could be called. She had simply announced her pending arrival to Damien Ruthven's secretary and then hung up the airport pay phone.

And she was very tardy, possibly unforgivably so, but she stood for a moment, in spite of the hour and the snow covering her in a damp mantilla, to look at the New York building where Damien Ruthven lived. Ruthven Tower was not the tallest skyscraper in the area—not by a long shot—but it had certainly captured the neo-Gothic feel of several of its larger brothers, which was to say that it was very gray and vertical and loaded with fanciful man-reptiles that leered down at passing pedestrians with their forked tongues and hooked ears. It also had what looked like an unrailed stair circling the middle floors in a dizzying spiral that would have tempted the choreographer, Busby Berkeley—had he been able to get insurance for such a dance number, which seemed unlikely.

Somehow, that seemed fitting. The current owner of this building was a literary showman who spent a lot of time sneering down at the authors whose books he reviewed, any number of whom had probably passed beneath him on these very streets.

There were three stories at the base of the building and thirteen stories above, though Brice knew from a quick bit of online research that the top three stories were actually all one open area where Damien Ruthven lived. Not that the real estate stopped there. His great-uncle had also cleverly manipulated the zoning law so that he and his heirs owned the airspace above the building and the airspace above the two buildings on either side. The next block might grow upward, but there would be no nearby skyscrapers obstructing the view.

She wasn't sure if she thought this foresight was admirable or grasping. Maybe it was both.

Jostled by a harassed Christmas shopper with her many packages, a cell phone and a cooling latte, wisely fleeing the snow that weathermen were predicting would worsen, Brice took up her suitcase and headed for the tower lobby.

The interior was about what she expected: lots of dark marble that made it look a bit like a tomb, though it was almost certainly supposed to be patterned after Napoleon's impressive palace at Compiègne. It probably did an equally effective job of intimidating anyone who didn't have a good and sufficient purpose to be visiting.

A security guard looked hard at her snow-covered suitcase as she approached, making Brice wish that she had taken the time to check in at her hotel, or at least to have invested in some less frivolous luggage. Hot pink and purple herringbone seemed to displease a lot of people. The guard's snooty stare set her teeth on edge, but she kept both her voice and expression polite as she asked after Damien Ruthven. The guard blinked. After a moment, he had her sign a logbook, then handed her a magnetic card which he got out of an envelope that had her name on it, written in an elegant hand with which she was now familiar. He directed her to a pair of elevators, where he told her to take the one on the right.

The directory beside the brass doors told her that the building was also the business home for a number of accountants, lawyers, computer software firms and one e-publisher. None of this information made her feel welcome, or happy about getting into the elevator. The airplane here had been packed, and she had had enough of confined spaces.

Fortunately, the elevator was roomy enough to not provoke her claustrophobia when the door slid shut. The private elevator to Damien Ruthven's penthouse was quick, and silent in its arrival.

There was no formal foyer on the penthouse floor. The elevator doors opened directly onto a gigantic space that now functioned as an office and reception area. The only screens that blocked the elevator were twin banks of lush houseplants that had been allowed to turn feral.

She stepped carefully around them. There was no sign of thorns on any of the plants, but she was in enemy territory now. It behooved her to be cautious.

Brice stepped into the open and took a deep breath. She found the interior of Damien's home rather more inviting than the arctic foyer below, though no less grand. The floor was of a lovely rose marble, softened further by Persian rugs roughly the size of your average Middle Eastern country and probably made when Persia still *was* Persia, though she couldn't swear to it since they showed no signs of wear. There was also a lot of glass on the wall in front of her, though it was mostly covered in sheers woven with golden thread and opera-house drapes of deep red velvet.

The only exception to the curtained look was the window directly behind an ancient desk where a woman—presumably the secretary Brice had spoken with so briefly—sat looking out the naked glass at the tumbling snow beyond.

The desk the woman was barricaded behind was a piece of furniture large and elegant enough to be called an historic artifact. Someone, or maybe several someones, of vast importance had undoubtedly used it while deciding the fate of nations. It was, Brice was certain, designed to deter interlopers like herself—not that it would work! No desk would keep her from Byron's memoirs.

Since she was unobserved, Brice took her time looking around. There were also some lovely and—naturally—large paintings on the walls. She was no expert, but she was certain that at least one was a Matisse. It sat above an enormous fireplace, which was unlit but laid with kindling and logs.

Brice put her suitcase down with a decided clunk, and, not caring if it made her seem crazy or rude, she did a silent 360-degree inspection of the room. It was all much the same—tasteful, expensive, large—except for a narrow iron staircase in one corner that spiraled dizzily up toward a frosted-glass ceiling. It looked a bit like a dinosaur's skeleton and would be as difficult to climb as a giant's ribcage. There were two other corkscrew staircases that rose up from other rooms, metal cyclones that reached for the distant ceiling.

The flights of curved steps ended in a catwalk affair that ran around the room, its decorative iron rail broken up by a series of torchère lamps that were probably a lot larger than they looked from where she was standing. She wasn't an expert, but something about them screamed *Tiffany*.

There was a second ring of balconies, also lined with books and reached by even narrower stairs. Beyond that was a glass dome, either made of white glass or else frosted over by the snow. The effect was rather like standing inside a giant wedding cake—a very expensive wedding cake.

If Brice had harbored any fears about Damien Ruthven being a starving working man just doing a nasty job to get by, they were now laid to rest.

"Ostentatious, but I could learn to call it home," she muttered, then flinched when the room picked up her words and amplified them.

"It does take some getting used to," a pleasant voice answered from behind the grand desk. "But after a while it actually feels rather homey."

Brice turned and looked again at the secretary. The woman was turned her way now. She was young and blonde—though not adolescent, Brice was relieved to see. She also seemed friendly, though there was a definite measuring quality in her gaze that mirrored the looks Brice had received in the lobby. Brice wasn't used to inciting so much curiosity. Perhaps she was the first writer to ever brave the dragon's lair.

"You must be Karen Andersen," Brice said, and then ruined the coolly polite greeting by sneezing violently. "Darn it!"

"Yes, and you are Brice Ashton," the blonde said warmly. "May I take that case for you? Or do you have more manuscripts for Mr. Ruthven?"

Brice stared at her in confusion, then started laughing. She fished a tissue out of her pocket.

"Please, take the case. There is nothing in it for Mr. Ruthven. My flight was delayed by the weather, and since I was so late, I came here directly instead of stopping at the hotel." While she explained, Brice slipped off her coat. She quickly stuffed her tissue in a pocket.

"Well, let me put these over by the desk and take you in to Mr. Ruthven. He was just about to have tea. However, he delayed to take a call from an associate, so you have made it in time for tea after all."

Brice gave up trying to be formal and dignified and smiled. "Thank you. That would be lovely. I asked for tea on the plane, but it was a lost cause. I finally used the teabags as eye compresses and gave the water back so they could finish washing the dishes in first class. They served some sort of fish up there, and the odor would *not* go away. I fear there will be stories of food poisoning on the news tonight."

"Well, I can promise you a wonderful pot of Darjeeling—and scones too. And not a single fish." Smiling, the secretary ushered Brice toward a set of French doors carved of dark rosewood. She didn't attempt to knock—all those angels lounging on fruit would destroy her knuckles—but simply opened a door and said: "Your guest is here."

And there he was: the literary critic, the creature many

suspected of having a soul of clay, if not being a golem himself.

Brice studied him warily.

He looked wrong for the part, she decided immediately. After hearing so much about the fire-breathing Damien Ruthven and listening to his secretary and the security guard refer to him as *"Mr. Ruthven"* in tones of utmost respect and even awe, Brice expected to meet a man of advanced years and impressive demeanor. But though imposing enough—*and those eyes! Good God! They were as black as anything she had ever seen*—he appeared to be no more than forty years of age. He also wore his hair long and had an earring.

Not certain if she found this lack of stereotypical fashion to be reassuring, she advanced slowly.

"Damien Ruthven?" she asked, wanting to be sure that she had the right man.

"In the flesh," he answered in a cultured voice, which held the hint of a British accent. He rose from behind his desk—it was an artifact too—and walked toward her. His eyes looked her over carefully. It was too much to say he sounded surprised, but Brice sensed that she had somehow astonished him. Perhaps he had also been expecting someone older. "And you are Miss Ashton."

"Yes." Brice couldn't help but continue to stare as he offered his hand. It was complete foolishness, a wild fancy brought on by jet lag and dim light, but he looked a great deal like the later portraits of Lord Byron, when pain and war had toughened his features into something nearly piratical.

Their fingers met and then their palms. A slight tingling passed through her skin, almost as though she were receiving a series of slight shocks. Brice was also aware of the heat rolling off of him. She wondered if she was especially chilled or if he had an abnormally high body temperature, or perhaps was ill.

Damien's eyes widened, as though he, too, could feel the shock of the flesh, and he continued to stare at her. His expression was partly delighted and partly puzzled.

"Have we met?" Brice asked, and then wished she hadn't. Where were her verbal filters today? She could feel herself blushing under the mobile brow that elevated at her question.

Maybe he wouldn't notice, since she was already flushed with cold.

"No, I'm certain not," Damien answered, finally releasing her hand. He added graciously, "But I understand why you ask. I, too, had a moment when I was sure that I had seen you before. But perhaps it was an author photo."

"No, I've never had one done," she answered.

She did not protest when he laid a light hand on her arm and guided her toward the desk, where there was an enormous vase of gold irises and very little else. No phone, no computer—no thumbscrews or iron maidens either. Other than a small desk lamp, there was no sign that the twenty-first century had penetrated his domain.

There was also no tingling when he touched her—not with the fabric between them—but she felt his warmth through the wool of her sweater.

"I have not had one done either," he confessed. He gestured to a chair near the fire. The fireplace in his library-cum-office was smaller than the one in the reception hall, but it was also hung with equally expensive art. This one looked to be a Goya. She stared at the portrait with disfavor. It was one of Goya's crueler paintings, done when the lead poisoning had eaten away at his brain.

"We are both somewhat shy, it seems," he added.

His column always appeared without a photo. Brice's writer friends had speculated that it was because Damien Ruthven hadn't been able to find a way to hide his horns and forked tail. That was ridiculous, of course, but there was definitely something about him that made her think of black magic.

She nodded to herself and tried to organize her face back into polite, professional lines while she studied another painting. It was a portrait of a pair of terriers and a monkey dressed as a Moorish slave. Byron was rumored to have had such a painting done while in Greece. It was fascinating to think about this possibility, but slightly less intriguing than her host, so she saved her questions for later.

"Perhaps we are merely private," she suggested when the silence strung out and she reluctantly admitted that it was her turn to say something. "We may not care to have strangers feeling a high degree of intimacy with us when we don't want intimacy with them."

Unable to keep her eyes away from him any longer, she looked back at Damien. He was smiling, but it wasn't an entirely reassuring expression; she sensed that it was prompted by amusement at her reaction to him and his surroundings rather than by good manners.

"Did you know that I'm a mind reader?" he asked, proving her suspicions.

"No." She cleared her throat and glanced at the large mirror behind the desk, wondering if her expression was giving her away. But she looked normal, even if she felt odd. She went on the offensive. "Wouldn't that be discomforting at times?"

"At times. For some people," he answered, deliberately misunderstanding her. "But to answer your unspoken question—yes, that is the painting that Byron commissioned. An ancestor of mine bought it many moons ago. He thought it was the perfect whimsical touch for an otherwise serious office."

"He seems to have bought a lot of things for the place," Brice retorted, and then blushed again. This time there could be no doubt that he saw the stains on her cheeks.

"You are correct. The Ruthvens were here at the birth of the industrial era and enthusiastic participants in the legal pillage of this nation's natural resources. The name Ruthven is not as well known today as Rockefeller or Dupont, but we went to many of the same parties. I hope you won't hold that against me, though. Truly, my taste in art and sense of civic responsibility are much improved over that era."

The door opened, and Karen entered, carrying a tray loaded down with a teapot, cups and saucers, creamer, sugar bowl, scones, clotted cream, lemon curd and jam. One whiff of the pastry and Brice's stomach began to grumble in loud, rude tones.

"You've apparently arrived in the very nick of time. Our guest requires immediate sustenance," Damien joked.

Karen smiled at Brice; then her eyes darted toward Damien where they widened. "The food was as bad as the tea?" she asked Brice sympathetically, though her eyes remained on her employer.

Brice was a student of human nature. Having seen Damien Ruthven and felt the effects of his charm, she could well imagine that Karen Andersen was smitten with her employer and not happy to see him appearing so invigorated by the presence of another woman. Brice half expected Karen to look at her as if she wished her in a bed of banana leaves with a roast apple stuffed in her mouth and cloves studding her hide. But there was nothing but surprise and—damn—more curiosity in the woman's gaze when she turned back. Clearly the fungus of envy had not set its spores in her. Either she was not romantically interested in her employer or she did not perceive Brice as a threat. Karen was curious, though. Very curious.

"Worse by far. And I couldn't even use it for compresses," Brice said finally, returning Karen's smile. Her stomach rumbled again. She might have blushed more, but that didn't seem possible.

"Just don't spoil your appetite. You're in for a treat tonight." The secretary poured a cup of tea and handed it over.

"I am?" Brice accepted the cup, looking from Karen to Damien. Karen's eyes were twinkling in an alarming manner. Damien looked vaguely annoyed at the pronouncement, but also resigned. He was apparently used to his secretary being well acquainted with his affairs.

Was it another hint of long-term intimacy?

And why should she care? Really, she shouldn't.

Still . . . Brice found that she did care. Damien Ruthven was *her* find. She didn't meet many intriguing people, she told herself, and she wanted the opportunity to get to know this one without interference.

"We have reservations for dinner at seven—if you are not too tired," Damien added as an afterthought. "I hope you like Italian and French cooking. There is a small place near hear that does some wonderful fusion cuisine."

"I adore them both—singularly and collectively," Brice said, but inside she was thinking hard. Was dinner with this man a good idea? For that matter, was being in his home at all wise? It had seemed a good idea when she'd thought it up, but it was looking less sensible by the moment. The line between home and office was only a doorway wide.

"Good. I couldn't let you come all this way—and in such bad weather—and not take you out for a proper meal." He was still smiling, still looking vaguely amused.

"The car will be here at six-thirty," Karen reminded them as she departed.

"And speaking of the reasons for me coming all this way . . ." Brice set her cup aside once Karen left the room.

"Certainly, let's speak of that. But have a scone first. They're wonderful. Do you like clotted cream?"

"Yes, actually, I do," Brice admitted. "But perhaps we should—"

"Excellent. And try the lemon curd. It's made fresh and is absolutely ambrosial."

Brice's stomach squawked again, and she gave up trying to resist the pastry's lure. Nothing had gone as planned today and she hadn't much dignity left anyway. Damien might as well see her eat like a starved wolverine. It would make an interesting sidebar in his column if he decided to write about her visit.

Their hands touched as he offered her the dish of lemon curd and she felt the now familiar electricity and then a small moment of vertigo. Brice pulled back. She blinked twice and the room stilled.

Hunger—that had to be it. And travel lag. And weariness. She hadn't slept well the last couple of days, being plagued with dreams of terrible storms and screams in the cold darkness.

Probably, once fortified with some stick-to-the-ribs food, she would be more up to the task of being sly and subtle when she asked about Byron's memoirs. Just now she didn't have the weight to step into the ring with her opponent, and she was just barely awake enough to know it.

Shall I tell you what renders love dangerous? It is the sublime idea which we often appear to have of it.
—*Letter from Ninon de Lenclos to Marquis Sévigné*

Man's love is of a man's life a thing apart. 'Tis a woman's whole existence.
—*Byron*, Don Juan, *canto I*

Critics are like children who can whip horses but not drive them.
—*Molière*

It is true from early habit, one must make love mechanically as one swims. I was once very fond of both, but now I never swim unless I tumble into water. I don't make love until almost obliged.
—*Byron (letter, September 10, 1812)*

Chapter Four

The snow that greeted them when they stepped out of the limousine still felt like laughter, but Brice thought it had taken on the quality of something closer to sly and sinister hilarity now that the day was dying and the sun burying itself on the western horizon far beyond the city. There was hardly any time to worry about this strange feeling, though, because Damien whisked her indoors before more than a handful of seconds passed.

The ceiling of Di Serrano's was high and beamed, lending the room a warm feeling in spite of its size. Torchères of stained glass shed softly colored light on the linen-clad tables and rough plaster walls where vases of elegant calla lilies were mounted in ornate brass sconces. In the background a pianist played softly. Brice couldn't place the tune, but it wasn't "That's Amore."

There wasn't a wax-covered Chianti bottle or red-and-white-checked napkin in sight either.

"It's 'Viens, Mallika' from *Lakme*," Damien murmured, inclining his head, answering her unspoken question and proving that he was, in some circumstances, very much the mind reader he claimed to be.

His warm breath made Brice shiver.

They were shown to a table near a large window that looked out on the street filling steadily with snow. She knew it would change quickly, but for now the world looked pristine and untouched even with the street ablaze with Christmas fanfare. And it was dazzling. The city's already formidable collection of lights had been augmented with lavish seasonal displays, and the cold air made the light sharper than diamonds.

Damien took over the task of seating her, but he allowed the man he called Antonio to whip out the brocade napkin with a practiced flick of the wrist and send it fluttering into her lap with the lightness of a butterfly alighting on a flower. Brice smiled at the swarm of men who appeared carrying all sorts of salvers and bottles which they left, and candelabras which they removed.

"I don't like candles at the table," Damien explained. "One sees the naked fire and never the light in a guest's eyes."

He probably didn't mean his words to be romantic, but they were.

Brice's senses continued exploring. Her fingers told her that the upholstery on the chairs was real velvet and the menus were bound in real leather. The scents told her the food would be truly exquisite, and it was probably a more effective way to lift the spirits than any antidepressant on the market. Sighing with delight, she smiled at Damien and opened the menu that Antonio put in her hands.

Maybe she was supping with the devil, but she didn't care. She'd just ask for a long spoon.

"And let the games begin," Brice said softly, taking in the many pages of appetizers and entrees. "What? No Jell-O salad? No meatloaf? No French fries? I bet they don't even serve parsley garnish. Oh—*flan aux poire!* And *les champignons violets*. I didn't think you could get these any time but April in Paris."

Damien laughed softly. Perhaps it was a trick of light, but for a moment it seemed that his eyes blazed with gold fire. "A fellow gastronome. We are so rare in this day of carb-counting. Let's celebrate our meeting of appetites, shall we? How do you feel about pâté? Would it fit the mood?"

"Like spandex shorts," Brice said before thinking.

Damien laughed again. In that moment she could see some wickedness in his gaze, and a lot of sex. It was as though something had switched on in his brain when they sat down at the table. Food took some men that way.

The name of the restaurant was Italian but the cuisine crossed many borders. Brice hardly knew where to start. Damien seemed inclined to order one of everything so that they could sample at will. Brice vetoed the idea, saying that she would feel like a *cochon*, a pig, and feared ending up on the menu herself.

Damien acquiesced. They didn't stint too much, though. They began with pâté, artichokes in hollandaise and *les champignons violets*. Neither being fearful of strong flavors, they rounded out the appetizers with some baked goat cheese. The edge knocked off their appetites, they readied themselves for the subtler flavors of the main course by cleansing the palate with lemon-fennel sorbet.

Damien had squab with roasted shallots and lingonberries as his entree and Brice the *salumon a la Griggia* with roasted asparagus. Throwing caution to the wind, they ordered both the Puligny Montrachet Latour and a Chateauneuf du Pape Beaucastel. As expected, the wines and food were all excellent.

For dessert, they shared berry ice cream cake and a praline bombe with rich espresso and brandy. It was decadent, a pleasure to cause guilt—hell, with the sorts of calories she was consuming, Brice decided that it might even be a mortal sin in the world of cellulite. She wasn't treating her body like the temple she was exhorted to worship in; she was using it as a combination wine cellar and candy kitchen.

She looked up once while savoring a last spoonful of creamed sin and caught a glimpse of someone in a tarnished mirror that hung on the wall, mostly masked by a spray of white tuberoses. The person in the glass looked vaguely familiar, and stared quite pointedly as Brice studied her. Puzzled, she stared harder at the woman, trying to place the face. It was her own reflection, of course. Yet not. There were differences. This woman's eyes were focused, her cheeks flushed with something other than cold. And she was half smiling, as though fighting to contain some excitement that she wasn't quite ready to share with the world. It was, she realized, the face of a younger Brice Ashton, one who hadn't lost faith in miracles.

Oh, no! she thought. But the face just kept smiling.

Brice looked away, feeling a little terrified as well as thrilled.

"Ready for a walk?" Damien asked as he signed the bill. There was nothing so vulgar as an exchange of money or plastic. "Or shall I call for the car? A meal like that can be as effective as a dose of Nembutal."

Normally, Brice would agree, but not that night. She, like the girl in the mirror, felt energized and wanted to walk off some of her dietary excess. "A walk would be lovely, but I'm afraid the best I can manage is a waddle. Do you still want to be seen with me now that I've gained twenty pounds?"

"Of course. Put on a coat and no one will suspect there is a *petit cochon* underneath."

"I hope not. There are probably laws about pigs roaming the street at will." She smiled and said sincerely: "That was delicious—thank you."

Antonio appeared before Damien could answer, bearing their coats and many best wishes for their evening and for their swift return to his restaurant. Damien allowed him the good wishes, but opted to help Brice into her coat himself. His hands lingered a moment at her shoulders, stroking the cashmere of her dress. She would guess that he was a sensualist as well as a gourmet.

"Where shall we go?" Brice asked as they stepped out into the snow, which wasn't yet deep enough to be a hindrance. But once outside, she was again bothered by the idea that the weather was laughing at her.

"We are quite close to Macy's in Herald Square. Have you ever seen the windows at Christmas?" Damien asked.

Feeling like a kid offered the world's biggest lollipop, Brice answered: "No. I've never been to the city at Christmas before. Though, of course I've seen *Miracle on 34th Street* many times."

As soon as the words escaped her mouth, she wondered if the wine was making her silly. But Damien merely seemed pleased by her answer. Perhaps he was feeling a bit tipsy too. Certainly he looked younger and happier than he had only a few hours before.

"The windows are worth a look. And if you are interested in architecture, the old wooden escalators are still operational down in the basement. The original marble floors are still there too. The sound is fascinating—like nothing else you've ever heard in a department store."

They strolled only half a block and encountered a dazzled crowd gathered outside of Macy's in spite of the falling snow. Brice thought Damien had rather understated things. The windows at Macy's were absolute wonderlands of color and whimsy that made her lust for things she wouldn't need on January second, but wanted just the same.

Seeing her delight in the bright displays, he obligingly peered in every one and even offered to take her up to Santaland so she could speak with the head elf himself about her newly discovered wants and needs.

Brice actually considered it for one moment, but then she decided she had behaved enough like a tourist for one night—which she said to Damien. She also figured that the sorts of wants and needs currently on her mind would shock the dear old elf—which she *didn't* say to her host. Damien shook his head at her refusal and laughed in his peculiar, quiet way. He said she should be a tourist for just a while longer and they would go see the ice-skating rink and Christmas tree at Rockefeller Center.

"And you must see *Prometheus*. It's my favorite statue in the city. We go back a long way."

Suddenly the hair of her nape lifted. Brice caught a glimpse of something—someone—of odd posture and proportions reflected in the dazzling window. The shape

56

seemed to be stalking toward them. She spun about hurriedly, but nothing was there and no one unusual was nearby.

"What is it?" Damien asked, stepping protectively in front of her and scanning the crowds around them.

"Nothing. I think I was anticipating a pickpocket. Or maybe the ghost of Christmas past sneaking up on me. I have to admit I've been a bit of a humbug the last few years."

"Isn't it the ghost of Christmas future who is so frightening?" he asked, turning toward her.

"Not for me," Brice answered flatly. Then she changed the subject before unhappy memories could crowd in and ruin her evening.

As they strolled, Damien acquainted Brice with the city and some of its Christmas traditions, beginning with the literary world but expanding into tales of invention and commerce. She laughed when he told her about the first Macy's Thanksgiving Day parades and how they used to release the balloons at the end of it.

"But then there was a near collision with an airplane and a few hysterical reports from ships at sea about flying monsters attacking New York. That put an end to the practice."

"Cost would probably have ended it eventually," Brice commented. "Those balloons are expensive."

Damien nodded, but she knew he was thinking that the expense was worth it, and that he would choose to give the balloons their freedom if he ran the parade. She wasn't certain that she could be so frivolous, but wished to be. Life would probably be a whole lot more fun if she could sometimes do things and not count the cost.

Brice was surprised to learn that her favorite children's

author and illustrator, Maurice Sendak, had gotten his start decorating the wonderful windows at F.A.O. Schwarz.

"And would you believe that I actually played Father Christmas at a party once?" Damien asked. "It was at a fund-raiser for the Met," He shook his head as though still stunned with disbelief.

"Er . . . is this a trick question?" Brice responded, feeling a smile tug at her lips.

"Not at all. A rhetorical one, maybe. I tried to live up to the part—I swear I did—but my 'Ho ho ho' was a bit inadequate and the adhesive on the beard gave me an ear-to-ear rash that had me scratching in an embarrassing way that made a woman ask me about head lice. There is nothing like a persistent itch to make one grouchy. I'm afraid I spent the night scowling."

Brice nodded gravely. "Holidays! I obviously never played Santa, but I dressed up as an elf at a book-signing once—and to this day I strongly suspect the costume I was given was inauthentic."

"How so?"

"Any elf who wandered around in a skirt that short at the North Pole would end up with frostbite on her— southern regions."

"I see." Damien smiled. "But was the signing fun otherwise?"

"Hardly! I got pinched black and blue. There are a lot of perverts in this world. And apparently, some of them read."

"Indeed."

They strolled along, arms almost touching, not feeling the cold or noticing the people, so wrapped up were they in conversation. A small part of Brice held back from the fun, observing herself and Damien. She found it fascinating that he didn't appeal to her nurturing instincts, such as they were. There was no shy little boy in him. He was, in fact, the most adult man she had ever met. Self-contained, self-sufficient, and yet not self-absorbed.

He also didn't seem the type of male who flirted automatically because it was an easy way to have his ego stroked. They passed many pretty women who smiled at him, but he was never more than polite.

In spite of this, she remained alert. He said nothing, did nothing that wasn't completely polite with her, but Brice had a sense that this man had made up his mind—somewhere between the pâté and the lemon-fennel sorbet—to seduce her. If not tonight, then soon.

It wasn't until they reached the trumpeting angels that lined the plaza leading up to Rockefeller Center that either of them became aware of the drastic increase in snow and a peculiar smell of ozone floating in the air. The wind abruptly changed directions and thrust its icy blades through the crowd, penetrating clothing and flesh and burying the cold in the marrow of their bones.

The crowd shuddered and began muttering. The festive mood was shattered.

"Enough," Damien said, his eyes again scanning the crowd. He did so with what seemed unusual attention.

"I'd never much believed that old saying that freezing to death was a peaceful and pleasant way to go," Brice gasped in agreement. The sudden arctic blast had all but taken her breath away. "Now, all questionable testimonials aside—I'm sure it's untrue."

To both her delight and trepidation, Damien put his arm around her and pulled her into the shelter of his body. It slowed their progress, but it kept the worst of the wind off of her. It also brought them close enough that she could feel the warmth of his spent breath as it hurried by her ear.

"We'll be out of this in a moment," he assured her in a calm voice.

"Have you seen a weather report? Will the storm get much worse?" Brice asked, shuddering at the feeling of cold—a million invisible ants boiling over her skin. She *hated, hated, hated* being cold.

"Yes, and quickly, but we won't see the lightning for another forty-eight hours," Damien said. He looked excited and suddenly energized. Pulling a strange device swathed in rubber from his coat pocket, he pressed a button and called for his car, telling the driver where to meet them. Seeing her curious look, he told her: "I can't use a cell phone. Something about the magnetic field of my body scrambles the signal. It's worse in lightning storms. So I use a walkie-talkie when I must be out."

"Oh . . . are you sure about the lightning?" Brice asked, wanting to talk about his *magnetic field*, but deciding it was a bit personal.

"Yes. Sometimes, if we're lucky, we get just the right combination of atmospheric conditions for a light show. The roof of Ruthven Tower is mainly made of iron, and it attracts the electricity."

"And this is a good thing?" Brice asked. She allowed him to guide her through the crowds, keeping between her and the street and making sure that no one touched her.

"Yes, oddly enough. You can't imagine what those gargoyles look like with Saint Elmo's fire dancing over them. In a really big storm, a sort of aurora-borealis effect happens as well. Such storms are rare—but I think we may get one for Christmas."

"You can tell?"

"I have a sort of inner barometer when it comes to the weather," Damien answered. He paused at the curb, and his black sedan rolled to an all but silent stop in front of them. He quickly ushered Brice into the quiet warmth of the car. "Miss Ashton?"

"Brice," she corrected, relieved to have hot air washing over her chilled skin. He seemed to forget that she preferred to be called by her first name every time he got lost in a moment of reflection or inner debate. The habit made him seem very English—and charmingly old-fashioned.

"Brice." Damien turned to her. His expression was pensive. "I have a suggestion to make. I fully realize that it is very forward of me, and will understand completely if you would prefer not to accept."

She nodded encouragingly when he paused, but her heart had began a heavy beating. It seemed that she'd been right about the effects of pâté.

"Would you consider being my guest tonight? I mean, staying with me rather than going to your hotel?" He waited, head tilted to one side. "For that matter, please stay as long as you like. If the weathermen are correct, travel during this storm will be all but impossible."

Brice blinked, willing the delightful fog of wine to retreat just a bit so she could give the matter some thought. Before she could answer, he went on: "I have a large library filled with rare and unusual reference material which I would be reluctant to let out of my possession, and it might be that you would find working there more comfortable than being at the hotel and having to commute through this weather...which is getting worse," he added, looking out the car window and frowning at the thickening snow.

Oh—he was offering his library!

Brice swallowed, feeling foolish. Then she was staring into his heated gaze and reconsidering what he was saying.

His library! That was cheating! It was the perfect lure—way better than the clichéd, *Come up and see my etchings.* He knew her too well.

Brice made herself stop the words of acceptance from hurrying off her tongue and to think carefully. Her impulse was to say yes—*yes!*—yes! She felt very at home with Damien Ruthven now, and absolutely lusted after the contents of his library that he dangled as a lure.

But she also seemed to be lusting after the man, and quite possibly he after her. There was an attraction between them that didn't appear to end with the respect of one intellect for another of close kin. She realized, with a small shock of revelation, that her physical desire over the last few hours had actually become a low-grade fire that burned the nerves just beneath the skin. And it intensified every time they touched. Did he feel it too? Looking into his eyes, she had to believe that he did.

Perhaps it was mostly the result of her hormonal cycle and a long period of abstentious behavior, but there was also something about Damien Ruthven that fueled these flames and made her feel recklessly impulsive.

Maybe she was incinerating brain cells to fuel her libido, and that was why she wasn't receiving any inner warnings that she should be cautious even when she gave herself time for reflection.

As though truly able to read her mind, he said: "You hesitate—but ask yourself how often will you have this chance. You don't want to spend Christmas alone in a hotel anyway. How dreary that would be."

No, Brice admitted, she didn't want to stay at the hotel. She wanted to spend the holidays in front of a roaring fire in Damien's library, drinking hot mulled wine and talking about Byron with this handsome man who seemed to truly understand him, and who didn't think her peculiar for being fascinated by the dead poet.

And supposing—just considering the improbable— that something did happen between her and Damien, would that be so terrible?

No, her body answered emphatically.

"Can it be that you doubt me? Do I need to reassure you that my intentions are honorable?" His dark eyes were suddenly dancing.

Brice thought unexpectedly about what Caroline Lamb had written in her diary after Lady Westmoreland's ball where she had first encountered Byron. *Mad, bad, dangerous to know. That beautiful face is my fate.* Brice had always had little sympathy for the spoiled, neurotic creature who had chased Byron shamelessly, but she finally understood what the woman meant. Though Brice had always doubted tales of love—or even of overwhelming lust—at first sight, she had to admit that if she were younger and less wounded—or simply more romantic—she might similarly be thinking of Damien as her doom.

"Does your silence mean yes, that you have reservations? If so, I believe I can dredge up a proper speech to reassure you."

She wasn't at all certain that she wanted to hear that he would be a gentleman, so she interrupted him before he could make any such declaration.

"No speech is necessary. I'm not concerned about your . . . integrity. And thank you for the offer," Brice added, her manners coming to the fore. "I gladly accept—on condition that we actually talk about Byron. That is what brought me here, after all."

"Oh, we will, I'm certain." And then, almost under his breath Brice heard him add, "Given his ego, there's probably no avoiding it."

"What does Ninon say about this?"

—*Louis XIV*

The night
Shows stars and women in a better light.

—*Byron*

"My honored father—I am eleven years old. I am big and strong, but shall certainly fall ill if I continue to assist at three masses every day, especially on account of one performed by a great, gouty, fat canon who takes at least twelve minutes to get through the Epistle and the Gospel, and who the choirboys are obliged to put back on his feet after each genuflexion. This all depressing, I can assure you. Well, I am done twiddling with the rosary beads while mumbling Aves, Paters, and Credos. The present moment is the one for me to inform you that I have decided to no longer be a girl, but to become a boy. As I am now a son, it is your duty to take over my education immediately, and I shall tell you how it is to be done."

—*Letter of Ninon de Lenclos to her father*

Chapter Five

Brice looked out of her bedroom window, marveling at the glow that suffused the city. The worst of the atmospheric violence was over, though not gone. The wind still howled intermittently, as though the sly storm were snoring and napping off the coast. She had the feeling that it was gathering strength for another assault rather than resting up before it moved on. If she were paranoid, she might even think that that storm was encircling the city, zeroing in on Ruthven Tower.

Brice had thought she understood about cold. She had a wool coat, a thick scarf, lined gloves, and a highly evolved mammalian brain that supposedly allowed her to prepare for a changing environment. But this storm was something different, a thing never encountered in southern climes. She might as well be a naked babe stranded on an unsheltered rock in a blizzard for all the protection her clothing afforded her. The storm felt like a killer, a vicious evil stalking the city. She hoped the homeless had found shelter before dark, because Death rode the frozen air and would happily gather up any souls left alone in the cold streets.

Yet it wasn't the cold keeping her awake now. It was her too-busy brain.

In spite of the freakish encounter with a suddenly hostile Nature, her evening had been wonderful, and Damien Ruthven had kept his word—or implied word— that he would be a gentleman while she remained in his home. When midnight crept around, he'd poured a brandy, shown her to her room, and left her with nothing more than a smile—and nerves that shrieked because she hadn't been given a good-night kiss. Or more.

Brice got back into bed and tried for a third time to get comfortable.

What was wrong? She'd had a hot bath and stepped into her favorite nightgown. Since her bed was a confection of down, comfortable and warm, and she was not usually of an insomniac temperament, Brice should have had no trouble dropping off to sleep. Yet here it was, three A.M., and she was still wakeful, in bed and then out again like a jack-in-the-box.

It was probably the library, calling to her. Rare tomes had a way of whispering when there was no other noise to drown out their honeyed words.

Brice rolled over, pulling the comforter over her ears, and tried humming herself to sleep. It didn't help. She felt restless, feverish. And Damien's face kept appearing before her even with her eyes firmly closed.

Something *was* calling to her, that was for sure. Deciding that it had better be the books and not her host, she finally got up. She slipped on a robe and quietly opened her door. Nothing stirred.

Satisfied that she was unnoticed, Brice padded down

the short hall that led to the first floor of the library. She'd find something to read—that was the ticket. Something boring and statistical.

She paused inside the opened French doors, listening carefully. The library had a cathedral-like silence, which was not to suggest that it was conducive to peaceful prayer. Any historian could tell you that murders happened in cathedrals too.

Something was waiting for her. Something that might be very good. It might also be very bad.

Brice shivered and cursed her too-active imagination. This was ridiculous. Nothing was here—nothing! But she decided—for no particular reason, she assured herself—against turning on the lights while she wandered around. Instead, she climbed carefully up the steep spiral stair, relying on the city glow from the tall windows to show her the way into the aerie.

In that eerie light the room looked vaguely familiar, and after a moment of searching her memory, Brice realized that the library was almost a duplicate of one in Newstead Abbey. It was even furnished in a similar manner to one of the paintings of the interior done during Byron's life.

She looked about quickly for a skull cup, like the one Byron had made of the monk's skeleton he had found in the garden as a child, but there was none about.

Of course not. The similarity might even be an accident of taste. Newstead Abbey was a mansion built on the graves of the dead. She had never liked its setting. Who could live in a cemetery? This place wasn't like that at all. Well, perhaps a little. It was just that the spiral stairs reminded her of something—maybe a scaffold in the moonlight—and the placement of the windows that brought Byron's ancient home to mind.

Not pausing again until she reached the final tier of books, she climbed carefully up the last curving stairs and began inching along the catwalk. The railing reached her waist, but she suffered some strange form of vertigo so that it didn't seem high enough to provide safety.

Brice was only half surprised when she reached a set of glass doors and saw her host standing outside, looking over the city.

His "magnetic" field had probably called her up here.

Or maybe she was actually still abed and dreaming all this.

She wasn't taken aback, but the longer she thought about it, the more his being outside seemed peculiar. For one thing, the weather was still bitter. No more snow fell, but the temperatures was below freezing. Damien's occasional breath was actually turning to frost and falling down about his feet.

Brice exhaled sharply, making her eyes focus. *Bare feet?* Damien wasn't wearing a coat or shoes. Also, he wasn't so much standing as squatting on the ledge, a careless hand resting on an iron chain. He looked more than a little bit like the large gargoyles he perched between. As she watched, steam began rising from his body in a cloud, and it swirled about him in a slow counterclockwise cyclone.

Torn between the temptation of opening the door and asking him why he was out in the night, and stealing away before she was noticed spying on him, she hesitated in the shadows.

He was beautiful, as beautiful as any midnight that had ever been. And it was not just his body that was appealing. She had found her prejudices dying out one after the other as they dined. Brice had barely noticed when the first small lie fell out of her mouth. She was used to social fabrication, but usually felt at least a small qualm when she involved herself in one. But not last night. And what should have been social lies, social politeness, had soon turned out as truth: She'd come to trust him—to actually want to speak her mind to him without reservation. And, lacking her previous distaste and wariness, resistance to his native charm was proving much harder to come by.

But he was also very odd, and—at least for her—maybe dangerous. She knew this, though she couldn't say from what direction danger would come. However nonspecific, she believed her intuition. As sure as the sun would show up in the east tomorrow morning, she knew he would be trouble for her if she allowed herself to get any closer.

Or maybe it was guilt speaking. Could it be that simple?

Brice exhaled slowly and thought hard about the possibility.

Former friends—all well-intentioned people—had often said to her in smug, self-congratulatory voices that they, too, had suffered loss and yet survived to go on to better lives. They said she was clinging to her grief because of guilt—guilt that didn't belong to her—and using it to push people away. At the time she had thought it nonsense. But were they right after all? Had she used tragedy to keep the world at bay?

On the few occasions when she had been confronted with this theory, Brice had firmly resisted the urge to tell these people that their losses—whatever they were— were unlikely to have carried the same terror and sense of helplessness that came from being trapped upside down in a car while an icy stream rushed in through a shattered windshield. That, while it was sad they had lost whomever, they had never watched the person they loved most in the world drown while they looked on, unable to help because their own broken body was pinned in place by a crumpled dashboard and a root-choked riverbank with branches sharp as spears.

She hadn't said anything then, but she had been angry. And only those who understood her need to grieve—and, yes, to feel guilt for surviving when Mark hadn't—had remained her friends. All others had been dismissed from her life.

And once the first anguish passed, she had adjusted. Mostly. There had only been one time, a black midnight when she had been very lonely and more than a little drunk. She didn't like to think about it, but that February night she had almost been tempted into the suicide tango; a short, passionate dance with death that seemed to offer the only quick and easy way out of the guilt and grief and loss.

But a kindly Fate had intervened, and She had come in an interesting guise. At the moment that Brice had reached for the bottle of tranquilizers on her bedside table, she had seen Byron—or rather, his photograph—staring up at her from the pages of a book of poetry. His eyes were intense, his lips slightly smiling. *Leaving so soon?* he seemed to ask.

The great poet had looked better than the Grim Reaper—braver and kinder—so she had danced with him instead.

Brice exhaled slowly. Her breath was shaky and irregular. Even now, the memory of how close she had come to giving up frightened her.

They said that some sorrows grew sweet with time, and that bitter fruit could ripen into something beautiful. But that hadn't been true of her loss. Still, she had thought she'd managed to keep the bitterness from poisoning all of her heart and the rest of her life. Was it so strange that she could never look back and think there was some silver lining to what had happened? Was it strange that she never looked back at all, period?

Brice shook her head sharply.

Enough.

It was true that she rarely felt entirely free. And very little happened in her life. Very little that was exciting or dangerous, that is—idiocy and annoyance happened all the time. But these days, though she wasn't carefree, she was rarely lonely either. Reawakened curiosity about Byron was always with her. The fascinating questions—and sometimes even more fascinating answers—were her constant companions. They kept the shadows away while the old grief and guilt slowly diminished in size and lost the cruel fangs and claws that tore at her dreams. And if she still had some problems with being confined in small spaces, at least she wasn't having panic attacks anymore. She *was* healing.

But she had to admit the memory of her grief was still there, deep in her once-broken bones, and sometimes—like at Christmas, and perhaps especially now that she had met a living man who fascinated her—those bones were bound to hurt.

She looked out at Damien, so still that he seemed made of stone, so beautiful that he stole her breath away, and so distant that he didn't seem human. Was that why she liked him? Because he wasn't anything like the man she had loved and lost?

"Bah," Brice said softly. "It's all psycho claptrap. I'm just coming down with a cold."

She touched a hand to her face. Yes, there was fever. She was ill and probably hallucinating. At the very least, she was exhausted and her judgment was therefore impaired. The throbbing in her body was not desire, it was sickness. What she needed was sleep, the kind to be had in the solitude of her room.

Sighing, half with self-disgust and half with regret, Brice retreated along the catwalk, staying in the shadows as she returned to her room.

She hadn't opened the door to join him. It was probably just as well. Though she appealed to him with those eyes that studied everything so intently while her brow furrowed and she rested her small chin in her delicate hand, he needed to be wary, to think things through.

Naturally, her open admiration of him—of Byron; he needed to be clear about that—was a lure. It was difficult to resist a woman who spoke of him with such passion and intensity, whose adoration and longing shone like a candle in the winter night that had become his soul.

But he needed to practice caution for that very reason. She wasn't the first wounded woman who had called to his tender side, and he hadn't forgotten that such affairs, when rushed, nearly always ended in tragedy. Even when allowed to develop in the fullness of time, they still often ended badly—in heartbreak and hatred and death, if they went far wrong. And cruel indifference and apathy, even if they did not. His memory was a graveyard of dead loves, and he still mourned them on the occasions that he allowed himself to pass by.

No, it was best that she had turned away tonight, that she hadn't ventured out to see the wildness in his eyes and the network of scars on his chest, and started asking questions. What she had witnessed was odd enough behavior in the hours just before dawn.

Perhaps she would think it all a winter's dream and not ask difficult questions in the morning.

Damien wasn't at all sure what he'd been doing outside anyway. Yes, he always enjoyed storms, and this kind of storm was particularly rare and invigorating, but it was too cold even for him. And though he was feeling uneasy, it didn't seem likely that he would actually be able to spot any danger from up there.

Danger.

He couldn't see anything, yet danger lurked nearby. In spite of what the private detectives had told him, he knew in his bones that peril lay ahead. He had developed a sort of sixth sense that warned him when doom was closing in. It had saved him more than once—from financial disaster, from an earthquake, several times from ambush, and once from a drug addict set to rob and murder him for the price of a fix. That instinct said mortal peril was near.

Brice had seemed to sense something, too, while they were out in the streets.

Damien hoped passionately that the warning was not also directed at her. Because he wanted Brice Ashton close by. He wanted to learn her secrets, her desires, her dreams. And he was fairly certain that he was going to make love to her eventually as well. The attraction was so bloody strong. He might even show her who he truly was, even if it was the most reckless thing he had ever done in his long, long life.

It was a terrifying thought. But it could happen—and easily. He knew himself, knew that the old longing for companionship she stirred would eventually overwhelm him. Frustration and loneliness had been a growing shadow on his spirit. In time it began to stain the soul as surely as the blackest of the deadly sins. Damien wasn't a glutton—*usually*, he amended, thinking about the dinner he'd just shared with Brice. He did not envy, did not lust after others' possessions. He wasn't even slothful. But he did hunger for companionship with the appetite of a starving man. He thirsted for a chance to be honest about who he was.

He wanted to give his heart again.

From the moment of his transformation, he had held back from people—from his lovers especially. Always he was wary. Always he held back his heart. And the secret of his identity, and his unnaturally long life, was as safe as the day he had received it from Dippel and the gods. But this time, Damien was sure he'd tell the truth to Brice.

Because the truth will set you free? an inner voice asked, mocking his romantic sentiments.

Perhaps. There were good reasons why men confessed their sins.

Damien jumped down from the railing and turned to the doors where Brice had stood. Her perfume lingered in the air. He could smell it on the hard, cold night.

And even if the truth didn't free him completely, he would let himself lose his heart to this woman—and do so before he lost his nerve and again pulled back from the warmth of life, and possibly even love, that she offered.

But he shouldn't do anything until he knew it was safe to share his information with Brice. He would wait. For a while. He had to.

All men are intrinsical rascals. And I am sorry that, not being a dog, I can't bite them.

—*From the letters of Lord Byron, October 20, 1821*

Rochefoucauld told me once that a man of sense may love like a madman but not like a fool. In this I agree.

—*From the letters of Ninon de Lenclos*

Like a lovely tree,
She grew to womanhood, and betweenwhiles
Rejected several suitors, just to learn
How to accept a better man.

—*Byron*

Chapter Six

Brice pressed into the frosted glass, looking downward. Yesterday afternoon she had seen lots of people scurrying by. Many of them wore bright knit caps with their black coats, and they had looked a bit like the world's biggest bed of asters pushing through the snow. This morning there were fewer pedestrians, and they walked hurriedly, postures hunched, telling her that bitter cold had settled on the city. There were no cars either. The plows hadn't been out yet to scrape away the snow left by the freakish storm.

Frowning, she pulled back from the cold glass. The scene seemed somewhat sinister for Christmas Eve, but wasn't that because she hated the cold and didn't know how to cope with it? Maybe this air of desertion was perfectly normal for the city. Perhaps its inhabitants were all at home by a fire drinking eggnog. Or at Macy's, doing last-minute shopping. Brice didn't celebrate Christmas now that her parents and husband were gone, but others did.

She pushed her bleak thoughts away and turned her mind to Damien instead. Which reminded her of something that needed seeing to. Brice reached into her cosmetic bag and brought out her birth-control pills. She was glad that she was still taking them. She had tried giving them up twice after Mark's death, but had been reduced to a nervous wreck who cried at the slightest provocation. The choice had been to take the pill again or turn to antidepressants and tranquilizers. After her thoughts turned once to suicide, hormones had seemed safer. And now . . . useful?

She swallowed the pill, chasing it with a mouthful of tap water, then turned to the rest of her travel arsenal.

Brice was vain enough—and attracted enough, in spite of last night's odd show—to dress carefully for Damien. She just hoped that she wasn't too obvious in her selection of clothes. She didn't want to appear as desperate for attention as an S.O.S. from a sinking ship. She also wasn't looking to get eye-fucked by any other person who happened to be passing by. Eye-fondled maybe, but nothing more than that.

Brice heard herself giggle. The sound was startling in its giddy youthfulness. It made her sound as if she had suddenly dropped thirty critical I.Q. points. She couldn't help it, though. Imagine using such a crude expression in front of Damien! She could see his eyebrows darting upward and his lips compressing in disapproval. The thought was hilarious.

Still, she was a grown woman now. She didn't giggle like a teenager, even at amusing things. Especially not when it made her sound stupid.

Not that she had reached the point where she was chasing after the fountain of youth with collagen injections and Botox, or throwing pennies in wishing wells and saying prayers to the evening star that age be gentle with her face and body. However, sometimes she did wear makeup—especially when she wasn't well rested and needed a lift. Which she most definitely did need this morning. The previous night had been anything but restful.

Shaking her head, she broke the seal on a new tube of mascara. She leaned toward the mirror, opened her mouth slightly and did her best not to blink while the mascara wand was near her eye. The only thing worse than botched mascara was crooked eyeliner. No one looked good with asymmetrical eyes. She stroked carefully, making small humming noises. Finally, satisfied with the effect on her right lashes, she moved to her left eye.

Of course, most men didn't understand what a compliment it was for a woman to wear heels and mascara for them. They didn't appreciate that a woman who wore them was really saying, *very well! I don't expect you to do the impossible and want me just for my mind. I will give you something for the eyes since you like that part of me more.* And, sure enough, though she always hoped for more, they usually didn't look beyond the packaging if it pleased them sufficiently. They figured that beautiful women were like beautiful weather, or the Detroit Lions finally winning a game, or a cold beer with baby-back ribs: things to be enjoyed and not questioned.

Certainly her last few blind dates had been with men who seemed barely bright enough to know which end of the spoon to eat with. They'd been sufficiently handsome and reasonably good-natured, but not the sort of choice a woman would make if she liked her men complicated.

The last one—*Luke? Duke?*— had been as easy to read as a nametag, and about as interesting. He'd smiled a lot because he liked her legs, liked her breasts, and generally liked that she was a woman. He was okay company for dinner, too, if you didn't switch topics too quickly. You couldn't change conversational gears on a guy whose brain had a bad transmission—not if you wanted him to keep up. Yeah, Luke, Duke, or whatever his name was had been extremely simple.

They almost all were. Even the less pleasant ones who picked on waiters and cabbies. The picky, whiny ones who usually looked great, but who could be offered a place at the right hand of God and still find fault with the seating arrangements. There was plenty of nastiness there underneath those expensively toned bodies and fake tans, but even then there was no depth.

But Damien Ruthven was not most men. He might notice her efforts and understand. Would that be good? Bad? Did she want a man who could actually read her thoughts and guess her intentions?

Maybe. For a while.

Brice blinked at her grinning reflection, again distracted from her unpleasant thoughts by Damien's shadow, which hovered constantly at the back of her mind.

Should she wear perfume? Did he like it? Perhaps just a tiny spritz, misted into the air while she walked through it.

Her heart began somersaulting the moment she walked into the library. Her tread was more measured than her thoughts, but even so, because of her heels, there was a definite swish in her walk. Until she saw Damien. After that, her knees got a little shaky and she had to brace herself.

She supposed the feeling of being unbalanced could only be expected when her stomach was doing back-flips and her emotions were standing on their heads, but she didn't care for the way the cardiac palpitations made her sweater jitter over her heart. She had seen Damien doing a gargoyle impersonation last night, hadn't she? And she'd been alarmed? Thought it abnormal?

It seemed hard to credit the memory this morning. He was dressed as a professor might be, in a tweed coat with the obligatory suede patches at the elbows. Yet somehow, in spite of the sober clothing, he failed to look like a scholar.

It was the eyes, she decided. He looked like Don Juan misdressed by an amateur costumer who did not know what play he was supplying.

Actually, with his hair drawn back and tied with a velvet band, Damien looked exactly like portraits she'd seen of Lord Byron, except for a comma that fell over his brow.

Brice almost groaned. *Not again.* She had gone over this all last night. She had Byron on the brain. It had to be pheromones. Or hormones. Maybe she should just sleep with Damien—let him seduce her before she lost all reason. She had a feeling that resisting him would be an impossible test of willpower, a test she was bound to fail soon if the mascara and heels were any indication, and probably without a great deal of regret. Why not embrace the fall and get her brain back right away?

Brice felt her lips part, but her voice failed when Damien looked up and smiled. That small bend of his lips didn't help her heart at all. Her sweater fluttered more violently.

"Come in. There is someone I want you to meet." He held out a hand to her. "Did you sleep well?"

"Yes, thank you," she lied, looking around the room and seeing no one. She didn't take Damien's hand, since her own was trembling, but she didn't pull away when he laid it on the small of her back and urged her around the desk.

"I'm afraid he's shy. The poor chap persists in hiding under the desk when strangers are here."

"Oh." Understanding at last, Brice smiled and knelt down, pretty sure that she knew what awaited under the writing table.

"His name is Mace. He's mostly Karen's dog since I travel so much, but she has allowed me to be the godfather."

"Mace? Strange name." Brice offered her hand, being careful to move slowly toward the small, dark ball in the shadows. "Hello, sweetie. Will you come out to say hi?"

Reassured by the soft voice and slow movement, the tiny beast crept out into the light. Her first sight of him made Brice gasp softly. The poor creature was a mass of scar tissue with odd clumps of hair growing in uneven patches on his head and body.

"Well, he is rather repellent-looking, don't you think? Poor chap got caught in a fire. His family died. He's mostly blind now, so nobody else wanted him. No one else thought he'd live." Damien's voice was brisk, demanding she not comment on any sentiment she suspected might lurk in his bosom for this maimed animal.

Brice also wondered if she had just been tested. If so, had she passed?

"You poor angel," she whispered, caressing the terrier's stubbed ears and earning a small lick in reward. "What a brave doggie you are. How sweet and good."

"We have some excellent brioche and coffee," Damien

said after she and Mace shared a couple more caresses. "Mace likes his with lots of cream and sugar."

"You have brioche and coffee every morning?" She smiled up at Damian. He looked good even from that angle.

"Not every morning." Damien helped her to her feet. His hands were warm and gentle. "Sometimes we have croissants and tea."

"With milk and sugar, though," Brice guessed, feeling her smile widening. Somehow, the dog's presence had—probably ridiculously—reassured her about Damien's character. So what if he had the semi-suicidal habit of sitting on the parapets of a high-rise? He couldn't be all bad if he loved this wretched scrap of a canine.

"Of course. Mace is now an English dog. He takes his tea in the proper manner."

"I see. And Karen doesn't mind you teaching him bad eating habits."

"I know the Heart Association would not approve, but we figured that Mace faced down an almost fatal fire, loss of his family, and a long, painful recovery that amazed his vet. Cholesterol doesn't scare him."

"And I face literary critics at breakfast. Cholesterol doesn't scare me either. I hope you've saved some for me," Brice teased, taking the saucer of milky coffee and torn brioche from Damien's hand and bending down to offer it to Mace.

The dog sniffed, then woofed appreciatively. The sound was barely a wheeze, and Brice realized that his vocal cords must have been damaged too.

She watched for a moment, enjoying the exaggerated care with which Mace plucked out the pastry. Each bite was followed with what sounded like a sigh of pleasure.

She half expected him to somehow pick up his saucer and slurp his tea, but though he was probably clever enough to manage it, he was too well-mannered for such boorishness. He lapped quietly.

"I can't tell you how overjoyed I am to have you facing me at breakfast. You are so much more attractive than my stack of manuscripts," Damien murmured, pouring out another cup and offering it to her as she stood. Before she could think what to say, he changed the subject by adding: "Now, there is absolutely no rush, but I have moved a desk in here for you and selected a few tomes that I think might amuse you."

Brice sipped her coffee, eyes rolling up in her head as she sighed with pleasure.

"Jamaican Blue Mountain," she said. "You hedonist, you! I have to special-order it—and then only on my birthday since it costs about the same as God's wisdom tooth."

"And how much are the Lord's teeth going for these days?" Damien asked, amused.

"Forty-eight dollars a pound. Plus shipping."

"Well, Mace insists on the best."

"And I adore him. He has exquisite taste." She let her eyes remain closed as she savored the scent and taste of the coffee. Brice couldn't be sure, but she was fairly certain that Damien took the moment to study her.

"I'm sure it's mutual." Slight amusement crept into his voice and made her eyes pop open. "I thought it was a man's heart that one reached through the stomach. For women it's supposed to be . . . what? Diamonds, that make her heart go pitter-pat?"

"I've never doubted that cliché," Brice answered, making her voice brisk. "In most cases, dogs are man's best friend, diamonds a girl's. But I don't see that a liking for one should preclude the other. Diamonds are, after all, merely an economic consideration left over from the days when women didn't work outside the home. In any event, it isn't my heart that the coffee has reached."

It was something a bit lower.

No, that's Damien, not the coffee.

Oh, shut up, will you? Brice pleaded with her chatty subconscious.

"You are suddenly looking quite thoughtful," Damien said. "Surely it is not all the contemplation of canines and gems that is making you frown."

"No, it isn't." Brice forced herself to smile and did some subject-changing of her own. "Look, don't simply be polite. Will it bother you if I work in here?" She hoped he would say no, but needed to ask. She was fussy about where she wrote and imagined Damien might well be too. She didn't turn to look at the books he'd brought. If they were wonderful, perhaps even Byron's memoirs, she would forget everything else, including her polite question about whether he really wanted her in his library. And Damien and his coffee deserved better.

She shivered. The books were beginning to whisper to her.

"Not at all," Damien assured her, his voice sincere. "That's why I moved the desk in. I look forward to spending the day with you. I have a manuscript that I need to start reading, but I'm entirely at your disposal otherwise."

Polite society pretended shock as polite society must, but it was only a thin veneer of morality that cloaked their own unwholesome deeds.

Brice looked up from her book sometime later, and seeing Damien's dark eyes on her she said: "You know, I feel as though I have lived with Byron for so long that we're married."

"So you are frustrated, affectionate and overly familiar with his irritating habits?" Damien's eyes twinkled.

Brice laughed. "Exactly."

"And how do you think Byron feels about you after this long association?" As always, Damien's odd questions seemed somehow important.

"I don't know," she answered, playing the let's pretend game fairly seriously. "If he is somehow aware of what I am doing, I hope he is pleased that I am putting much of the record straight. He's also maybe annoyed at the bits I've gotten wrong."

"Do you know, I think you are right. About him being pleased. So much of his life as known today is a collection of malicious tall tales."

"Still, it must irritate his shade that this matter has been left to me when he so clearly intended that his own words be published." Brice frowned. "It adds pressure. And there is the eternal frustration of making the thing on the page match the thing in my mind. And that presupposes that the version of truth I have in my head is one that he would recognize. Perhaps I've reordered the facts of his life to suit my own desires and expectations. I am, after all, female and a child of the late twentieth century. This has to have influenced my perceptions of his words and deeds."

Damien nodded, his expression oddly sympathetic. His next words were also revealing. "That is the plight of writers everywhere. If one is fortunate, the outlines of truth do eventually appear, and something inside tells us we finally have it right. Where many go wrong is in backing down from the truth too soon—taking the first easy answer that presents itself and not waiting for that inner confirmation. I suppose it's understandable. It is always frightening to look history in the face, because if you stare long enough, history looks back and the gaze is not always kind. Some of our ancestors were evil people."

So, there was something there—a hidden side to her host.

Carefully Brice asked: "Do you write? I mean prose? Or poetry?"

"Every once in a while," Damien admitted, but didn't specify which. He also didn't offer to share any of his writing with her.

Brice didn't ask again, but she was betting he wrote poetry. It was so intensely personal an undertaking that most poets never talked about their work. Certainly not with strangers.

The thought was intriguing. She added it to the list of possible explanations for the mysteries that she sensed made up the very complicated Damien Ruthven.

It was Damien who next interrupted the office quiet. He looked up from the manuscript he was reading and sighed heavily.

"Sometimes I fear for the English language," he said to Brice. "I suspect that many of these would-be writers use their dictionaries—supposing they actually possess them—as doorstops. Or maybe as stepstools to reach the stash of marijuana hidden in their bedroom closet, which they smoke in preference to attending classes or reading books."

"That bad, huh?" she asked understandingly, looking up from her notes. They were annotated photocopies of old journals, badly faded and written with very creative French spelling. "I don't think French is in any better shape—and it never was. The spelling in these old journals is absolutely villainous. I consider it an ancient conspiracy to keep me from understanding them."

"No, the French are probably not in any better shape. No one in the Western world is. And yet . . ." Damien shook his head and dropped the manuscript on the table. "I cannot believe that all this purposeless literary evil was brought about through nothing but educational laziness. Perhaps the freedom from grammatical tyranny will lead to the free expression of great ideas. I admit it hasn't happened yet, but perhaps some day."

"Perhaps."

"I always hated it when someone told me I must think a certain way because great men before me had thought in a particular mode, or used some accepted literary device. I refuse to approach my writing that way. I'd be bored to tears."

It took an effort to find something nice to say, because Brice was not in the habit of having charitable thoughts toward those who arrogantly presumed to tell the world what was literature and what was not, but she found that she could be approving when she thought about Damien's job from the viewpoint of a beleaguered reader in a superstore trying to decide what to buy rather than as a writer being flayed in print.

"There are readers who refuse to approach *reading* that way, too. That's why they look to you for guidance when sorting the wheat from the chaff," she pointed out, surprised and then ashamed that she had never considered that he might take pride in his work as a critic. But, of course, that was writing too, if of a different nature. "You would not be as popular as you are if you were just one more among the many, a voice no different from all the others. I don't want you to think I'm flattering you, but there are moments when you almost sound like Byron—supposing he was alive and writing literary criticism."

She didn't add that Byron had been a real opinionated bastard.

Damien colored at this praise and then nodded once. The gesture lacked his usual grace, and she sensed his deep perturbation, though she couldn't imagine why he would be upset by what she had said.

Perhaps he hadn't been talking about his reviews. Maybe he meant his other writing. Before she could correct herself, he spoke again.

"Thank you," he said. Then, changing the subject quickly: "Your own writing is rather brave. I suspect that you must bring your editor to elation. Or despair. His emotion is likely dependent upon whether he likes interfering with his writers' thoughts or not."

"He wouldn't dare." Then, against her better judgment and the unwritten rule about asking a critic why they like your work, she joked, "Why do you say I'm brave? Because I dare to use semicolons?"

"No. Because you dare to ask uncommon questions, dare to challenge history's hasty and often self-interested conclusions. Because you dare to tell the truth about the people you examine, regardless of entrenched dogma or the literary sainthood conferred on a subject. You dare to say that the emperor has no clothes." Damien's dark eyes burned with the same intensity as his voice, and she didn't doubt his sincerity. He added with a sudden smile, "Do you know how many people will be enraged by this biography?"

It was Brice's turn to blush. She'd often been told that she was beautiful, often told she was clever, often told she had a nice turn of phrase for a historian. No one had ever thought to compliment her courage in telling the unpopular truths that sometimes came to light when she investigated historic personages. It was thrilling to hear it now.

"Thank you." She cleared her throat. "I do know, actually. That's why I always try to be thorough. And fair. It wouldn't do to gore someone's ox unless they truly deserved it. Or to canonize them if they are really villains. And, those lofty considerations aside, I have to be able to face my critics too."

He nodded.

"Of course, I'm not so judgmental about people in everyday life," she assured him.

"But I'm certain you are," Damien answered. "We all are. It is just that you choose to accept many of society's standards as your own and therefore forgive what might otherwise annoy you. It is also probable that you don't bother to examine the people about you too closely. There are, after all, so many of them. And so many are boring."

Brice thought about that and then nodded slowly. "Anyway, who wants to know all the flaws in our loved one?" she said. "Relationships are difficult enough. It's best to keep a few illusions."

"You are working on a biography of Ninon de Lenclos?" Damien asked, again switching topics abruptly. She had the feeling that his agile mind had raced ahead without her. If she stayed here long, she'd have to find some sort of yoga for the brain so she could be more flexible in their conversations. "That is a bold move indeed—to attempt to explain one of the world's first feminists, who is also one of the world's great enigmas."

He leaned close, and Brice reflexively started to cover her notes, but then she decided she was being silly. He might be a critic, but he wouldn't judge her rough drafts—assuming he could even read her messy comments, scrawled in shorthand.

"Yes. I'm afraid that she is my other pet obsession, and I am finally writing about her."

"A worthy choice for an obsession." Perhaps sensing her discomfort, Damien leaned back a few inches. "And what do you find most fascinating about *la belle dame?*"

"Everything," Brice answered promptly. "She's a mystery. I know what she did, but not why or how she did it."

"For instance?" Now he sounded like a professor. Damien even steepled his fingers as leaned back in his chair. The leather creaked softly.

Brice's eyes narrowed, but once again she chose to follow his conversational lead and see where it might take them. She had never really had the luxury of having someone with whom to discuss her thoughts.

"How could this woman have managed to retain her place as the great beauty and lover—and thinker—of seventeenth-century Parisian society for all those decades without being burned at the stake? Especially when the queen and the church were both after her. Why, she even admitted she sold her soul to a 'dark man' so that she could enjoy eternal beauty. And in spite of this heresy, Molière, reluctant Voltaire—even the great Cardinal Richelieu wanted to know her and were influenced by her views. Horace Walpole called her *Notre-Dame des Amours*. Queen Christina of Sweden befriended her, even though Ninon ran a scandalous school for lovemaking. The highest members of society were honored to sleep with her, or at least receive training at her hands. Hell's bells! The last young man she refused as a lover, when she was *sixty-five*, killed himself!"

"That is probably because the Chevalier de Villiers was

her natural son," Damien pointed out apologetically. "It may not have been her charms that made him choose suicide. Finding out that the object of your desire is your own mother has had that ill effect before—as the Greeks will attest."

"So the rumors say. But even if it's true, it doesn't contradict my point. She was still beautiful and desirable at sixty-five. And in spite of this very odd life, was she not thought to be *the happiest creature who ever was*? How did she manage it? She wasn't sociopathic. Ninon had morals. She lived in an era of repression and yet thrived. And the legends of her beauty into old age! They didn't do plastic surgery back then. There was no Botox, no dermabrasion. I've heard talk of her skin potions, but no recipes were ever found. I don't buy this story of a dark man bringing her a magic elixir. Yet there must be some secret that everyone has overlooked. Certainly it wasn't clean living—though she did bathe every day, which was a novelty at that time."

Frustration colored Brice's voice, and she forgot not to lecture on her favorite subject. "The trouble is that the further I get from her, the more difficulty I have backtracking to the truth. It's like you said—history has built up a self-interested myth around her, and so far this cult of personality has pretty well defied direct investigation."

"I understand," Damien said slowly. "There have been biographies, of course—Dangeau's memoirs, for one— but they were written too soon after Ninon's death and by interested parties who were selective in reporting the hearsay. Even the well-intentioned works were saturated by the feelings of those who knew her, and were filled with secondhand reports of letters, events and so forth."

"They drip with feeling," Brice agreed. "Her students loved her—that is obvious. They wanted her memory to live on in gilded splendor. But women apparently loved her too. That's baffling and flies in the face of everything I know about my sex. And again and again you hear that she was a creature completely at ease with herself and the world. That she was honest—always. How could that have been, given the time and place in which she lived?"

"Her lovers' wives and mistresses appreciated her, one assumes, since they benefited indirectly from her teachings."

"One would think. Especially if the instruction came before marriage," Brice added. "After all, in those days, far too many men were raised by the-hand-is-quicker-than-the-eye method of foreplay."

Damien laughed, his dark eye crinkling at the corners.

"Or '*look, mum, no hands.*' The English were often accused of being bad lovers—cold ones," he said.

"But I don't agree that the trouble is climatic so much as cultural and literary," Brice said fairly. "The isle has produced more than its fair share of romantics—and look at the Scots! They have even worse weather, so we can't use that as an excuse."

Damien smiled. "I agree. If the French aren't thought of just as unpolished, but as lovers, I think we can thank the lovely Ninon for giving them such a splendid reputation. That is one part of her legacy that lives on."

"Probably. But how can we know? There is no direct evidence, no firsthand testimony that I can find. Not even a curriculum from her school. Of course, I should be used to it by now. The same thing happened with Byron when I began. All those early biographies are useless, concoctions of lies by people trying to profit from their association with him—sycophants, glory-stealers, would-be poets, women scorned."

When she paused long enough to indicate that he

should speak, Damien answered, "I agree." Again, as had happened once or twice last night, she sensed part of him was far away, looking at something related to the topic under discussion but not quite ready to share the insight with her. It was frustrating. She could eavesdrop on the dead through their artifacts, but not on Damien Ruthven.

"I suppose it is dumb to be irritated with the dead, but they muddied the water for us scholars. And I hate having to know people secondhand." Brice shoved her escaping hair back behind her ear. She had not mentioned her suspicions that Damien had a copy of Byron's memoirs, but she made an indirect plea for him to share his information. "It's like being a tourist. I am traveling through Ninon's life with a biased guidebook that never allows me the chance to get off the bus and experience, or even understand, who these people were. Even when I have a supposedly direct quote, there is no way to know if it is accurate, or in what context it was written or said. If only more of their letters had been preserved. As it is, these secondhand accounts are too diluted to be of much use. It gives me a rough outline, but the subtle shadings are missing. I need—want—more."

Damien's gaze returned to her face and his thoughts to the present.

"Would you . . ." He paused, then said to himself, "But perhaps it's unwise. It is early in our relationship to burden it with a matter of trust."

"Would I what?" she prompted. Then she added: "And please know that I enjoy being burdened with confidences. At least, historical ones."

"You would enter a conspiracy with me? You of the honest face?" He smiled a little.

"I know I don't look as if I could conspire against

poached eggs, but I assure you that I am quite able to participate in a discreet relationship." She hoped he would understand the double meaning of that remark.

Damien nodded, suddenly serious again.

"Miss Ashton, if I share this with you, you must never say where you heard this story or came by your material. I would need your promise."

Brice's senses came on the alert. "Brice," she corrected. "Yes. What is it? Something about Ninon? Or Byron?"

"Both," he said. "And I mean it. I want your word. I will let you have copies to work with, but you must think of some plausible tale of how you attained them that does not involve me. I do not want to be mentioned in any context. Academic attention isn't a complication I want or need. Frankly, I wouldn't share this material now, except I suspect you may have some insights into a matter that has eluded me, and I would value your opinion."

Brice thought about it for a moment, then reluctantly threw her passion for documentation to the winds. In spite of her flip words, usually she documented everything in painstaking detail and honesty. But if the material was worth it, she would lie about where she got it no matter how much pressure other scholars brought to bear. If it wasn't worth it, then she wouldn't even mention what she'd seen.

"Okay, I promise."

"I have some of her letters—or perhaps copies of letters that are supposedly hers. I cannot be entirely certain that they are authentic, though they are all done in the same hand." The words were fast and a little harsh, and Brice suspected a lot reluctant, even though he had been the one to bring the subject up. "It was not common knowledge, but Byron in the last years of his life conceived of a fascination with this woman, and he collected as many of her letters and as much of her writing that he could."

Brice checked to make sure she wasn't gaping. She then made sure she was still sitting down, because she suddenly felt faint and feared her knees would give way.

"What?" she heard herself ask in a faint voice. "You have this collection of Byron's?"

"It's been a while since I made a lady swoon. Usually I have to work a little harder," Damien said almost to himself as he watched her sway in her chair. "Dash off an ode to her eyes at the very least."

"You have letters from Ninon de Lenclos? Byron owned letters by Ninon de Lenclos?" Her voice was high, very nearly a squeak. "Byron was fascinated with Ninon de Lenclos?

"Yes to all three." Damien continued to stare at her. "You better take a few deep breaths. You've turned a shade of white that matches the snow outside, and I am afraid that my household—though old-fashioned in many respects—does not contain smelling salts."

Brice swallowed and followed his advice. She lowered her head to her knees. After half a dozen slow breaths she spoke again. This time her voice was almost normal.

"How did I not know this? Oh, God! What else have I missed about Byron? I have worked on this for nine years—how could I have missed this? There was only that one reference to her in *Don Juan*!"

"You didn't miss much," Damien answered quickly. "Not that I can see. So don't start ripping your hair out and wailing *mea culpas*. Very little is known about his time in Greece. It was probably in his memoirs, and everyone would know about this if the things hadn't been burned."

"I'd like to shoot Hobhouse and Murray. Really. I mean that." Brice sat up slowly. Her color was slightly better than a moment before, but she was still pale and didn't try to stand.

"Yes, the thought occurred to me more than once too. Ah—would you like some brandy? Or tea?"

"You have letters . . . It's like a miracle—more than I hoped for," she muttered, not hearing his question. "I know it sounds crazy, but it's as though Fate arranged this chain of events. You got my book to review. You decided, against all normal practice, to write to me. Against all normal practice, I decided to visit you. Then this storm trapped me here in the city. You happen to see my notes for the next book and . . ." She trailed off. "This is downright spooky. You do understand what this means? That a scholar could go her entire life and not get a break like this? There will be professors in the halls of academe committing suicide when they find out what I have. Everyone but the CIA will be frantic to find out where the information came from."

"It does rather look like destiny has taken a hand, does it not? And I am glad that you should be the instrument to share the knowledge with the world." Damien's tone was thoughtful and again a little amused. "There is one other treat waiting for you—a miniature of Ninon painted in a locket. I don't think it is what you are expecting."

"A portrait? You have a portrait? I'm going to have a heart attack," Brice said, lowering her head again and resuming deep breathing. "No one has a portrait—except that one that is always copied. And there is that one bad pencil sketch."

"Well, I have a different one. I'll be back in a moment. Sit tight and don't make Mace nervous. He hates it when people fall on the floor."

"Don't worry. I'm not going anywhere," Brice assured

her host in a voice muffled by the wool of her skirt. Hearing herself, she made another effort to sit up and look like a professional biographer and not some wild-eyed mystic offered a look at the original burning bush. Besides, she was going to smear her eye makeup if she kept rubbing her face like this.

Perhaps sensing her perturbation, Mace came out from under Damien's desk and curled up around her ankles, offering what comfort he could. He panted up at Brice until she leaned down to give his ear stubs a scratch.

"It was done in sixteen seventy-seven," Damien said as he returned to the room, opening the delicate mahogany box he had fetched from his vault. He took out a small velvet pouch, pouring the contents into his hand. Then he said: "Merry Christmas, Brice Ashton. No more touristing for you. Get off the bus. I give you a glimpse of the real Ninon de Lenclos."

Brice stood up, being careful not to disturb Mace, who had rolled onto his back and was giving a fine impersonation of a dead dog. She righted the locket and opened it slowly, taking in the face of the woman she'd decided to investigate since her Byron biography had been finished.

Speak to me, ma belle dame.

Brice stared at Ninon's portrait like it held a clue to the cure for graying hair. Ninon stared back, looking vaguely amused. Her eyes appeared oddly dark and contrasted strongly with the red-gold hair that framed her delicate face in ringlets that had been so trendy in the seventeenth century. Her mouth was shown as a bow with full lips—a real Kim Basinger pout—though such open sexuality was not the fashion of paintings of that era. And there was a definite cleft in her chin.

The nose was stronger than Brice expected. Ninon's

complexion was fair and of the peaches-and-cream variety, but seemed to be lit by a golden glow, much as though she had been painted by firelight.

Brice shivered, though unsure why. Maybe it was because she was looking at a woman who, though immortal, was nonetheless dead. It was something like encountering a real ghost.

"Her hair is very close to yours in color—a bit longer, though," Damien said.

"But she has eyes like yours," Brice remarked, glancing up. She added thoughtfully, as his gaze again arrested hers, "Until you, I had never met anyone with eyes so dark. I thought it unique. Yet it must be somewhat common, after all."

It was more than that. Both Ninon and Damien wore similar expressions of remote amusement.

"Not common, I think. But not something that is solely mine." He finally looked away and added, "There are other people who have such eyes."

Brice made an effort to stop staring. It was difficult, though, because the small hairs of her arms were standing on end.

"Did the artist flatter her, do you think? She would have been fifty-seven when this was painted." Brice's voice was filled with awe.

"Who can say? But by all accounts, as you said yourself, she was fascinating and beautiful to the end. There was even wild talk in Paris about her making a deal with the devil to preserve her youth."

"Seeing this, I can almost believe it. May I?" Unable to wait any longer, she gestured at the small chest.

"Please."

Carefully she laid the locket aside and picked up the

first parchment in the pile. She untied the faded silk ribbon that secured it and unfolded the document carefully. Her hands were shaking.

"These are well preserved, but I must make copies for you to work with. We can't risk damage to the originals."

Beneath her, as Brice continued to ignore him, Mace rolled back onto his stomach and then resurrected. He retreated quickly toward the fireplace, where he curled into a small ball and settled in for a nap.

The parchment in Brice's hands proved to be a letter from Ninon to the Marquis de Sévigné. Brice translated quickly.

"'Love! I feel thy divine fury! My trouble, my transports, everything announces thy presence. Today a new sun arises for me; everything lives, everything is animated—'"

"'Everything seems to speak to me of passion, everything invites me to cherish it.'" Damien finished the paragraph, demonstrating his familiarity with the material. "One of her few flights into romantic fantasy. They're not all like that, though. Many are essays for her pupils—lessons in love, the curriculum in which you are interested. There is also a fascinating and different account of her meeting with 'the dark man.' I shall be especially interested in what you make of that."

Brice sank down on the alpaca rug in front of the fire. The tremor in her hands spread fast and her quaking knees refused to hold her up anymore. Mace made a small noise, asking if she was all right. "Essays? There are essays?"

"Feeling faint again? Buck up, my girl. You'll need your strength for this next lot. They aren't exactly 'insert tab A in slot B' illustrated instructions of lovemaking, but they are pretty graphic even by today's standards."

102

Damien set the box down beside her and gave both Brice and Mace pats on the head. Brice was too stunned to protest. "I'll leave you to it."

"I can't believe it. Essays." Brice rubbed her face, as though she could scrub away the shock.

"They're intelligently written too—she had such a clear, fresh voice. And since the affairs of men and maids have changed very little in the intervening centuries, I believe that it would make an excellent modern-day entry in the sexual self-help book category if it were ever published—which I think it should be. It's a pity Ninon isn't here to see that it happens. I think it is something that would please her."

"I'm trying to be her voice," Brice said, still a little dizzy. "God knows I'm trying."

"And I think you'll succeed. Perhaps to a greater degree than you ever expected," Damien added cryptically. "But you'll have to dig for the answers. She won't surrender her mysteries without a fight."

On the night of her eighteenth birthday a stranger was announced and, being much alone, Ninon received him though he gave the servants no name. The man who appeared before her was very strange—old and yet ageless.

"My visit surprises, perhaps terrifies you. But be not afraid. I have come on this night to offer you a gift, one of three things: either highest rank, or immeasurable wealth, or eternal beauty. But you must choose which without delay. At the count of seven the opportunity will be gone forever."

"Then I choose eternal beauty. But tell me—what must I do for such a great boon?"

"You must sign your name on my tablet and never tell a soul of our secret compact."

Then, when Ninon had done as he said, he told her, "This is the greatest power that a person may have. In my six thousand years roaming the earth, I have only ever bestowed it on four mortals: Semiramis, Helen, Cleopatra and Diane de Poitiers. You are the fifth and last to receive this gift. Look for me before eighty years have passed. When you see me again, tremble, for you shall have but three days to live. And remember that my name is Noctambule."

—*An account of the meeting between the Devil and Ninon de Lenclos*

Ignite me, O fire of isolation!
It hath not been long since I felt thine ice
and my soul's ticklish tears upon my cheek.
I have burned before and stayed unscathed,
despite the draw of death . . .
　　　　　　　　　—*From* Le Chevalier sans Paix

Love never dies of starvation, but often from indigestion.
　　　　　　　　　—*Ninon de Lenclos*

Chapter Seven

"Good God! She didn't really plan to sleep with four hundred and thirty-nine monks, did she?" Brice demanded out loud, shocked by what she had just read. "Surely she just said that to piss off the queen."

Damien's lips twitched. Probably because of the word *pissed*. Polite as he was, it wouldn't ever be part of his intentional daily linguistic fare.

"I'm not sure. She might have made good on the threat—if the monks were worth it, of course. She did not lack courage and she did not believe in hell—at least, not the 'hell ever after' the Church talked about."

"Hmph! I guess I wouldn't blame her if she had done it. Listen to this brainless, sexist drivel from the queen's confessor," Brice demanded, and began reading aloud from one of the letters. Damien obviously had read through it already, but he listened attentively as she related first the priest's opinion and then Ninon's words about the slavery of marriage to an unintelligent man, in passionate if oddly accented French.

He responded, "It was an attitude of the time—this belief that women could not know honor or courage or reason. I think it is why Ninon so often dressed as a man." He spread his hands as he spoke. His words were measured and old-fashioned, as they often were when he talked about Byron or Ninon. Unknowingly, he seemed to need to discuss them in the language of their own eras. Brice found it fascinating. But then, pretty much everything about Damien fascinated her.

"Hogwash." She wanted to say *bullshit*, but didn't since her host set such an example of restraint.

"Yes, I agree. But, considered inferior, women were expected to submit to a man's will. And given the difficulties that faced any independent women and their children, many *wanted* to submit, since it was the lesser evil. Marriage at least had the benefit of social acceptability. And a wife was harder to cast off than a mistress."

"But not all men thought this way. Nor all women," Brice argued, holding up Ninon's letter. "Even in those dark days, some knew better."

"Of course. But as a rule, the exceptions to the community standards were punished harshly by society, which above all things loves the status quo." Damien grinned suddenly. "And understandably so. It is my experience that independent women can be fatiguing. There's nothing like them to disrupt a man's well-ordered life."

"I know. But it pisses me off. What a waste of so many lives. Their thoughts and dreams quashed before they ever blossomed—and all because of their gender." Then Brice thought about what Damien said regarding independent women, and that she had tacitly agreed by not speaking out against it at once, and glared at him. "Don't joke about it. You'll be burned in effigy if anyone hears you making remarks about independent women. Of course, you're probably roasted regularly anyway."

Damien blinked at her words, and Brice pointed at the newspaper. It was folded open to his latest review. He laughed.

"Alas, it's true! Hell hath no fury like that of a writer scorned. You're in good company with your views of women's bondage, though. It annoyed Ninon too. You can see it even in her most circumspect writing. To us it seems obvious, but remember that she was questioning what was the accepted philosophy of her day—what was the given, divine truth."

"I know, and that's what's so amazing. I think I can see why Byron was fascinated by her. It wasn't any sort of sexual fixation. Forget all that Don Juan, the great mythic lover stuff," Brice said, reaching for the last scone. They had missed lunch and were both hungry. Since Damien had been being a pill about her gender, she didn't offer to share. Busy with the scone, she didn't notice how Damien's eyes widened at her words.

"Aside from her mind, which was keen, she shared another common trait with him." Brice slathered on lemon curd with a lavish hand.

"Yes?" Damien cocked his head. "Her love of intellectual freedom perhaps?"

"That, too, of course. But I am thinking of something subtler. They didn't make a big fuss about it, but neither of them could abide cruelty—especially not when it was directed at the weak. Neither ever took pleasure in another's suffering. Not even that of their enemies. And they were not judgmental—which is not to say that they lacked judgment or moral fiber," she added. She waved a hand, searching for the best way to explain what she thought. "They just didn't feel that everyone had to make the same choices they did. They believed that people should be allowed to find their own intellectual paths whatever those happened to be. Nor were they afraid of the opposite sex, because they understood the genders very well and allowed for the differences. That made them far more forgiving of the world than the world was of them." She frowned, and her voice became soft. "I wonder if they were ever lonely. They were rarely alone, but . . . well, you know what I mean. It's the path not taken and all that."

Damien sighed. "They often were lonely, I should think. It takes brave people to truly befriend crusaders—especially in an era when society was so willing to destroy people for having aberrant views. Friends would have been few and far between." Damien looked her in the eye. "Not that things have changed that much. We still do that with the misfits and rebels."

" 'But it was only a thin veneer of morality that cloaked their less wholesome deeds,' " Brice quoted softly as she looked out the window. She was glad that they couldn't see where the World Trade Center had once stood. "The *ton* was made up of such bloody hypocrites. And they were all so cruel."

"Yes."

"Things have changed—for most of us," she said softly, arguing against Damien's stated assumption that people still were hypocritical and repressive. "Fanaticism of this stripe is the exception, not the norm. At least in the Western world."

Again, for some reason the observation seemed to affect Damien, who nodded in polite agreement but looked away. His troubled gaze suggested that he saw something painful in his past. She wondered what it was. He turned back to her and said suddenly: "Have you ever made a wassail bowl?"

Brice blinked. Damien had a way of surprising her with strange non sequiturs. She didn't understand how his brain worked sometimes, but it nearly always led somewhere fascinating; she was quite willing to follow.

"No, I haven't actually. I've read recipes, of course."

"Well, come along. Time for a hands-on history lesson. We are going to make Byron's favorite wassail bowl." Damien stood up quickly. "I do hope we have dark ale in the house. That's the start of all excellent wassails."

Mace made a small complaining noise from under the desk.

"Soon," Damien promised the dog. He explained to Brice, "This is the time of day when Mace and I ride the service elevator down to the basement, where we have a visit with the janitor. It turns out that Mace has a real taste for thrill rides. We've tried the regular elevators, but they are too tame. Mace prefers the near free-fall of the older deathtrap."

"I see," Brice said. But she didn't. She couldn't imagine finding any pleasure in an elevator, let alone one that could be classed as a thrill ride.

The kitchen was fabulous, which was only to be expected. What was surprising was that Damien seemed to know his way around it. For some reason, she had thought that there would be a cook in residence, and maybe even a butler and footmen.

"Obviously, this was designed by a man. The counters and cupboards are so tall," Brice commented as she ran a finger over the professional range.

Damien turned, smiling broadly, and somehow she

wasn't shocked when he put his hands around her waist and boosted her onto the counter as though she were a child of four.

"Usually there is the cook—Mathilda Jones—but I gave her the week off. Her family lives in California." Damien plucked out some crab apples from the bamboo bowl on the marble counter. "Where is the sherry? We need that, and lemons too."

He went to the door and stuck his head out.

"Karen," he called. "Where is the sherry?"

"Have you tried your desk drawer?" His secretary's dry voice floated back down the long hall.

"Damn! She's right. I left it there for Mace."

"Mace likes sherry?" Brice felt herself smiling at the sheer ridiculousness of the notion.

"Every evening at five," Damien confirmed, turning the oven on and throwing the small apples into a white baking dish.

"Shall I go get it?" Brice asked. "Mace will share with me, won't he?"

"Would you mind? Second drawer on the left. Tell Mace I'll return it promptly."

Brice nodded and slid off the counter before Damien could lift her down. She hurried back to the library.

Pulling open the second drawer of the desk, she found the tall, skinny bottle. She also found a sheet of folded paper with Lord Byron's signature on it. She froze.

Could it be a letter? The draft of an unknown poem? A piece of his memoirs?

Hands trembling, but not hesitating, she slipped the sheet out of the drawer and unfolded it carefully. It was a poem, *Le Chevalier sans Paix*. She scanned a few lines, amazement growing as she read:

Warm, salty splashes on oars
deeper and deeper they sink, trying—
praying desperately to banish the flames
which light the poles; the sails have torn
free, flapping about thy shoulders
and yes! You are there my love—

She looked again at the name. She checked, but there was no date. What was even stranger, the paper seemed very modern. It was of good quality, and it showed no signs of age. None.

The hairs at the nape of Brice's neck began to rise.

There was a leather book underneath the paper. It was tied shut with a faded blue ribbon and looked promisingly old.

"Did you find the sherry?" Karen asked from the door. "His lordship grows restless. He is a good chef, but not a patient one."

Brice jumped and let the paper slide back into the drawer. She closed it quickly.

"Yes. It's right here." She hoped that, if she was flushed, Karen would blame it on her being stooped over and not on guilt from being caught snooping.

She patted the curious Mace on the head. Her hand was unsteady.

"I wanted to tell you how much I love your dog. He must be good company."

"Better than my ex, that's for sure," Karen said, retreating from the room. "Though he is a bit disloyal. He seems to like my employer more than me."

"It's probably the brioche and sherry."

Karen's voice was fond. "Quite likely. You wouldn't know it to look at him, but Mace is quite a glutton."

"It's the company," Brice suggested. "I've been eating like a pig since I arrived."

"Fortunately," Karen answered, turning away, "neither you nor Mace show it."

Giving her cheeks and brain a moment to calm, Brice walked slowly back to the kitchen.

What could that leather-bound book be? Probably nothing—heck, it didn't have to be a journal at all. She was crazy to imagine it was Byron's memoirs. By all accounts, those had been loose sheaves of paper anyway. And Damien had already shared his greatest Byronic treasure with her. Also, Ninon's letters and portrait were priceless; why would he hold out on her about this?

He wouldn't. She was just being greedy and wishing for the moon.

"Got the sherry?" Damien asked as she re-entered the kitchen. "The apples need to marinate in it while they roast."

"Yes, sorry I was so long. I stopped to pet Mace. I think he expected some sherry, but I didn't see any glasses." It was only a small lie.

"We'll give him some wassail instead. He likes that too."

"I take it that Mace isn't afraid of the long-term effects of alcohol." Brice boosted herself back onto the counter and watched Damien quarter lemons on the cutting board. When he motioned to her, she took over chopping.

"Not from fine wine and ale," he agreed. Opening the oven, he poured sherry over the hissing crab apples. He then went to the stovetop where dark ale was heating in a glass pan. "He has also been known on occasion to touch the demon rum."

"I like rum myself. It's a component in many of my favorite summer drinks. I love trying silly-sounding beverages that come with paper parasols."

"Don't we all? Not that this is at all a frivolous beverage."

"Of course not," Brice agreed without smiling.

"Now, one of the other keys to good wassail is only using glass when you heat the ale," Damien said, assuming a lecturing voice. "Metal pans alter the flavor."

"I've heard the same about mulling wine," Brice commented. "Is this enough lemon?"

"One more," Damien answered, looking back at her small pile. "And now it's time to add the honey. One must never let the ale actually boil."

He poured in a generous dollop of honey and then began squeezing lemons into the brew. Lastly, he upended the sherry bottle and poured the rest of the golden spirits into the pan.

Brice watched Damien work, liking the way his long fingers made everyday gestures acts of grace. She smiled a little at his lecture too. In spite of his unvarying politeness of expression and his puttering in the kitchen like a contented *hausfrau*, Brice was willing to bet that in other situations he was alpha male all the way.

What remained to be seen was whether he liked alpha mates, or if he had to dominate everything. The fact that he used charm first didn't mean anything except he wasn't stupid or a bully. What was the saying? *Violence is the thinking man's last resort, and the ignorant man's first.* Damien was—above all things—a thinking man.

And a proud one. He would be insulted if he knew she had looked through his desk.

Brice understood. She would be insulted too. Her actions made her squirm. Would he despise her if he

114

knew what she'd done in a moment of weakness and surprise? The thought of his anger or contempt left her stricken.

But that was ridiculous. She cared too much what he thought of her. She barely knew this man—how could his opinion already count for so much?

A word she didn't want to hear popped into her head.

No! There was no such thing as love at first sight. Lust at first sight, definitely. Lust with strong potential for a future relationship—probably. But love? No, nothing that constructive and supportive came out of instant attraction.

And sexual arousal was the enemy of productivity, Brice reminded herself when she felt herself losing the argument. She knew her shortcomings. A new lover, on the rare occasion she took one, left her distracted, almost amnesiac. And in the end, what had she to show for these affairs? Usually nothing except a rushed deadline brought about because she hadn't been able to concentrate.

No, at the end of the day, no matter how wonderful the sex, Brice had no interest in men who refused to learn, to grow beyond their past failures. And none of them ever had. They were all trapped in their pasts, uncommitting to the future because of fear of failure. They enjoyed a fairy-tale passion, she learned their few charming quirks and mysteries, and then they got boring.

It was depressing to think that this was all there was. People got stuck at times—all people—nailed in place by painful events. The smart ones, the brave ones, eventually moved on. But those were sadly rare.

Byron had managed, in spite of his losses. That was part of what made the poet so appealing to Brice. And part of what made so many other men *not*.

She wasn't a wildwoman, an emotional kamikaze who took frequent risks with her heart, but she had once tried to not let fear hold her back. If a *right* man came along, she wanted to be ready to love him.

So, what about Damien?

Yes, what about Damien? Wasn't it time to start asking herself some critical questions? He had no wife, no family. Was he one of those arrested souls, one who could never commit?

No.

There was definitely something beneath that civilized exterior. He was an unstill water that unquestionably ran deep. Whatever had kept him from marriage, Brice didn't think it was fear.

Damien looked up then and smiled. His grin pulled her out of her brooding thoughts.

"Now for the crabs," he said, opening the oven and letting the delicious smell of baked apples into the kitchen. "Just listen to them whistle when they hit the ale. That's why they call it *wassail*. The apples are singing."

Brice giggled as the first apple hit the punch. "It sounds like a cat with adenoid problems."

"Clearly you have no poetry in your soul." Damien sniffed and said loftily, "That is the sound of distant churchgoers trudging through snow and singing to keep their spirits high."

Brice shook her head. "Adenoids."

Damien ladled out some punch, pouring it into a Toby mug and handing it to her. The helping was more than generous.

"Drink. I promise you'll hear heavenly hosts after you get that lot under your belt."

He ladled out two more mugs and a small amount into a shallow dish.

116

"Come on. Mace and Karen will want some too."

Feeling quite warm after only a few sips of the potent brew, Brice followed obediently.

"Damien . . ." she began, wanting desperately to ask about the old book and the piece of paper in the desk, but knowing she shouldn't.

"Yes?" He looked back. The hall was shadowed, but steam from the mugs seemed to wreathe his head in a golden halo. And it was truly earned. Damien had been an angel to her, sharing his treasures and his home.

She felt more guilty than ever.

And more attracted.

"Nothing." She took another sip of punch. It was heady stuff. Better than demon rum. "I was just going to say that I'm having a lot of fun. Thank you for inviting me to spend the holidays here."

He grinned at her. The smile did funny things to her blood pressure.

"Oddly enough, I'm having fun too. So don't thank me. I am being amply compensated."

Men are more often defeated in love by their own clumsiness than by a woman's virtue.

—Lesson in Love *from* Carte du Tendre *by Ninon de*
Lenclos

Talk to your lover about herself, and seldom of your own self. Take for granted that she is a hundred times more interested in the charms of her own person than in the whole gamut of your emotions.

—Lesson in Love *from* Carte du Tendre *by Ninon de*
Lenclos

Nothing can confound a wise man more than laughter from a dunce.

—*Lord Byron*

She knew—
For quickly comes the knowledge—that his heart
Was darkened with her shadow.

—*Lord Byron*

Chapter Eight

Brice didn't usually like handsome men, not if they were aware of their beauty and cultivated it at the expense of their minds. Men who routinely traded on their looks seemed weak, even effeminate to her. It was such a female trick. It wasn't that she didn't enjoy seeing handsome men—far from it. But she preferred that the men in her life be men: rough, competitive, proud of their physical skills and their logical, even cold-hearted, judgment. If they were extremely intelligent, so much the better. She didn't like having to slow down and explain things to those who couldn't keep up.

She'd been told that she was retrograde in her tastes. Maybe that was true. She hadn't any use for brutal men, but she wasn't fond of whiny, pacifistic males either.

Damien seemed quite perfect—alpha, graceful, intelligent.

And she had probably drunk entirely too much of that

wassail punch. Perfect? A man? That was a heretical thought.

It was getting late, too. Karen and Mace had left hours ago. She should make some pretense of retiring to bed; she just didn't want to. There was too much pleasure to be had in Damien's company, and time was running out. She couldn't stay at his home indefinitely.

"A penny for them," her host said, finally putting aside his manuscript. The soft light from his desk lamp again surrounded him in a golden halo. He didn't look angelic now, though, unless one was thinking of the fallen one. Hadn't Lucifer been the fairest of them all?

"I'm surprised that I'm able to work here," Brice said. And that was true, as far as it went. Usually when she was working, she needed a routine. She was like a high priestess performing a sacred rite. Any disruption and she was left distracted and wrathful. Searching through the paper remains of the dead was a hard, lonely business. She was surrounded by people when she went to the great archives, the living and the dead, but she was not part of them, was simply a witness to their actions. The people she studied were like actors in home movies, ghosts going on with their lines, unaware that someone was eavesdropping on them from the future, watching, taking notes on everything they said and did and thought. Being such a witness required silence and meditation.

But here she was frequently interrupted by Damien— or Mace—and it didn't bother her in the least. In fact, she looked forward to hearing his voice, to feeling his touch at those moments when they traded papers, or when he helped her from a chair.

And petting Mace was okay too. She found she liked having a warm body lie on her toes. It was companionship without distracting conversation. She would have to think about getting a dog.

"I'm not all that surprised that we should rub along tolerably well," Damien answered. "As you said, it's as though destiny took a hand in our affairs."

"Yes—but destiny isn't always so tidy. In fact, I can't recall anything ever going so smoothly. It makes me nervous, if you want to know the truth." As soon as she said this, Brice realized it was true. She did feel nervous.

"Perhaps Santa has brought you an early present." Damien frowned suddenly. "Too bad he didn't bring you a new laptop as well. The drive in that thing sounds asthmatic."

"I know. Maybe next year, when I get my next advance. For now, this will have to do. I need the thing too badly to abandon it. Human memory is a terrible record keeper, you know. And my handwriting qualifies as villainous. I take copious longhand notes when I can't bring the portable—and have to transfer them to disk while I can still read my own writing," she said, typing the last entry into her laptop and then saving the file to both drives. That part of her routine had not changed. After a bad experience with a hard-drive crash where she'd lost almost a hundred pages of work, she had become religious about saving her written labor at regular intervals. Her new first commandment was: *Thou shalt back up files*.

Brice chuckled suddenly, and before she could reconsider the wisdom of introducing the topic she said: "The brain does manage to keep track of some peculiar things, though. Take this fact about the Etruscans I read fifteen years ago. They were supposed to race into battle sporting full erections. It was thought to terrify the enemy, and was part of what made them such great soldiers. I suppose that might have worked. However, I have a bad feeling that it might have made me giggle instead of quail. I mean, picture it. They wore those silly little tunics, and there they'd be, bobbing along like the gentlemen of the chorus. Would you find that terrifying? Or, if you were a fellow Etruscan, inspirational?" She shook her head. "I'll never be able to write about them, you know, because I just don't get it. The whole society is an enigma."

Damien's teeth flashed. "Hm. Interesting strategy, I must say. But the Etruscans have rather died out. I wonder if there's a connection. Battle can't be the safest place for an erection, not with all those nasty swords and maces being swung around."

"That's exactly what I said to my history professor when he brought it up."

"Did he agree?"

"I don't know. He just sniffed." Brice shook her head and confided, "A lot of us had doubts that Dr. Knowlton actually knew what an erection was. Frankly, we weren't sure he knew what an Etruscan was either."

"Was he male?"

"We were never entirely certain. Usually I can tell, though." She peeped at him over her screen. "For instance, your gender is quite evident."

"I'm so glad to hear it."

Brice smiled. Picking up the next letter of Ninon's she unfolded it carefully. Damien took up the manuscript he was reading.

She was becoming accustomed to the idea that he was a critic and doing his wicked work in her presence. Damien was a reviewer, but a scrupulous specimen. She had learned that there was nothing personal motivating him, nothing beyond his taste and somewhat exacting standards—and heaven knew that she had those idiosyn-crasies too.

Damien Ruthven and his arrogance went together like truffles and foie gras—which was not a common com-bination but probably should be, now that she thought of it.

On that consideration, Brice bent her head back to her work.

"You're grinding your teeth," Damien said a short time later. The storm was again raging outside.

"Am I?" Brice exhaled heavily. "Sorry. I sometimes do that when I'm angry."

"What's annoying you?"

"Oh—the usual. Life lessons presented when I don't want to think about them." Brice sighed again.

"Such as?"

She waved the letter in her hand. "Ninon seemed to manage to be it all—sex goddess, mother, writer. . . . What's my problem? I wonder sometimes if not marry-ing again and not having children have led me to a life of intellectual self-indulgence and cowardly isolation. In a word, I have become a *writer* more than a woman. I should go to the DMV and have the gender on my license changed."

"That seems drastic. I am quite certain that, writer or not, technically you are still female." His words were playful, but his mood was not. He could feel a frown plucking at his brow.

"Yes. But only technically. I've been transformed into something sexless. I mean, is what I do so important? Am I wrong to close out the world in favor of work?" Brice chuckled suddenly, her face losing its scowl. "Is the fact that I'm asking this question of a virtual stranger a sure sign that my lifestyle has made me self-centered and narcissistic?"

Her earlier words hit him. "You were married?" he asked, surprised. The idea had not occurred to him. Probably because he didn't like the idea that she could have ever loved anyone else or been some other man's wife.

"Yes, briefly. He died in a car accident. At Christmas." Her voice was calm, not unhappy, but not as lively as it had been. Her explanation was succinct and said more about her lingering grief than her facial expression.

"Do you still miss him?" *Do you still love him?* he meant.

"Sometimes. Not so much anymore. It happened many years ago." Her head was bowed and she shuffled absently through the papers.

"You've healed well," Damien commented, wanting to say something else entirely but wisely refraining. He added, "One would never guess at such a huge tragedy in your life."

She shrugged. "I drag around as much emotional baggage as anyone else. Maybe more," she admitted. "The trick to getting on with things is to make sure that those bags are on wheels. The right work helps too. Everyone should have at least one magnificent obsession. It's a life jacket when the ship goes down." She gave a wry smile.

He nodded once, liking the analogy. She had emotional baggage—no surprise. All interesting people did. And he knew all too well that some emotions, some memories, couldn't be left behind, no matter how one longed to abandon them. The only thing to do was to learn to travel with them. What Damien liked most about Brice was that she didn't seem to expect anyone to handle her heavy baggage for her.

"Pain is usually an excellent teacher. It is fortunate for

the human race that most romantic lessons don't stick. Without this amnesia no one would ever love more than once," Damien said. "Certainly, one would never marry a second time."

Brice nodded back, her eyes thoughtful. "You can pull up the drawbridge and turn crocodiles loose in the moat, but eventually loneliness compels most people to open up and try again, I suppose. But not me. Not marriage. At least, not any time soon. It's like I said, I take copious notes and they remind me of what I need to know. And I think I'm with Ninon on this one." She leaned toward her screen and read the translation aloud. " 'Women have always refused to recognize what most marriages are. Wives are slaves to their husbands. Even the convent seemed better to me. I am not saying that we should not love—to fight against nature's passions is to invite a life-long torture. Yet a woman must consider carefully before she sets a legal seal on her deeper emotions. Passion is fleeting; marriage is not.' "

Brice looked up. "Perhaps I am fortunate not to have faced such disillusionment. Mark died while I still loved him."

"So, you are not looking for marriage?" Damien wasn't sure how he felt about this. Once upon a time, it would have been the answer to his prayers. Now, he wasn't certain that he liked this unwillingness to commit.

"No. Not at the moment," she said firmly. "And maybe not ever."

"And what about passion?" he asked, knowing his voice had gone deep and smoky. "Are you looking for that? Have you been searching?"

Her deep blue eyes studied him. She looked more serious than he'd ever seen her.

"Do you know, generally speaking, I don't mind desire

suggesting a course of action," Brice said slowly. "But I have refused in these last few years to be ordered around by it. The heart and soul have greater needs, and most men did not seem worthwhile."

"But this time?" he asked directly. "Do your instincts say that I would be worth an investment of time?"

"This time . . . I've decided to take the suggestion under advisement. It's why I'm still here."

Damien looked at her. He could see himself reflected in her spring-colored eyes. His own were shining, but he knew they were as black as the endless midnight that was now part of him. "Is that wise?" he asked, knowing it was only fair to give her a chance to back away.

"Hell, no." She shrugged. "But you know what's rarer than a first edition of *La Coquette Vengée*?"

"A second edition," he suggested. He smiled slightly. Even while being enticed, Brice continued to be more intellectual than passionate. She was interested, but was still hiding behind her barricades. Others might not notice, but Damien saw them for what they were because he had his own barriers that kept people from pressing too close. Brice carefully armored herself with books and research and other intellectual distractions—and thus far they had served her well.

Brice had also blithely admitted to not replacing a broken answering machine, and she refused to carry a cell phone, so that she could get lost when it suited her. She even had a house that was remote enough to discourage casual visitors.

Damien's own defenses were more obvious: a huge library where he did unending research instead of spending time with friends, security guards to keep the unwashed masses away, a secretary to keep known but unwanted associates from interrupting. And he had a home at the top of a citadel that had only one entrance, which he controlled with electronic keys.

But he had let her inside his fortress, had allowed her to pry enough to catch a glimpse of who he really was. And he had enjoyed it. It was time for her—willing or not—to return the favor. Stripping her layer of protective reason away so she could deal in pure emotion would be half the fun of seducing her.

Damien felt his smile widen. Brice smiled back warily and shook her head.

"No, it's true desire that's rarer." She answered the question she'd posed. Her voice was low. "Not the simple kind where you can satisfy the physical longing with any nonrepulsive person. I'm talking about passion—a specific, complicated, dangerous and insane desire."

"And you are feeling complicated, dangerous and insane?" he asked. His voice was very deep and he could feel his pulse like a trip-hammer in his throat. He wondered for a moment just who was seducing whom.

"Yes."

Damien stood and walked around the desk. He stepped in front of the lamp where it outlined his body in perfect detail but left his face in shadow. His own passion was rising, fed by both Brice's words and the storm, and it might be best that she didn't see him in direct light. The physiological changes would be hard to explain.

"What delightful news."

She smiled. "Are you sure you want to get involved with someone who admits to insanity?" she asked, turning the tables. He wondered when shyness or caution would intervene in their conversation. Surely it would. Her nature was reserved, dignified. Wasn't it?

He stared into her eyes. "I've known true insanity. This is just a touch of divine madness. In any event, there's some grand fishing to be had in the deep waters of the psyche," Damien joked.

"Perhaps. But maybe this is a very shallow pool," she responded. Casting the stack of letters aside, she rose. "Maybe there isn't enough water of thought here to raise mosquitoes, let alone game fish. Dive in at your own peril."

"Give it time. The tide rises quickly."

It was dark, but Brice saw Damien smile and reach out a hand. Should she take it?

There were compelling reasons to do so, and equally compelling reasons not. She couldn't sensibly choose between them, because one set of arguments belonged to the realm of reason and the other to emotion. She *wanted* to touch him.

She looked up, seeking an answer from heaven. But heaven wasn't visible. The lamp didn't light more than the desk. It couldn't. It was a 150-watt bulb, but the vaulted ceiling was high and the light lost heart before reaching it.

She was alone here—just her body, her heart and her mind.

Brice noticed no odor of smoke, and yet the room seemed haunted by the lovely scent of pipe tobacco, so faint that it was little more than a memory. There was another familiar perfume too, but there was no time to hunt down the elusive knowledge of where she had smelled it. Maybe it was the ghosts of those people immortalized in the journals and letters she was reading. Had they turned the tables? Were their spirits now watching their watcher be seduced?

Damien touched her. It seemed that all the heat in his body roared through his hands and stabbed through her skin. It entered every fiber of her body, spreading fire. But it didn't burn; rather, it melted. All senses fled and Brice's muscles weakened. She did not resist when he drew her into his arms and then laid her down on the desk.

There was time for one last thought. She'd done it now—broken several personal rules. She was caught up in her own rather gothic romance with the lord of the manor. All that remained to be seen in this piece was whether Damien was a hero or a villain.

Her hair lay over the edge of the desk in a red-blonde rope. Lovely, but he wanted it loose. He reached down and unraveled it quickly. As he touched the strands, soft now, like her expression, he was immediately awash in a surge of emotion that was close to religious ecstasy—not the barren worship he had been raised with at the emotional necropolis that had been his home, but something pure and almost holy and entirely alive.

He sighed happily. Yes, this was what he had sought, what he longed for.

One didn't need to touch to appreciate Brice's beauty and the beauty of the moment—but the touch certainly added to the pleasure of the instant. And he needed to know that she agreed.

He looked into her eyes, waiting for assent. At her smile, he began.

He undressed her first, enjoying the tiny buttons of her sweater that revealed her velvety skin by slow, tantalizing inches. She wore a bra, a confection of maroon and lighter rose lace that was more teasing than useful. He kissed around the edges and coaxed the straps down, pushing the lace away.

His fingers explored. He loved the delicate articulation of the muscles beneath her creamy skin. Ah, the beauty of the female body! There were no knots of muscle, no hard bulges, just the smooth, almost liquid flow of movement when she shifted that was so sensual.

Perfect! She was perfect. He took her left breast in his mouth and nibbled with the edge of his teeth.

She tightened like a bowstring and moaned as if the breath were being ripped out of her. She turned her head and bit his shoulder. Such animal response was both thrilling and a warning. Some men liked docile, domestic women, pussycats who purred and cuddled, and certainly the sweet ones had their attractions. But tonight he wanted the tigress. The hunger rising between them was not of the usual sort between a man and a pretty woman. The appetite was immense, an implacable lust that could be sated only if they did not hold back. They needed to feast.

She made a noise that was part moan and part growl. It had no words, but he knew what it meant: *Here lies madness. Beware.*

So, he had been warned twice. He didn't care. Especially not when her hands reached up and began undressing him.

She worked efficiently but without haste. As the layers were stripped away, her eyes filled with wonder and questions and heat. She peeled his shirt off slowly, revealing the soft net of golden scars that covered his chest and back. They would become more pronounced as his arousal grew.

He moved toward the light, intent on dousing it, but she reached out quickly and stayed his hand.

"No." Her voice was soft but definite. She went back to undressing him, unbuckling his slacks and pushing them away. "I'm not afraid to see. You should know that the only way I ever do things is with my eyes wide open."

She reached for him, but he caught her hands. He held them still for a moment and then kissed them.

"Patience." His voice was rough, filled with the energy of the storm outside.

"Why? *You* don't look patient."

Byron followed her line of sight and looked down at his penis risen to attention. He laughed once. The show-off! Selfish, inconsiderate, gluttonous, always desiring its way—and immediately. But it was as reliable as the tides when it wanted something. And it wanted Brice Ashton very much.

"Damien?"

He realized he was still smiling as he held her hands, and Brice was now looking a little concerned. Laughter was an inappropriate response at the moment, but storms always left him feeling a little high and wild. And the storm would only grow. Windy fists, harbingers of that assault to come, struck the glass, their power only slightly lessened by being diverted around the buildings of the city. He should leave Brice until the storm had passed. Failing that, he should reassure her somehow.

Then he realized that she wasn't staring because he was laughing. She was staring at the vein that pulsed just beneath the skin of his organ, and at the foreskin—such an anomaly in this day and age—that was laced with a mesh of golden scars which were now quite evident.

"It looks like lightning," she murmured, marveling and not appalled. The hair on her head began to stir as static electricity crept through it.

"It is."

Could she also see that he hummed like a tuning fork? That his muscles had taken in an electrical charge, drawing from the atmosphere of the room and the storm without, and they were begging for a chance to expend that energy in some physical activity?

"I wish I could say that I feel respectful, for you deserve it." His voice was low and rough as he looked into her eyes. "But you must settle for libidinous reverence rather than esteem."

"The strongest emotions don't respect what is proper and decent and nice." She again managed to sound reasonable, in spite of the pulse hammering in her throat—and he loved that too.

"No—and thank God they don't. What's the point of spontaneous sex that isn't mindless and crazy?"

"I haven't a clue," she answered, though of course they both knew what else it could be if emotion was allowed to intrude into the proceedings.

Brice tugged her hands free, and this time he didn't stop her when she reached for him.

He crouched, ignoring the crisp sound of crumpling paper beneath her on the desk, and lowered his mouth to hers. It was like kissing lightning. Power poured from his mouth to hers, mixed with her own divine fire and then rebounded, stabbing through his nerves where the charge redoubled.

Her hands were cool on his skin, but not enough to stop the heat rising in him. No, not nearly enough, as her hands slipped around his flanks and traced the cleft of his bottom. He could feel her exploring, one hand sliding over his buttocks and then between, the other roaming around to the front of his body. Her touch was gentle, soft as a fall of apple blossom as she coaxed the foreskin up his shaft, but he felt every stroke, every nerve. In that moment he was all sensitized flesh.

"Your halo is so bright," she whispered.

He knew she was right. Only, it wasn't a halo. He could feel the lightning beginning to dance over his skin. The reaction was too intense. He should stop, or think of baseball, or—

"So beautiful," she whispered, and then turned back to his lips. He didn't mind that her kiss turned harder, less refined. She cradled him in the relative coolness of her body, accepting his heat—even demanding it.

He moved down to her breasts, suckling strongly and drawing another moan from her as she curled fingers into his hair and pulled it forward toward her lips. He went lower, biting the underside of her breast with enough force to mark but not break the skin. Then, distracted by the weight, he lost himself in the sensation of smooth, cool skin gliding over his face.

Though she resisted with her handholds, he slid lower. Her scent aroused him, a patchouli that was universally feminine and yet specific. He had been humoring her earlier when he talked of Fate—and yet it almost seemed that destiny *had* taken a hand. Pheromones couldn't have reached him all the way from where she was in South Carolina—unless perhaps they had clung to her manuscript . . .

He stopped thinking, explaining. This was something that just was.

Damien's hands flexed on the muscles of her thighs, urging them to open. She writhed under the exploration of his fingers, crying out when his thumb flicked over her and then slipped inside. Her legs moved restlessly, shifting the drifts of antique paper and spilling some onto the floor.

He set his mouth to her, enjoying how this flesh also changed. He wanted to devour her, to climb inside; he was going to detonate, perhaps electrocute them both.

The electricity dancing over his skin was visible now and pouring onto Brice as well.

He had to end it immediately; it was too dangerous to wait. Such play could come later when the first burst of arousal had passed and the storm calmed outside.

Damien slid back up her body, and her legs whipped around him as though securing him against another escape. She was ready. He slid into her. The tempest was on him immediately. There was a flash of light, a sheet of whiteness that passed down their bodies in both directions from where they were joined. Brice screamed once when the shock threw her into erotic convulsions, and he followed immediately. He found release.

He collapsed on her when his muscles unclenched. The small lightning of last desire danced over their skin and died out slowly, a last fizzle of eerie, incandescent light. Brice's eyes were mere slits, and Damien wondered if she had seen what had happened.

And if she had, what she would say.

After a moment he shifted off of her and onto his side. "That was wonderful," she whispered, sounding a bit stunned. "It was also really weird."

So she had noticed. Well, what had he expected? They had just lit up the room like a searchlight.

"More wonderful than weird?" he asked, bracing for the next question she would ask.

But, as always, she surprised him.

"I'll let you know in a minute. I'm thinking wonderful, but my brain isn't working right."

"Please, don't let me rush you."

"You couldn't, not at this moment." She turned her head and closed her eyes as though exhausted.

Damien, who felt energized rather than drained, took the opportunity to drink her in. He didn't care for the

134

modern obsession with hair removal, particularly not the strange goatee achieved by the Brazilian bikini wax. Brice did not have this issue.

He ran a finger along the edge of her inner thigh, outlining the soft blonde curls. Yes, he would play here again. When it was safe. When there was no storm outside. Or inside.

"That tickles." Brice's eyes cracked open, She looked down at his hand and blushed slightly. "I know. It looks a bit like a merkin. But I assure you it isn't a wig."

Her words startled Damien to laughter. He had forgotten about the old craze for pubic hair wigs.

Brice smiled wryly. "I wasn't planning on seducing you, you see. Not tonight. Obviously. I would have shaved." She added, "And I would have chosen a better location for seduction. As it is, I think I have a stapler embedded in my back."

Damien, manners finally recalled, helped Brice off of the desk. She stood slowly and then, with a frown, started peeling off the papers that perspiration had glued to her body. Damien looked on with interest. The photocopies' ink had transferred to her buttocks in a sort of reverse print. The left cheek said *The Collected Letters of Marquis Sévigné*. The right cheek was harder to make out but said something about the philosopher Saint Evremond.

"The two men were never so close," he murmured.

"What?"

He reached for her, turning her back to the giant mirror that hung on the wall. "Look."

Brice peered over her shoulder and made a disgusted sound as she tried to rub the print away.

"Please tell me there are no security cameras around here. This isn't something I want preserved for posterity."

"None. There are the wages of sin, though. You can't hide from them," he told her, shaking his head with mock sadness. His eyes danced, still sparkling wildly.

"Then it's your lot to help cleanse my . . . soul." She put the damp papers carefully aside. "I'm just thankful it wasn't the originals. I don't know what I was thinking!"

Spoken like a true historian.

"Your soul?" he asked, relieved and yet perplexed that she hadn't asked him any questions about what had just happened. Surely she was puzzled by what had occurred at the moment of climax.

Her next words confirmed that she understood part of what had occurred, that she understood the lightning that had swept through them.

"My soul, and anything else you messed up with your lustfulness," Brice said, taking his hand and towing him toward the guest bathroom. She added thoughtfully: "I hope we don't end up brain damaged from making love in water. Do you think that could happen?"

The corpse was dismembered and the dissevered limbs cast into the pit where they continued to move about for an entire day, only gradually losing mobility. My assistant called it an abomination—and perhaps it was. But all I could think of were the applications in battle. Imagine an army where the soldiers could be killed, have limbs struck off, and yet continue to battle. What would such a warrior be worth?

—*From the medical journal of Johann Conrad Dippel*

I should, many a good day, have blown my brains out, but for the recollection that it would have given pleasure to my mother-in-law. And even then, I might have carried it through if I could have been sure of becoming a ghost and haunting her.

—*Lord Byron in a letter to Thomas Moore*

Not quite adultery, but adulteration.

—*Byron*, Don Juan

Chapter Nine

A while later, when they were curled up by the fire in the library, sipping at some horrendously expensive brandy, Brice finally got around to the subject of their unusual lovemaking. But even then, her methods were indirect and delicate, guiding the conversation yet giving Damien room to answer or not as he chose.

"That's some physiognomy you've got. It seems to work like a dynamo. Still, if it always has that effect . . . ?"

"Nearly always," Damien confirmed.

She smiled a little. "I guess you like winter a lot, then."

"This winter," he answered, his hand running down the curve of her waist, wanting her skin but settling for the soft flannel of her nightgown. He liked the way her hair looked when it was slightly damp. It fell into messy ringlets that glowed in the firelight.

"Does it ever get embarrassing?" Brice asked curiously. "I'm thinking especially when you were a teenager."

"I've learned to control it," he said and then frowned.

"Except during very particular kinds of storms. But I remain home for those special events. When the raging outside is no match for the one within, it's best to stay indoors and away from temptation."

"I would think so."

"Anyway, I didn't have this . . . *condition* when I was a teenager."

She nodded calmly. After a moment, obviously coming to some decision, she said in her most reasonable way, "Many people don't know it, but intuition is really the most sophisticated sort of reasoning that humans have. It comes from both the conscious and unconscious, putting together many clues buried in both sides of the brain. I think everyone has it, but few choose to listen when it speaks. Perhaps that is because the same process causes imagination—which is usually embarrassingly wrong about what it conceives."

"Your intuition is speaking?" Damien asked. His body tensed slightly but he didn't turn away. This was what he wanted, wasn't it—someone to finally understand?

"Yes. Or else my imagination." She rolled over to face him, then draped an arm over his waist. She kissed the part of his chest that peeped through the V of his shirt. "Whichever it is, my gut is telling me something that should be impossible. But I don't think it is. Which presents me with an intriguing problem."

"And what is that? The impossibility, I mean."

"Do you really want to know? To have it out in the open?" she asked gently.

"Yes. I think so." Then Damien frowned. "Hell! I don't know. Tell me anyway."

Brice looked at him for a long moment, then sat up. She went to the desk. First she selected and opened a book that contained a copy of one of his handwritten let-

140

ters, back from when he'd been George Gordon, Lord Byron. Then she leaned down and slid open the second desk drawer where the sherry had been. She pulled out a piece of folded paper. She closed the desk carefully and brought both to Damien, who had risen and was adding wood to the fire.

She compared the signatures before she handed the book and paper over.

"Are you a forger?" Her voice was slightly unsteady. "You could tell me that, and I would make myself believe you because my imagination is vivid and I have been wrong before. Once or twice."

His heart stumbled. Of course she'd had indications of the truth—provocative ones. Yet nothing individually, or even collectively, should have been enough to lead her to this conclusion. Not so quickly. Yet, somehow, she had made this leap of intuition and faith, and arrived at the correct answer.

That was what he wanted, wasn't it? he asked himself again. It was why he had kept her here, revealed Ninon's letters, seduced her during a storm. He could have stayed quiet about these things, could have locked himself away for the night. But he hadn't.

"No, I'm not a forger. Just careless, apparently." Damien turned back from the fireplace and put up the tongs. He took the proffered tome and paper, but barely glanced at them. Instead he watched her face.

"Are you . . . well, *are you?*" she asked.

"Yes. I am." He waited for her reaction.

"But how?" she asked, believing and yet clearly baffled. "How can this be? Is it connected to the . . . the lightning?"

"It's a long story," he said. Then, looking at the window where the wind still screamed, he added: "But, then, it seems that we shall have a long while for me to tell it. The city will be closed down by morning. I can't recall the last time that happened. It rather reminds of another storm long, long ago."

"Never mind the weather." Brice knelt on the rug and reached for his hand, tugging him down beside her. There was still some current, some inner heat that made his skin tingle, but it was mild now, safe. For a while at least.

"I had epilepsy caused by a lesion in the brain," Damien began, gaze and voice remote as he visited a past that he would have preferred to forget. "And every year it grew worse until I was certain that I would die or be made an idiot from the increasingly violent seizures. I worked feverishly at my poems, but . . . Fate slung ever shorter years at me like a volley of arrows, shooting them by too quickly for me to see, and yet leaving great damage in my body and brain. I needed more time for my work. For my life."

Brice murmured encouragingly as he began his tale. His voice had changed, had become more . . . British. Her heart was beating a bit wildly. But then, these last few days her heart had beat faster and harder than ever before, pumping not just blood but expectation, desire, even hope into every fiber of her being. And it was all because of him—George Gordon. Lord Byron. *Damien.* It was confusing, because she thought of him now as both men. It was because of him that she felt alive. He'd done this for her—given her back the pulse of a living, vital person, reminded her that she could have a life that wasn't as plain—as boring—as the stale soda crackers she crumbled into her canned soup every day at lunch.

And now she was taking a journey with him back in time, and she was about to learn something no other living person knew. Talk about getting off the tour bus! She wasn't just seeing—she was *finding*. She was thrilled and terrified, and her heart jittered as it bounced between the two extremes of rare emotion.

"My wife was alarmed and repelled by my seizures, and she feared that the condition was hereditary and that we would have idiot children. She shunned my bed, and eventually her fear grew into hate. Few know this, but her increasing revulsion was one of the real reasons I left England."

Brice strove to keep all traces of pity from her face, to not speak ill of his wife. She knew that not everyone was brave when it came to challenging Fate, which was so much bigger and meaner than mortal man or woman. And back then they hadn't understood about epilepsy, nor had they known effective treatments for it. When the bully of illness had sneaked up on Byron's wife, it was understandable that the woman had quailed and fled.

Yet Brice despised her anyway. It was just one more way in which the woman had been a coward. And that fear had made her into a liar who maligned her husband, hurting him even after his death.

"On my journey to Lake Geneva, I happened by a castle where I took shelter from an especially terrible storm—a notorious castle later visited by the Shelleys." Brice couldn't help but stiffen, and her movement made Damien smile slightly. "Yes, that's the one. Understand, it was not a place I would have sought out voluntarily. It was an inhospitable and lonely situation, but night had fallen early. A cold white cloak of stinging mist that carried a strange clinging snow had settled on my hair and shoulders. It was periodically torn away by a raging wind when we emerged from the tract of woods, but always it returned, colder, deeper, more tenacious and smothering.

I realize now that it stank of formaldehyde because we neared the castle and Dippel was hard at work.

"You have to imagine it. The air in the open was merciless and battered everything. Even the clouds were ragged and bruised, unable to hold their shape. I feared for my mount and also for the coachman and those horses that hauled the carriage." Damien exhaled slowly. "Anyhow, we took shelter at the castle, and it was there that I met Johann Conrad Dippel. And it was in his presence that I had my most violent seizure. It was also that night that he made me an intriguing—but what I then took to be insane—proposition."

Damien looked out into the night.

"You don't mean . . . ?"

"Yes, that's it exactly. Of course, I did not accept his offer right away. And as soon as the storm passed, I continued on to Villa Diodoti—in the carriage, for I was very ill. I got on with life as well as I could. It was only later when the Shelleys visited and I again had a terrible seizure which nearly ended my life that I finally gave in to their entreaties and sent for Dippel. The seizures were coming hourly by then. I consented to his treatment."

"And thus a legend was born," Brice whispered. Her eyes felt enormous and probably were. "It involved some form of electroshock therapy?"

"A form of it, yes."

Logs crashed in the grate, and the sound broke the worst of the spell of Damien's strange tale.

"I don't know why I've told you this now," he said at last, focusing his dark eyes on her face, his voice returning to its present day intonation and accent. "Perhaps it is because I see in you many of the traits that existed in me when I was young—first and foremost, a hunger beyond the understanding of most men, a thirst for knowledge that reaches beyond the present and into the past where history was born. You also have a logical mind. This makes me believe that you can perhaps understand why I did what I did."

Brice nodded—not in agreement, but simply in acknowledgment of his words. She was not certain that she did understand or agree. Perhaps she had been conditioned by too many horror films, but she found his story as appalling as it was fascinating.

As though guessing her conflicting thoughts, he added: "That intellectual hunger is an odd thing. At first it was satisfied with investigation, with the exploration of other great minds, with expressing my inner thoughts through poetry. Then one day I looked up and truly understood that the river of time only runs one way, and that it is always flowing, carrying us farther from our goals and closer to death. Every year we lose precious brain cells. Every year we grow weaker. Yet even then, armed with this knowledge, I probably would not have considered this sort of life had not my own been in danger of ending prematurely." Damien got up and began to pace, his thoughts clearly causing some sort of agitation that required physical expression.

It was probably at least three parts regret for having confided his greatest secret in her. Brice remained still, not bothering to attempt reassurance. Not yet. He would know if she lied or spoke out of ignorance, or pity, or any heated emotion.

"I had very nearly made my peace with my early demise when this extraordinary coincidence happened. It was a gift, a dare from the gods! A chance to heal my brain, to extend my life—indefinitely, I suppose, though at the time I thought I was only reclaiming what would have been mine if disease had not plagued me." Damien paused in front of his desk and touched the manuscripts piled there. "There are those who said—and perhaps will say if they ever know the truth—that I was wrong to accept the challenge Fate threw at me. That I am unnatural because of what I've done."

"Mary Shelley?" Brice asked softly, speaking for the first time in a long while. "Was she one of those who did not accept?"

"Among others. Polidori left me soon after, you know. Dippel horrified him. He should have horrified me too. He knew what he was doing, after all. He *knew*." Damien's head turned in her direction and his dark eyes burned. "But I still count it as a gift. A dark one, to be sure. But it is not a bargain I too often regret."

"A bargain? Then there is a price attached to this"— she hunted for a word as she tried to snuff out an image of Daniel Webster dealing with a devil in a lab coat— "this immortality? What did you have to pay Dippel? Your firstborn son?" The attempted joke came out flat.

"In a way, yes. There is always a price, you know. Can you possibly doubt that? Especially when one is purchasing his life?" He pushed up his sleeves, showing the fine network of scars. But they both knew there were higher costs than the marks on his body.

"And that sometimes-regretted cost is . . . ?" she asked softly.

He spread his hands wide. "Where do I begin? Never writing poetry again for fear that someone would discover it and ferret out my identity." Brice made a small involuntary sound of pain, but Damien went on relentlessly. "Re-creating myself every two or three decades because, even in this age of plastic surgery, people do notice when you fail to age. Living a life that has at its core a secret that leads to vast deception of the people around you. Never being able to have true, lifelong intimacy with another human—not with a friend, not a lover, not a wife. And certainly not children. For almost two hundred years, my best friends have been dogs." He shook his head, for a moment his face lined with pain.

"But surely if you wanted—"

"No. I have buried children before—I will leave no other orphans behind wondering what became of their father, nor some woman wondering if her missing husband is truly dead. I see the question in your eyes, but think! Assuming they could survive the process of conversion, how could I ever bring them with me? It would be forcing them into an unnatural life of lies and secrets before they were old enough to truly understand. And what if any of them refused? Would they not be bitter if their mother and siblings aged and died and their father remained young? Would it not grow worse as they also aged and I did not?"

Brice swallowed all the questions and arguments that were welling up. It took a moment, but she asked calmly, "So, even with all this, you do not regret what you've done?"

"No." He paused. "At least not often. Though sometimes I wonder if Tennyson had it wrong—is it better to have loved and lost than to have never loved at all?"

She thought of the losses he had known. Many were well documented. But how many more had the next centuries brought? How many lovers had he turned away? How many lives and offers of happiness had he rejected because of his secret? How bad could the cumulative losses be? she asked herself. How could she measure it, given her own brief life?

Then Brice remembered an incident from her childhood. When she was twelve, her father had been trapped in a building that collapsed in an earthquake in San Francisco. He had ultimately been found and rescued, and had not suffered any permanent harm, but in those dark hours while she and her mother awaited word from the rescue squads, she had known the agonies of the damned. A part of her had never felt entirely safe after that.

She'd had other losses too—but only one lifetime's worth. Those losses had been hard to bear, the disappointment of loves that weren't great loves after all, and the one great love that had ended in death—a pointless death caused by a drunk driver on an icy road. Then the loss of parents, both to cancer. For a time she had been so sad, so lonely, that it had hurt to breathe because every inhalation reminded her that she was alive and in pain. And she'd decided then not to love again, not to care—at least not to care about anyone who was still living.

But, of course, in the end she always did care. Not caring was too much like being dead. You marinated in your grief long enough and you became the very heartache you wanted to escape. Then you turned into a ghost, and then into nothing at all. Surely it was the same for him, only on a vaster scale because he'd had centuries, lifetimes, to love and then lose. She'd never lost a child, but could imagine the pain of it. How could she judge him, or question any decision he made in order to survive?

His dark, compassionate eyes watched her, perhaps guessing what she was thinking.

Brice cleared her throat. "Sometimes I've felt guilty for being alive when Mark isn't. My parents too. They died so young. And though life has been good, I've wanted to go back and savor the lost time that I never realized was so precious," she confessed. "Sometimes I've felt like I would give anything to have it all back so I could do it better."

He shook his head. He wore the darkness well, and by the firelight he looked like he was one of the elements of the night—moon or star or even a dark angel. That was fanciful, of course, but the flickering gold light revealed the fantastical in him.

"There's no going back except with thoughts and words," he said. "Do not deceive yourself. I can't give you that. No one can. This is not magic. Yesterdays—yours and mine—are gone forever. We can never go back to where we were, when we were, who we were. I did not realize until later just what I had gained, and lost, forever."

Brice stared, unable at first to voice the new question that his words had given life. She was both fascinated and horrified.

"You can't give me that? But you can . . . ? Are you saying that you actually know how to . . . ?"

"Yes, I am breaking my rule of silence and secrecy. I am telling you the truth." He spread his hands wide. "It is just possible that I could give you many more tomorrows than you ever planned. Time to know all you wish to know about Ninon or myself or anyone. To achieve everything you want." He added almost to himself, "And perhaps that would be enough for you."

"You could give this to me?" she repeated. "Really?"

He backed off. "Perhaps. Theoretically. I've never attempted it before."

"*Perhaps?* But how, exactly? You actually know what Dippel did? The process?"

"Yes, I believe so. The process was more elaborate and

painful than the one I must go through now that I've changed, but I could probably duplicate it—if someone were mad enough to want me to." He again turned on his heel and paced the length of the room. His gait was only slightly marred by the surgery he must have had to correct his club foot. Any scars he might have as a memento of the old birth defect were too fine to see by firelight.

"I almost can't believe it." In fact, she couldn't.

"Understandable. You recall my mentioning that there was a price."

She nodded, returning her gaze to his face. "Yes." When he didn't look her way, she added, "Something besides emotional isolation and all the rest of it?"

"Yes. There is also a physical risk and permanent bodily changes. I risked the peril because my epilepsy was worsening and I couldn't bear the thought of it damaging my mind, killing off my intellect with every explosion in my brain."

"What is it that you did then?" she asked, eyes a little wide, breathing a little fast. She'd seen too many Frankenstein movies, and the horrible images of stitched corpses stolen from looted graves buffeted her mind like a flock of evil black birds. She was repelled and desperately hoped that he wouldn't tell her anything too awful to accept.

"I embraced death," he said simply. "I went to the gods in an iron cage, by stopping my heart with lightning. And then, in the place of agony, I grabbed their fire, praying that though it killed me their power would again return me to life." He stopped in front of her. "And it did."

"But?"

"But there were many others who were not so fortunate. Dippel had many failures. Maybe they didn't want life badly enough to fight through the pain."

"I see." In spite of the blaze in the fireplace, she felt a chill. A part of her wanted to make some sign—perhaps to cross herself, or to make some gesture to ward off the evil eye that must surely be watching.

"Read about it, if you want." He went to the desk and took out the old journal she had seen earlier. He hesitated a moment and then offered it to her. "I've improved upon the method he used, but fundamentally it's the same process—a mix of stimulants and electrocution by an iron plate clamped over the heart and charged with Saint Elmo's fire."

"You have been doing this to yourself?"

"I have to in order to keep the epilepsy at bay. Once in a while. It isn't a yearly event."

The paper of the journal had yellowed badly. She thought at first that it was age but then realized the paper had been exposed to intense heat. Some pages were even singed.

She squinted, reading the first few lines:

10 Dezember, 1731
Das Tagebuch
Johann Conrad Dippel.

She shivered again, her breath stopping as her heart constricted and then forgot for a moment to go on beating. This ghost would speak to her freely. He would be very real after this. If she took the apple from the serpent, would he always haunt her?

"My German is rusty. Does that really say that it's the daily journal of Johann Dippel from December of seventeen thirty-one?"

"Yes." Damien waited, hand outstretched, offering her a chance at knowledge.

Afraid and yet unable to resist, Brice stepped closer and reached for the journal.

It hit her at once: the same sensation of heat that had charged through her when she had opened Byron's letter. It was a passion driven by a mix of adrenaline and the knowledge that she was seeking, if not forbidden fruit, then the fruit of knowledge that had been denied most men. It felt a lot like desire, and a bit like terror, and it made every other emotion seem pallid.

She couldn't refuse it, whatever ugly thing she learned, even if the knowledge banned her forever from the innocence of Eden, she had to know.

Eyes very wide now, and face too pale, she looked up at her mentor. Finally, as the world began to gray at the edges, she remembered to breathe.

"I am in so much trouble," she whispered. Then she gave a small, inappropriate gasp of laughter that was two parts joy and three parts hysteria.

"What? Out with it," he said, sitting on the edge of his desk where he had made love to her. "I'd like to know what there is to laugh at in this. So far, it seems very unamusing."

"You're wearing jeans," Brice said, throwing up her hands.

His lips twitched. "I see. And?"

"Given what we are talking about—what you are suggesting—I am just so relieved that you don't smell like something that's been taxidermied." The teasing words came out against her will.

"Or cooked?" he suggested, starting to smile. Perhaps that was the only thing to do in this situation. He reached out and took her free hand, slowly drawing her toward him. The small band of flesh at his wrist was crisscrossed with the golden net of scars. "And here I have been romantically thinking of myself as a phoenix, not the main course at a barbecue."

"If you're a bird, you could be roasted or stuffed," she pointed out, allowing herself the joke. It was odd that his touch excited but also calmed. He was a man, a special man, but still human. Much of her supernatural fear died away.

"The first response that comes to mind at that observation is entirely too crude."

"I just can't believe it," she said.

"That I can be crude?"

She shook her head. "That I'm holding hands with history."

"Ah! It's more exciting and strange than you guess. Go read," Damien said, standing up suddenly and guiding her to her borrowed desk. He switched on a light. "Later, we will talk about the rest."

"There's more?" she asked, amazed.

"Yes. Dippel's story—and his evil—is not ended with that journal. Unfortunately."

Brice, head swimming with too many experiences, sat down and began to read at the place where the journal was marked. Damien opened his desk and pushed something. Soft music filled the room. He didn't bother trying to read or scribble out a new review, but sat watching her attentively.

A few minutes later, Brice lifted her head and glared.

"What?" he asked, his voice virtuous, his expression innocent.

Brice didn't want to admit that his gaze bothered her, but she heard herself saying, "I can feel your eyes inching up my nightgown."

"And that's a bad thing?"

"It's a damned distracting thing. I'm trying to read

about the greatest scientific experiment known to man here."

Damien smiled, but obligingly turned his gaze to the manuscript on his desk.

Two hours later, when the fire was nearly dead, Brice shut the journal. Byron put his manuscript down too. This time, neither of them smiled.

"I don't know if I believe it," she said. She rubbed a hand over her eyes. "But then, I have to believe it, don't I? This madman's ravings actually prolonged your life."

"No, you don't have to believe. You can let yourself suppose that this is all a dream. Or that I am a pathological liar. Or deranged. There are many options if you can't accept it," he answered.

Brice shook her head. "No, I can't believe any of that. Could you?"

"Honestly? No. I've never had the capacity for vast self-deception." He added, looking closely at her face, "I'm sorry. I should have waited to tell you about this. It's shocked you."

"Literally." Brice finally smiled. "I'm still tingling, you know."

"I don't actually feel bad about that part," he confessed, eyes heating. "The attraction between us all but danced in the air. How could I ignore it?"

"Why should you feel bad? I enjoyed myself hugely. But, Damien . . ." she said softly, then paused. Her brow furrowed. "What should I call you now?"

"Damien is best," he answered. "You must not think of me as being anyone else. It wouldn't be safe. You see, there's a lot more that I have to tell you about this situation. Until you understand, Byron must remain dead."

"There's a lot more?" she asked unhappily. Brice knew

she was in deep and would eventually have to know the truth, however terrible. A few hours ago—yesterday, even—she would have said that she had no expectation of this affair being more than an exciting interlude of escape from her work. It had been years since she had allowed herself to hope for anything more from a relationship than that there would be a quick mercy-killing when it came time for it to end. But that had all changed. This was the man of her dreams. And more. Hell's bells! He had loved several lifetimes and she was certain they had each been dangerous and exciting. And someday she would want to hear all about it. But not tonight.

"Yes, there's further to go in this tale. But that's for later. You've had enough dark stories and warnings for one night."

She nodded, face again sober, brow creased with concentration.

"Your intuition is speaking again?" he asked.

"Maybe. Was Ninon de Lenclos one of Dippel's . . ."

"Experiments?" Damien suggested.

"Patients," she corrected. "Don't make it sound so bad. For heaven's sake! You were seeking medical treatment, not an audience with the devil."

Damien didn't look convinced that so harmless a concept described what Dippel was doing, but he nodded without arguing.

"I've been thinking about the stories of her endless youth, and also her eyes. In early portraits her eyes were pale, but in that locket, her eyes are black. Your eyes only changed after . . . ?"

"Yes. Mine were blue. It was only afterward that my eyes became so dark. It is one of those physical changes I mentioned."

"I'm thinking of that mysterious man in black who

brought her that elixir to mix with her bathwater. Could that have been Dippel and not the devil?"

"I've wondered." Damien began searching through the papers on his desk. "There is another version of the story that she recounted to Abbé Scarron, claiming that the dark man appeared three times in her life. The dark man was said to be able to produce thunder and lightning at will. Ah! Here we are! Read this. Right before Ninon's eighteenth birthday she and Gentilly sought out a dark magician living on the outskirts of Paris."

Brice took the letter and read aloud in French. Her accent was improving with practice:

Upon entering the village, we enquired after the building where there lived a famous necromancer; and a guide presently presented himself to lead us thither. After proceeding five minutes along an underground passage, we found ourselves in a circular chamber hewn from the heart of the mountain.

I stared at the figure on the throne before us, a dark man, oddly scarred, with eyes as black as midnight.

"Approach!" he cried in a terrible voice. "What do you wish?"

Brice stopped reading aloud and scanned the rest of the letter. "Amazing."

"Yes. It reads like bad fiction, right down to their being blinded by lightning. And there are several other intriguing incidences. Twice in her life, Ninon's hair began to fall out, and twice, after she retired to the country for a rest, it grew back completely—in a matter of weeks. The second time it happened, she went to England. It was when she witnessed the execution of Charles the First—a king who had been lame as a child but who was miraculously healed as an adult. A king whose eyes had also gone dark."

"Charles the First?" Brice's voice was awed. "He was Dippel's patient also?"

"Maybe."

"I recall this story about Ninon. Rather than wear a wig, she arranged her short curls in a style called *se coiffeur à la Ninon*. It was very popular. But everyone in Paris marveled that her hair grew back so quickly. I think they were dismayed at finding themselves with such short crops when her own hair grew in so rapidly. Do you think that this is when she . . . *renewed* herself?"

"It's suggestive, isn't it? But as for it being Dippel's brand of eternal youth, I don't know. I always suspected it but could never be sure. Reason says Dippel couldn't have done it. Not if he was actually born when he said he was."

Gooseflesh raced up Brice's arms. She put the letter down carefully. "But was he?" she asked. Then, shaking her head: "But Ninon eventually died. There was a funeral, and many people saw the body."

"I had a funeral too—several of them, in fact. And people thought they saw my body as well," Damien pointed out. "Services and burials really don't mean as much as one assumes. I have a lock of her hair, so DNA testing would be possible—and I've had French lawyers petitioning to have the body exhumed so a comparison can be made, but the odds of them ever granting the request aren't good. And so far I haven't been able to bring myself to try grave-robbing."

"Has there been any sign of her? Any . . . anything?"

"No. Not that I've found. But I still think it may be possible that she survived beyond her nineties."

"I think my brain just imploded," Brice said weakly.

"I'm sorry," Damien apologized again, genuinely contrite. "It's all a bit much, isn't it?"

Brice suddenly wanted noise, everyday noise—a vacuum, a telephone, traffic, voices—anything to break the weird spell that surrounded them. But there was only that eerie wind that pawed at the windows, and the last soft crackle of ashes falling in the fireplace.

"Such a fierce expression. What are you thinking?" Damien asked.

"That I know very little about you, other than you prefer your coffee mercilessly black. Also, it seems a pity that I can never tell the world the truth—that the immortal poet Lord Byron really *is* immortal," Brice finally said, forcing a smile to go with her understatement.

"Not immortal." His face was serious as he tried to explain. "Only indefinitely alive. Understand, I can be wounded. I can even be killed, though my body has a great capacity to heal damage. Frankly, in my more fanciful moments, I find this fact reassuring."

"How so? Afraid of eternal boredom eventually setting in?" The question just slipped out.

"Not yet." He smiled briefly. "No, my thoughts are actually more gothic, more morbid. I don't know that a twenty-first-century mentality can understand them."

"You worry about your soul," she guessed, certain that she was right. It would worry *her*, and she had not been raised in the nineteenth century when religion was treated more seriously.

"Yes. And it is odd that I should wonder about it now, for I never did when I was young." Damien frowned.

"And what have you decided?"

"It seems to me that unlike a vampire or fictional Frankenstein's poor monster—or Dorian Gray, perhaps—since I did not seek out this quasi-immortality, and since I can die, that I have not actually sold my soul for this gift of long life. And therefore, I have not rendered myself unfit for heaven."

"Do you often think about this?" Brice asked, feeling sympathetic.

"No, not often. In fact, until the last few weeks, I hadn't thought of the matter since April of nineteen sixteen."

"Why nineteen sixteen?" Brice asked. Then, guessing, she said: "Because it was the anniversary?"

A noisy buffet shook the window. The wind howled like a wounded animal and threw itself at the building, and like a wounded animal after its attacker, the wind seemed dangerous. She was glad that the glass was thick. Heavy shutters would have been even better.

"Yes, the centennial." Seeing her distress, he went to the window and pulled the drapes against the storm. "But suddenly I find myself thinking about these things again—and being watchful. Perhaps it is just this strange weather that has plagued us this winter, but I've felt as if Fate is closing in, that the wheel of life is turning in a new direction."

Brice shivered and made an effort to push back the tiny fear that was making the hairs on her nape stand on end. It was an atavistic fear, a sudden dread that reached out from the blackest night and the earliest primeval awareness of evil. Timeless evil, intelligent and calculating—though probably mad—was once again walking among men, and was stalking them.

Oh, bullshit. What evil? This wasn't intuition—it was just the storm. And Byron or no Byron, she'd had enough of the macabre for one night. It was time to turn the subject to happier things, like the miracle she had just made love to. A miracle who could answer all the questions she'd ever had about his life as a great poet.

She laughed softly.

"I heard a rumor that you gave Murray a bible—a very handsome one which he liked to display," she said. "Or he liked it until someone pointed out that in John 18:40 you had changed the verse from 'Now Barabbas was a robber' to 'Now Barabbas was a publisher.'"

"But can you blame me?" Damien asked, answering her smile. He seemed as relieved as she to have the subject turned.

Brice thought of her own situation with her publisher, which involved as much hate as love, and grinned wryly. "What of you going about London eating nothing but hard biscuits and soda water? I always thought your supposed creative diet was a sham or caused by a tricky stomach."

"Of course it was a sham, but it got me attention—and so many of those fools actually followed it, waiting for the muse to visit them. It was inconvenient, but I could eat other things at home—sparingly, of course. In those days, when my health was so fragile and I could not exercise, I was prone to fatness."

Lord Byron fat? Brice shook her head, still feeling more than slightly dazed.

"And the story about you swimming the Grand Canal in Venice with a lantern in your left hand?" She tactfully left out the part about him doing this after visiting his mistress.

"Well, I tried it the night before without the lantern and kept getting whacked by oars from passing gondolas. It turned out there was a law that everything in the canal had to carry a lantern after the sun was down. I was only obeying the ordinance." He was smiling easily now, more relaxed.

"And did you really keep a bear in your rooms while at university?"

"Only briefly. And only once. I quickly discovered the difficulties in sharing living quarters with the beast, and there were more convenient ways of expressing defiance of scholarly authority. I also got expelled for using the bear to tree one of the dons." He shook his head. "But that's enough of my past sins for one night. It's nearly dawn. Time you were in bed."

"I'm only going if you come with me," she said quickly, perhaps fearing that he meant to leave her to the storm now that his secret was revealed.

"I'll come with you—but only if you agree to stop asking questions. Your eyes look bruised. And I can see you're half dizzy with lack of sleep. I've not treated you well. You must rest."

"It's just the brandy that's made me tired," she assured him, wanting him to know that he hadn't hurt her when they made love.

He shook his head and then took her hand. Sparks flew, though they were invisible to the eye and comparatively tame. He began to lead her toward her bedroom.

"You won't be able to resist me," she predicted smugly. "Not with the storm still raging."

"We'll see," he answered. "I am certainly going to try. And you will help me."

"I will?" she asked doubtfully.

"You will," he said firmly.

"And what will happen if I don't? Will you spank me?"

He looked back, eyes amused. "Nothing that enjoyable. I'll just leave you to sleep alone."

"That's cruel. I knew you were an alpha," she muttered under her breath.

161

MELANIE JACKSON

"And I knew you'd be my undoing." His voice took on a stronger accent and he slid into his lecturer role. "Now, let's talk about something dull and un-arousing so you can sleep. Let's see. Victorians, they're the dullest of the dull. Frankly, I found the era of the nineteenth-century absolutists more depressing than anything that came before. It took the world a long while to shake off the Victorians, since they attempted to smother any new ideas at birth and precious few innovations survived to challenge their way of thinking. It was better in America, of course. At least here ideas were given a chance if they showed any hint of economic viability."

"I'm a historian. That's not a dull subject," Brice warned him.

"It will be," he promised. "And if that doesn't work, there's always baseball."

"Please! I know it's un-American, but anything but baseball."

And thus did I instruct my assistant: These volumes should be your study day and night, your familiarity with them sufficient that you should retain an understanding of the material that you may perform these experiments without recoursing to notes. Until such a time, no experiments should be undertaken, for this is not something to be enterprised lightly. We are treading in the realm of gods and must beware.

—*From the medical journal of Johann Conrad Dippel*

I am in terror. I have seen my man in black! The man with the red tablets bearing my name and the dozen bottles of elixir—the one who appeared before me seventy years ago. And I heard him say he has a son who will be called St. Germain and the world shall know him and be filled with awe and dread.

—*From the letters of Ninon de Lenclos*

Now hatred is by far the longest pleasure;
Men love in haste, but they detest at leisure.

—*Byron*

The reading or non-reading of a book will never keep down a single petticoat.

—*Byron, letter to Richard Hoppner, October 29, 1918*

Chapter Ten

Brice dreamed as she never had before, her weird, nightmarish visions played out before a sewn-together backdrop of strange emotions, memories and wild imaginings, where frightening things both real and unreal happened over and over again. The only difference in each performance of the nightmare was that the stage grew progressively dimmer and the mood more ominous.

She came awake in a rush, alarmed. "What's wrong?" she whispered, her voice raspy. She wasn't her usual bushy-tailed self after only a couple of hours of sleep and the lingering terror of the dreams made things worse.

"The power's out," Damien answered, his voice also hushed.

Brice glanced at the clock on her nightstand. It was dark in the room but not completely so. She looked quickly toward her door. Out in the hall, there was a small red light up near the ceiling. It blinked periodically.

"The smoke detectors have battery backup," Damien

said, guessing her next question. "Just sit still and listen for a moment. There should be light soon—if this is just an accident. The security man at the desk knows how to turn on the backup generators."

They waited for what seemed an eternity, staring at the small red dot—*danger, warning, spilled blood*, it said—then Damien threw back the covers.

"*If*, you said. You think this isn't an accident?" Brice's voice was barely louder than the wind outside. The storm had worsened while they slept.

As though hearing her thought, Damien went to her window and pried it open. The wind rushed inside, hurling snow at them. The bitter confetti latched onto the drapes and carpet and clung with icy claws.

Brice thought of the story Damien had told her about the unnatural storm that brought him to Dippel's castle. She shuddered, pushing the memory away.

"It's dark over the entire block. But only this block. Damn," Damien said. "Get dressed, Brice. I have a bad feeling."

Brice scrambled after Damien, her skin crawling with more than cold. She had a bad feeling too. She rushed to the window and looked down before he could close it, half expecting to see something evil waiting there in the fierce night.

The streetlights were out as well, but she could see that there were tracks in the snow leading up to the building's main entrance. It was difficult to tell, since more than one person could have walked the same path, but she counted at least three distinct trails. And there was something ominous about them.

"Who would cut the power? Could it be street gangs?" she asked, allowing Damien to pull her back and slam the window shut. The question should have surprised her, because it came out of her subconscious, bypassing reason. It didn't, though. She felt very in tune with Damien and knew what he was thinking.

Brice shivered. The magic bubble of new love—or at least new lust—that surrounded them had burst. The dark that had been romantic only hours before was now sinister. And she was standing naked with a man who was, if not a virtual stranger, then at least still very strange to her. However, the death of romance did not mean her mental connection with Damien had ended. If anything, it was stronger than before.

"Trust me, it's no one you want to know," Damien said grimly, dusting her off with his crumpled clothing and then pulling on his dampened shirt. "You recall when I said that there was one other thing I needed to tell you? One other danger connected with my prolonged life?"

"Vaguely." She remembered more clearly his passionate description of her body by moonlight.

She reached for her boots, then decided she had better put on her pants first. She turned to the dresser and pulled open the top drawer, grabbing clothes by feel alone. She hated that she was always a little slow upon waking, that part of her mind seemed tethered in the dreamlands and she had to reel it back in before being fully functional.

"Well, there are actually three things you need to know," Damien said. "One, Dippel probably isn't dead. For the longest time I thought he was, since the peasants in his village did a real torch-and-pitchfork number on his castle and supposedly killed everyone in it. But I have recently begun to suspect that it is otherwise. Two, I know of two others of his former *patients* who have come to a bad end. I wasn't close with them, you understand, but we knew of each other. One lived in France, one in Florida. Both died early last year in suspicious fires. I didn't find out about it until this fall, though. The will of my acquaintance in France took a long time to probate, and the small instruction of informing me of Jean's death was overlooked for months. And Paul had no will."

"And three?" she asked, keeping her voice level. It required an extreme effort, because she was beginning to shake violently. The snow was off of her body, but not the chill.

"I hired a firm of private investigators to find the man I suspect to be Dippel, and to determine if he had anything to do with the deaths of Jean Perregaux or Paul Holmes."

"And?" Brice pulled on a sweater, hoping she had it the right way around.

"There was no proof one way or another. But the man who sounds a lot like Dippel has vanished from his bunker in Nevada—which also conveniently burned— and one of the investigators turned up dead, again burned in a car crash when his vehicle ran off the road."

"Was it an accident?"

"The police report says so." Damien moved toward the door. "But I don't believe it. Not now."

Brice grabbed her coat and moved behind him. As always, he didn't seem to feel the chill.

"I think I'm frightened."

"Come on. We need to get to the library. Just stay close and be quiet and everything will be fine." His voice was brisk and reassuring.

They ghosted down the hall, their way lit by the distant city lights bleeding through the iced-over windows and by the intermittent red light of the smoke detectors.

Damien stopped by a small table and lifted the receiver of the antique telephone.

"It's dead. It could be the storm." He didn't bother to put any conviction in his voice.

"Uh-huh, and pigs may fly. Do you have a cell phone somewhere?"

"No, I told you. I can't get a signal off the bloody things. In fact, I wreak havoc on lots of machines. Do you have one?"

"No. Remember? I told you I can't stand constantly being interrupted."

"So . . ." Damien turned and continued down the hall.

"I think we have to assume that we're really in trouble," Brice said as she followed.

"Yes, I believe the expression is 'in deep shit.'"

Brice almost laughed. The phrase sounded ridiculous on his lips.

"Yes—but how deep?" she asked. "I'm not sure I understand, or even have the scales on which to measure our difficulties. What does Dippel want? To kill you? And if so, why?"

They walked quickly, being careful to avoid the desk Brice had been using. There was still a faint glow of embers in the fireplace.

"That remains to be seen, though I suspect you have the right of it. He wants me dead—if not, why not just send a Christmas card or phone for an appointment?" He asked abruptly, "Can you use a gun?"

"Yes," Brice answered without hesitation. She didn't ask if he could. Lord Byron had been a noted marksman. It wasn't likely that he allowed his skills to deteriorate.

"Good." Damien opened a side panel in his desk and extracted two pistols. She didn't recognize the make of either gun in the dark, but they were heavy, and hers was warm—almost hot. She began to be aware of how warm Damien really was. His body temperature had been normal while resting, but standing beside her, he radiated heat like a fully stoked iron stove. His elevated body temperature had heated the metal in the few seconds he held the gun.

"It's loaded," he said. "Just point and shoot."

Brice turned toward the window and sighted down the barrel. She checked to see where the safety catch was and then opened the gun and looked inside. It held eight bullets. She hoped that would be enough.

"Aim for the face," Damien said, tucking his weapon into the band of his pants. "It may not kill them, but it's hard to chase someone with your eyes shot out."

Them? Dippel's monsters, his undying soldiers. All the horrors she'd read about in that leather-bound journal. So she hadn't been wrong about the ominous prints in the snow and what Damien was thinking.

Brice swallowed and nodded, trying not to feel like Alice down the rabbit hole. It was difficult, because in spite of what Damien had told her, the proof she had seen with her own eyes, and what she had read in Dippel's own journal, she hadn't really believed most of it. She still didn't. It was easier to think that any invaders were conventional thieves or drug dealers.

Brice dropped the pistol into her coat pocket. She thrust her hands in as well. She didn't want to see if they were shaking.

"Okay, here's the plan," Damien said. His face was harsh in the dim red light. "We are going to climb down the ladder in the elevator shaft to the floor below. After that, there are stairs we can use. We are making for the fifth floor. That's where the security office is."

"There's more than the guard in the lobby?"

"There should be at least one other on duty even at night. Hopefully, he hasn't been incapacitated yet."

"And if he has?" Brice asked, even though she was sure she wouldn't like the answer.

"Then we take any weapons we can find in the office. And we come back up here and I lock you in the vault while I take care of this mess."

"No," Brice said immediately. She didn't like the sound of the vault or of Damien "taking care of this mess." Both sounded potentially fatal.

"It has an inside latch. You'll be able to get out if you need to," Damien said, understanding that she was objecting to being shut up in the vault. He started for the foyer where the elevator was.

Brice thought of all those not-so-accidental fires that Damien had mentioned and shuddered. If the building went up, escaping from the vault wouldn't help her.

"No. We don't split up. Not for any reason. They always split up in the movies and it's always a bad idea."

"Yes, we do split up—if the guard has been gotten at," he argued. He looked back at her. "Unless you've done a lot of mountain climbing in the snow?"

"No." Their footsteps echoed in the hall. She asked, "Why would that matter? You said the elevator had a ladder. And there are stairs." She could do stairs, even in the dark. The elevator . . . well, she would manage somehow. A shaft wasn't like a car, and she rode in elevators all the time. Well, a lot of the time. When she had no other choice.

"If Dippel's gotten to the security room, then they are in the building—using the stairwell probably. If I'm to get down to the generator and see about reconnecting the phones, I'll have to go down the outside of the building.

171

In good weather, it would be a hard climb. In this hell broth? No, I couldn't let you risk it."

"No." Brice repeated. Again, she didn't ask about who "they" were. It made some sense that Dippel wouldn't come alone. And there were those tracks—so at least three people were here. "No, absolutely not. Look, I have a better idea. If they've gotten to the security guard, we burn a match under the smoke detectors and set it off. That'll bring the fire department. They can call the police if we need them."

She didn't think about the fact that Dippel might have a similar plan, only one that involved actually burning down the building. That was too horrible to think about.

"Good plan, but it won't work." Damien stopped in front of the elevator doors and began working his fingers into the crack. He shouldn't have been able to force the car open, but he managed it quickly. "The smoke detectors only alert the security room. If there really is a fire, the guards call the fire department. I had to do this because I kept setting the damned things off every time it stormed or I had a nightmare. And you can bet the phone lines have been cut for the whole building, not just on this floor."

Damien finished opening the metal door with one hand. Brice could only stare at him and wonder how strong he actually was. Had Dippel's treatment done more than extend his life and turn him into a human furnace?

"Let's try it now," she urged as he swung into the dark shaft. She could smell grease from the gears and cables and began to feel a little dizzy at the thought of stepping into the black hole. She didn't like confined spaces. She never had, and it had gotten worse since the car accident. The petroleum smell rolling out of the dark didn't help, either. "If the guard is there, then he'll call the fire department and help will be here in no time."

"The ladder is to the left," Damien said. "It's stable, so don't worry about falling."

"Damien, damn it! You aren't listening."

"Look, we can't do that. If Dippel has taken over the security room, then this will just alert him to the fact that we're up and know he's here. We might as well lay out the welcome mat and shout *'yoohoo, over here!'* Anyway, I'm not sure we want the police and fire departments. This would be awfully hard to explain, and I don't much fancy becoming anyone's medical marvel—which is bound to happen if anyone with an ounce of medical training gets a look at me." His voice was getting fainter. "Brice, just wait for me up there. It's safe for now, and I'll be back in five minutes."

"Damn it." Brice reached into the dark, feeling for the ladder. The smell choked her, but she forced herself to ignore it. "I'm coming. Slow down."

"Wait there. And be quiet a moment. I need to listen for them," Damien said, and there was the fading sound of another set of doors being forced open.

Brice waited, breath held, listening with Damien for any reverberations that suggested he had walked into an ambush on the floor below. But there was nothing. And after another moment, she realized that there wasn't any Damien either. He had gone on without her.

"Damn it!"

Though she was not in the shaft yet, a sort of claustrophobia set in. Suddenly she became aware that the building, though comparatively huge, was actually finite. And therefore not big enough. Not while a killer might be on the loose, not while death stalked. And try as she might, she couldn't shake off the idea that there could be something there in the dark, something dead, creeping toward her up the ladder she still couldn't find with her groping hand.

The walls of panic started closing in. She pushed back with all her might, shoving, sweating and swearing in her brain, using all her willpower to hold the claustrophobia and fear at bay. It was no use, though. Brice finally pulled her arm back, shuddering violently. She couldn't do it. Not alone.

It was such a small thing, but she couldn't look into the dark pit and not sense monsters waiting there.

"Damien, damn you."

The Ninety-first Psalm suddenly popped into her head:

> *You shall not be afraid of the terror by night, nor the arrow that flies by day, nor pestilence that walks in darkness, nor destructors that lay waste at noonday. A thousand may fall at your side, and ten thousand at your right hands, but it shall not come near you. . . .*

"Yeah, sure." She forced her voice not to quaver, but fear was creeping over her, bringing a chill to her skin. "Santa, if you're listening, cancel that order for a new laptop. All I want for Christmas this year is for us to make it out alive."

Damien knew from experience that there were two kinds of time. One was the stuff that made up days and nights. You marked it with minutes and hours on a watch, or by weeks on a calendar.

Then there was the other kind, the type that went too swiftly for the consulting of timepieces. It was the type that rushed at you in moments of danger. That was where he was now. His body was recalibrating to this faster internal clock, sending adrenaline to his muscles, speeding up his heart so he was prepared for the shift into battle.

Another minute and he was ready. He had discovered long ago that he was willing to lose his life in combat, but not his nerve. Not his honor.

Gun ready, Damien stepped out of the elevator shaft and sprinted through the dark for the security office.

It was too much to hope that he'd find the security guard rocking back in his swivel chair, hands folded across his lap as he napped, unaware of the power outage. Or that perhaps the backup system had kicked in and the guard was now watching over several screens filled with universally peaceful scenes. Or, if there was something fishy on the screen, that he would be able to whip out some exotic weapon that could be used remotely, and only on the lower floors—perhaps something like a knockout gas, which could be sprayed through the ventilation system.

Actually, he'd better hope there wasn't any knockout gas around. There was no guarantee that it would work on Dippel, and Damien didn't fancy being caught napping by his old friend.

Damien jogged right and then got up close to the wall as he inched toward his goal.

Under other circumstances, Damien might not have known where the security offices were located. Having no mania for law enforcement, he did not habitually seek out knowledge of this sort. But he had designed and overseen construction of Ruthven Tower, and had made a point of knowing about his tenants and any changes they made to the architecture.

The new security suite was down the hall from the elevators on the west side of the building. It took up the coveted northwest corner of the tower and was the only suite on this floor not leased by Birken, Birken & Thomas, Attorneys at Law.

Damien reviewed the building's new layout as he ran. Birken, Birken & Thomas's offices ran the gamut in sizes. There were ridiculously large suites for the senior partners, cubbies and lavatories for the legal researchers and assistants, and one palatial bathroom, heavily insulated, lined in marble and without any windows. It could only be accessed with an executive's key—which Damien happened to have. It would be a good place to stash Brice if she flatly refused the vault. It also had a fire escape right across the hall. This would please her, though he had no intention of using it or letting her set foot on it either. Dippel wasn't stupid, and he would likely have guards watching the fire escape and the stairs. She'd be an easy target out there in all that white.

Normally, the security office was locked with a card-reader that could read badges and also accepted codes punched into the key pad. But with the power off, the door unlocked automatically, enabling firefighters or paramedics to get inside in the case of an emergency.

Damien stopped outside the offices, breathing quickly, sickness in his heart.

It had been a long time since he was in a combat situation—not since World War I. That "war to end all wars" had killed his last remaining appetite for foreign crusades and bloodshed. Europe, at the end of his stay, had seemed to him a wasteland of barbed wire, starvation and shattered corpses, all caused by the endless and ultimately senseless shelling done by both sides. But the skills he had learned there and on every *other* battlefield where he'd shed blood had not deserted him. Damien had spent a lot of his time doing what they now called guerilla-style fighting behind enemy lines. In this place of *other* time, it was as though he had been in battle only yesterday. Damien didn't like it, but he knew what to do.

The door! Damien thought as his eyes focused, the thin strip of paler darkness arresting his unpleasant memories of past conflict.

The door unlocked in a power outage, but it didn't open itself. That took some outside agent. And guards were trained to always close the door after themselves if they left the office. It was possible that under these circumstances, the guard had simply forgotten. But it was quiet. Too quiet. *Dead* quiet.

Damien stopped breathing for a moment to listen for sounds from the office, creeping up silently on the crack in the doorway.

He began breathing again. Nothing. Except a certain unpleasant smell—also all too familiar.

Damien walked into the room, gun in hand, but no longer pointed it straight in front of him.

The guard was dead. Two deadly blossoms of crimson were unfurled on his chest, the handiwork of a high-powered rifle discharged at close range. His eyes were open, his mouth too. There was nothing subtle about this assault; Dippel wasn't making an attempt at stealth. He wasn't trying to make anything look accidental. And he wasn't sparing innocents. They were simply bait, things to goad Byron with.

Maybe he saw this poor man as a gauntlet that he could hurl in Byron's face.

"Bloody hell."

Damien noticed on the desk a small white box in a nest of red wrapping paper.

There was a fish tank on the desk as well, quiet now that the bubbles were stilled along with the other electrical appliances. The neon tetras still moved about, but cautiously, as though frightened into an unnatural stillness by what they had witnessed.

Knowing it was pointless, Damien still knelt down and felt for a pulse in the guard's neck. He noted more details about the uniformed man as he touched the chilled skin. The guard's face was colorless now, but it had normally known a more healthy tint, the man being of Hispanic descent. He wasn't a young man, but not old either. He should have lived another thirty years.

He'd also presumably been someone with dreams, someone who could laugh, who probably occasionally drank too much at parties, played basketball, maybe cheated on his taxes. He was someone's son, maybe someone's lover, maybe a father.

And now he was nothing.

Well-known bitterness filled Damien's throat, and he had to choke back a cry.

At least the man had gotten to open his present before he died. A watch. Gold gleamed on the man's thin wrist, the hands moving in the lighted face. It was a good watch, then, shock resistant, and it went on telling the time of normal life though it was now meaningless to its dead owner.

The watch had an alarm, too, and it began to chirp as the hands reached the hour mark. It sounded a strident alarm, but too late to save the man who wore it. Damien quickly shut it off.

Familiar anger, the rage of the battlefield, though an emotion not felt for more than ninety years, began to fill him. The berserkers, the dark, dangerous parts of his personality, dormant for almost a century, awoke and prepared themselves for war. Wasteful death—and a death meant for him—had been visited on this innocent man. It didn't matter that Damien hadn't known this guard. Donne was right: Every man's death diminished him, when the loss was not meant for the person who suffered or died. The one responsible for this would pay—and pay horribly. Pay eternally. It would be Damien's pleasure to see to it.

A small snarl rose from his throat and rumbled in the dark. The sound was shocking. Inhuman.

"No," Damien said into the cold room, denying the beast. "Don't go there. It won't help."

A part of him wanted the rage, though. It felt wrong to stay calm, and it was disrespectful to the man who had died in his place. Still, Damien killed the anger immediately. He knew what the rage could do, and it was one of the few things he feared.

He'd felt it the first time as a boy, when he'd found that stupid workman flogging a lamed horse. Trapped between the toppled wagon's traces by the long wood poles and his own broken leg, the beast had been entirely at the man's mercy. By the time the young and limping Lord Byron arrived, the creature was streaming with sweat and blood and screaming in pain and fear. He'd nearly killed that man, had actually taken pleasure in wresting the whip away from him and turning it on the sadist, beating him as the man had beaten the poor animal, stripping away cloth and then skin and then muscle.

Damien shuddered at the memory of his own savagery. He hadn't cared that others looked on, hadn't heeded the man's screams for mercy. If others hadn't eventually intervened, he might have beaten the man to death. As it was, he had still nearly turned his pistol upon the man after he put the horse out of its misery.

The guard deserved to be avenged as much as that horse, to have someone rage against the wrong done him.

But hot anger made all men careless. Worse, Byron's rages had always blinded him, made him impulsive and foolish. He couldn't afford that now. Dippel wasn't some ignorant, brutish farmer who couldn't defend himself. He was clever, and he was expecting that Damien would be as impulsive as he had always been.

Sometimes revenge was indeed a dish best served cold.

"Dippel, why have you come here?" Damien asked the night. "Why aren't you dead, you whoreson? Didn't the pitchforks and torches do a good enough job? What will it take to send you to hell and keep you there?"

There was no answer.

He stood. Damien didn't allow himself to feel—not anger, not fear nor even alarm. There wasn't time for that. Dippel was probably busy trying to find some stairway up to Damien's suite, but the murderous doctor would soon give up on that and think about using the elevator shaft. Damien had to get back to the apartment and get Brice to safety before Dippel found a way up there. She would hate the vault and hate him for putting her there, but it didn't matter now. No one else was going to die for him tonight. Especially not Brice. He would not let her be martyred. He'd kill to stop it. He'd even die to save her.

Damien had a quick look around the ruined offices. The security cameras were as dead as the guard, and by the same weapon, it seemed. The lights and the telephone were lost as well, and there were no weapons. There may have been some in the desk, which had been broken open with some sort of pry bar, but if so, the guard's killer had taken them when he departed.

"Bloody hell."

A noise came. And then another—it was faint, unidentifiable, but out of place in the silence of the abandoned floor, and therefore ominous. He had no proof, but everything inside him said it was Dippel and that he was not alone.

Damien turned toward the door and sprinted for the elevators. His flesh was now hot enough to leave a vapor trail behind him. The rational part of his mind had rejected his rage, but his body still embraced it. Anything that got in his way tonight was going to be hit with several lifetimes of stored-up fury at the injustices perpetrated by the monsters of the world.

A woman who is through with a man will give him up for anything—except another woman.

—Lesson in Love *by Ninon de Lenclos*

If I don't write to empty my mind, I go mad. As to that regular, uninterrupted love of writing...I do not understand it. I feel it as a torture, which I must get rid of, but never as a pleasure. On the contrary, I think composition a great pain.

—*Byron*

Is it not life, is it not the thing? Could any man have written it who has not lived in the world and tooled in a post-chaise? In a hackney coach? In a gondola? Against a wall? In a court carriage? In a vis-à-vis? On a table? And under it?

—*Byron of* Don Juan *in a letter to Douglas Kinnaird, October 16, 1819*

Chapter Eleven

"Have you ever noticed that the best affairs are accidental ones? They are meetings not sought out but delivered up randomly like a message in a bottle washed up on a beach." Brice thought she had asked Damien that just before falling asleep, but if he had answered her, she didn't hear.

But she was hearing something now, a noise in the elevator shaft. Relieved and annoyed, Brice opened her mouth to call down to Damien, but then paused.

Probably it was Damien coming back up to her. Probably. But what if it wasn't?

Brice tried to still her breathing, so she could listen to the small, stealthy sounds that came out of the fearful darkness.

Something was definitely coming up to her. Something that wheezed. Something that smelled oddly chemical and could be scented above the sickening smell of the gear grease.

Her first impulse was to flee. Or maybe to shove a potted plant down on top of it, to kill the monster before it could get her.

But could it be Damien? Perhaps hurt?

But if it was he, why didn't he call out to her? If he didn't want to yell, he could whisper, or yodel, or hiss. Why hadn't they thought of a secret knock they could use? Like "Knock three times if you're human—and twice if you're not."

Maybe he was silent because something was chasing him? Or maybe he knew that something was already up there with her and didn't want to warn anyone he was coming?

"Oh, damn."

Now truly frightened, Brice retreated to a corner of the room and squatted down behind the screen of weeping fig, her eyes alternately fixed on the darker opening of the elevator shaft and the door into the library office. The hall to the kitchen opened up behind her and was blessedly silent. She was certain that nothing was hiding there, since it was the direction from which she and Damien had come. Thank heavens! It was her retreat. From there she could get to the kitchen, dining room, and then back around to the library and the staircase. She had avenues of escape.

As long as it was just one person coming up the shaft. As long as she was swift and silent.

"Please let it be Damien," Brice whispered to herself. "Please let it be Damien, and let him be unharmed."

Damien stood outside the elevator and listened. There were sounds in the shaft. A person, or persons, was climbing up from about the fourth floor. Unfortunately, he couldn't tell how many.

"Damn." The vertical tunnel wasn't a viable means of travel anymore.

He thought for a moment about shoving one of the sofas in the waiting room down on the climber and then scrambling for the upper floors before they could get off a shot. But what if it was Brice down there? That didn't seem likely, but maybe she had come after him and had miscounted floors. Had he even told her what floor the security office was on?

"Bloody hell."

Brice. She was probably still waiting upstairs, maybe even thinking it was her lover returning to her with the security guards. She could get caught waiting right by the doors. Could he count on her to use the gun he'd given her if she saw a stranger? She had accepted the firearm easily enough, but maybe she wouldn't use it. And she could get hurt if she tried to fight off Dippel and missed with that first shot.

She could even die.

He had to get there before anyone else! That meant being creative.

Damien ran silently back to the security offices. There was only one thing to do if he was to get back up to Brice before anyone else.

The door was still open, showing him the windows that looked out toward the river. They were the only ones on that floor that actually opened to the outside. The insurance company had insisted that functioning windows were a liability in a high-rise.

There was no way to gauge the wind outside the fifth-story windows, but the news couldn't be good. The cold wouldn't affect him right away, but it did affect everything he'd be using. Ice and wind weren't any sort of a plus when climbing freehand. Still, this seemed the only way to make on his own terms, without being surprised by any of Dippel's creatures.

Damien slowed his breathing and cleared his mind of all fears and memories of disaster. He began a small, internal pep talk as he stripped off his sweater. It was made of loosely woven wool and would be likely to catch on things and perhaps upset his balance. He'd miss the warmth, but it seemed a crucial trade.

Mountaineering without equipment—whether on actual mountains or buildings—required two things: strength of body and strength of mind. And of the two, the fortitude of will was probably more important—as long as one was in generally good condition.

There weren't a lot of rules to the sport. Just one, really: Don't look down if you want to keep yourself happy. He knew from previous experience that the sight of a long, steep slope of glass and stone could instantly diminish one's belief in his ability to be a human spider.

Looking up was another matter. The building had some obstacles that had to be negotiated, including a variety of ledges and inconveniently placed gargoyles that vomited gutter water. He'd have to avoid them. Fortunately, looking up did not cause vertigo.

This whole affair wasn't a happy proposition, but at least he knew that the drainpipe on the corner was secure. He had them checked all the time, knowing they were his tertiary means of escape in case of a fire. They could take his weight and then some.

If they didn't shatter in the cold.

And he wouldn't be seen because there were no windows close by.

The only danger in this venture, he assured himself, was losing focus during the climb.

Or a really powerful wind gust could lift him off the wall and take him for a short and fatal ride. Okay, and patches of ice might form when his abnormally hot body melted the snow and it refroze into ice slicks, which would be dangerous if he had to come back down again.

His impulse was to hurl himself into the night. But there was no need to rush, Damien told himself as he popped the latch on the window. He stepped out onto the snow-clogged ledge, which looked like a miniature polar wasteland, complete with crumbling ice cliffs and crevasses. Brice was probably safe. She had a gun. And even if she had been taken hostage, Dippel wouldn't hurt her. Not right away. The bastard would want her as bait.

Look at that ledge! Are you insane?

No. He was perfectly rational. All he needed to do was inch along the ledge for about twenty feet until he got to the drainpipe—and there was plenty of room on the ledge, a full seven inches. A climb of seven or eight stories was nothing. He could do it blindfolded and with one arm tied—well, perhaps not blindfolded *and* with one arm tied behind his back. But it was a short, easy climb up to the roof. He'd managed much more difficult feats in Venice—while drunk even.

Something hurtled out of the night and nearly struck Damien. Weirdly, unexplainably, a small brown bat flew by the window and then flew by again almost immediately. Which was impossible. That meant there were two bats out here in the storm, since no animal could circle around so quickly.

"I don't know what you want," he said to the retreating bats as they tumbled around the corner of the building, though he could guess what had drawn them. The gargoyles took on both an electrical charge and also an eerie resonance that probably wrought havoc with the bats' sonar every time it stormed. "Trust me, you won't find anything flying in circles. Anyway, can't you see it's snowing? Go home before you freeze or fry."

In reply, a gust of wind struck Damien like a hammer, driving his words back into his mouth. He turned his face from the onslaught and huddled against the wall, fingers locked around the window frame.

Seven inches of ledge. That was plenty. Really.

In the distance, lightning began to flicker—special lightning that brought out something like the aurora borealis and lingered like napalm on the buildings it struck.

Damien counted as he moved: *One-one-thousand, two-one-thousand, three-one-thousand, four-one-thousand, five-one-thousand, six—*

The storm had circled back and was moving his way, and quickly. He wasn't afraid of the lightning, as long as he wasn't hit directly, but it could be inconvenient since contact with it left him higher than a kite and sometimes gave him an erection. That wouldn't be so good on a seven-inch ledge.

Perhaps there was a need to hurry a bit after all.

"Bloody hell and back again." His frustrated words were barely audible over the crunching of the ice beneath his feet.

Damien scooted another three steps, kicking the snow away with angry feet, and finally reached for the drainpipe. Looking straight ahead, he started to climb the iron rope that was all that linked him to the roof.

One-one-thousand, two-one-thousand, three-one-thousand, four-one-thousand, five-one—

Thunder roared again.

Brice hadn't waited to get a good look at the person who came out of the darkened shaft. He was huge and he wasn't Damien. He also wasn't wearing a uniform—and that was all bad news.

On hands and knees, she scurried silently into the deserted hallway and then pushed upright once she was around the corner. She padded toward the kitchen on anxious feet. For some reason, she felt safer there. It was warm and beautiful and smelled of baking bread—like something in an architectural magazine. Surely no nightmare monsters could stalk among the marble countertops and the old stone sink and modern appliances. She'd be safe there until the lights were back on.

Her footsteps sent up small, betraying echoes as she crossed the floor. Brice ducked down behind the island where she and Damien had made wassail and tried to stay still.

Maybe she was safe, but where the hell was Damien? Surely nothing had happened to him. She had listened carefully and not heard any sounds of struggle or shooting. He had to be okay—just somewhere too distant to have heard the hulking thing climbing up toward her. If he had heard it, he surely would have come back to save her.

Wouldn't he?

Of course he would.

Brice shivered, and her legs began to cramp. She never had been good at deep knee bends.

"Damn it," she whispered. She couldn't stay here, squatting by the counter. Couldn't stay still and quiet while her nerves were firing, making her twitch hard enough to knock her off balance, and her teeth were chattering like a telegraph. She understood now what was meant by the phrase *thrill of horror*. It happened when you overdosed on adrenaline.

Brice stood up slowly, peering at the dark doorway that led back to the foyer. Her stomach growled suddenly, and she realized that she was ravenous—as hungry as she had ever been in her life. How long had it been since she'd eaten?

Her stomach growled again as loud as a lion's roar in the quiet of the echoing kitchen. Appalled at the noise, she grabbed a small bunch of fragrant bananas out of the bowl on the island as she ran through to the carpeted dining room. She had to shut her stomach up before someone heard it. She also needed to be someplace where the acoustics didn't amplify every sound.

The incongruity of her possible last meal being one of overripe fruit didn't escape her. It had a certain pathos that would appeal to a segment of the population, though it would never be used as a marketing tool. What would the advertisers say. *Bananas—the healthy deathbed snack? Bananas—for the dying woman who really, really doesn't have time for a meal?*

Brice crammed a chunk in her mouth and chewed hastily. She debated about throwing the smelly peel on the floor, wondering if it would really trip anyone.

She also thought, with a shade of justifiable resentment, that her last supper should involve bread and wine, if not a choice sirloin grilled with herbed butter and mushrooms.

Not that this would be her last meal. No way. She wouldn't let it happen. She was in a tight spot, but it wasn't hopeless. Damien had probably already rounded up the security guards and was coming back to rescue her. The power would come on any minute now. All she had to do was stay hidden and shoot at anyone who got too close.

Still, she would rather not shoot anyone while waiting, if she had a choice. She *could*—of course she could. She knew how. But retreat was definitely the better part of valor in this case.

But retreat to where? Where wouldn't Damien's horrible enemies go?

The smoke detectors in the kitchen and dining room blinked unhappily as they announced in periodic chirps, which could be heard even through the double-paned glass, that they were running on backup batteries. From the outside, the windows in the dining room showed as a set of flickering oblongs that stained the snow with sinister red light that looked all too much like fire.

Damien, camouflaged under a dusting of snow he'd acquired while scrambling over the ornamental railing at the top of the building, couldn't see any signs of movement inside the apartment. That was good.

Still, he was careful to stay in the shadows as he moved toward the windows. No point in making the job easy for the bad guys. This wasn't a night for taking chances. At least, not avoidable ones.

Brice's shadow fled ahead of her, stopping only when it reached a door of the library. There it reared up, an alarmed animal at bay. She listened closely to the sounds beyond the door—the weird bestial grunts and breathing she'd heard in the elevator shaft.

There was definitely something there. Not exactly wheezing, but . . .

Brice wanted to run away; she truly did. But just as she began to back up, the devil called to her again.

Brice, don't you want to know what's in there?

No, not really. Not this time.

Yet, slowly, reluctantly, she knelt down and put her eye to the keyhole.

Her gaze was immediately pinched and seemingly trapped by the narrow lock she peered through, but she saw enough in that gap to frighten her into stillness.

He—it—had a flashlight, which it held awkwardly as it searched Damien's desk, rifling through the precious antique papers with a carelessness that made Brice want to scream.

The light was dim, but she could see that its skin was a sour shade of bile, and was badly pitted. It looked more like an insect's carapace or a reptile's skin than something that belonged on a human. Brice realized suddenly that she was looking at scars, not pores or scales—the same type of scars that Damien bore, but which had turned septic and were overlaid many, many times until almost no undamaged flesh showed through.

Dippel? It had to be.

She stared, repulsed. How many layers of scar tissue were there? A hundred? More? How many times had Dippel inflicted electrocution on himself as he searched for immortality?

Brice shuddered. There was something else wrong with him too. His limbs were unbalanced, like those of a fiddler crab. His left arm was enormous, more than twice the size of his right and about eight inches longer, and it clicked like a crunching snail shell whenever it made contact with a hard object.

Brice had an impulse to spray him with insecticide, to see him crushed under a giant fly swatter or stuck to the world's largest pest strip.

As though sensing this sudden hostility, Dippel

turned toward the heavy carved door where Brice knelt, and he seemed to look into her widened eye as he cocked his head, listening to her breathe. The flashlight went out, leaving them both in darkness, but in that last moment of illumination she saw into his eyes and was terrified.

She froze as any prey animal did when the predator neared. Her heart beat harder, counting out her fears with every painful thump. Dread escaped with every breath. She was grateful her exhalations had no color. It was bad enough that she could feel it gathering around her in a clammy cloud; had it tint, she would have been stained yellow with cowardice.

Chirp went the smoke detector, breaking the silence. The red light flashed on and off, assaulting her eyes with its brief flare and perhaps betraying her to Dippel.

The monster didn't move. Neither did Brice. She stayed perfectly still, not blinking or even breathing, and eventually he looked away. The flashlight was switched back on and Dippel continued his search.

Brice slumped. She closed her twitching eyelids on the sudden outpouring of tears, trying to shut out the angry red light. But she couldn't hide from it. The red flash beat against her thin lids and her aching brain, giving her no relief.

Done being skeptical and logical and reasonable— perhaps done being sane—Brice gave in to the beginnings of panic. Reason said to stay calm and unemotional, and quiet, but damn it! This was *her* crisis. She'd speculate freely, marvel, thrill, and be terrified, if she wanted to.

She'd also have to find another way downstairs to the security office. If she could get to the surveillance cameras, maybe they would still be working and she could find Damien and the guards. Hadn't he said there was a backup generator that ran the emergency lights on the stairs? They needed light, and they needed to know how many people—how many monsters—they faced.

But where were the stairs? Surely Damien's building had to have some exit besides the elevator in case of a fire. There were codes, damn it!

Fire.

She looked up at the flashing fire alarm. Stupid! They'd been so dumb! There *was* another way out. Fire escapes were usually located outside—probably starting on the roof. And Damien would have one, even in the penthouse. Yes, it would be cold and icy and not the safest thing to climb in a snowstorm. But it was better than staying in the building with Dippel.

Brice took a deep breath and pushed the incipient hysteria away.

She had to go back around to the other side of the library where the metal staircase was and get up to the door that opened onto the roof. It was a bit risky, but the door and stairs were screened by a thick stand of weeping figs. Dippel was busy searching the desk. Maybe he wouldn't see her when she sneaked inside.

Maybe he'd even be gone.

Brice turned and ran away silently, grateful for the thick carpet in the hall that deadened her footsteps.

This time her shadow pursued her in the eerie red light, but it looked no less frightened running in the opposite direction.

Damien found himself thinking of strange things as he forced open the dining room window. Worry about Brice was a natural thought to be on his mind. But thinking about love—specifically and generally—was not.

Yet that was what occupied his brain as he stood in the snow, breaking into his own apartment.

Love, every time he'd felt it, had transformed him, and in ways he hadn't expected and sometimes hadn't liked. It was a brave person—or a foolish one—who submitted himself to such alteration when he couldn't know the outcome of the encounter.

He'd learned something else, too, over the course of the years: Egos couldn't love. Vanity did not adore anything but itself. Pride did not cherish. Intellect could understand but did not feel. When love came, it was from the soul. It *was* the soul. And it could not be controlled, calibrated or manipulated.

People spoke all the time of a fear of intimacy, but that wasn't the problem at all. People feared change—change of their circumstances, change of their personality, change of the soul.

He had feared, too, for a very long time. But not now. Faced with possibility of disaster, the only thing he dreaded in this moment was that he would lose Brice before he had a chance to know if he truly loved her. And if she loved—or could ever love—him in return.

Frustrated with the frozen lock, Damien slid his shirt over his hand and put a fist through the pane of glass nearest the latch. The small tinkle of glass spilling onto the rug was barely noticeable. Or so he hoped.

Damien reached inside, not being particularly careful of the glass's rough edges. He would heal. Brice might not.

"Which other cities do you favor with your noble presence?" Brice had asked Damien last night when they ran out of boring Victorians to discuss and had moved on to more personal material. "You know I'm from Charleston by way of Savannah—by way of San Francisco?"

"I'm glad you're adaptable," he said, tucking her hair behind her ears and encouraging her to snuggle closer. "Frankly, outside of New York, I avoid the East Coast. Too many of the Puritans' descendants about still trying to burn sinners. I like New Orleans and San Francisco primarily. It's fun living in cities where instead of *purging* oddballs—the self-proclaimed vampires and witches— they give them cable-access television shows and treat them as tourist attractions."

"When were you last in San Francisco?" she asked.

"I was there in the sixties."

"The nineteen sixties?" she clarified.

"Yes, but I was there in the eighteen sixties, too, back when it was the Barbary Coast. Anyone with an ounce of dash put on a loud tapestry waistcoat and went west."

It sounded like a joke, but Brice was now sure that he'd meant it.

She was also sure that she felt like bursting into tears as she inched her way up the library's cold iron staircase, feeling her way in the dark. She was being dead silent, though the room now seemed empty.

Was this really happening? Couldn't I still be asleep, caught in a nightmare?

She didn't like small spaces, but a part of her wanted to hide in the dark, to just stay in some deep, safe shadow until it was day, because surely normal people would come soon. Even with the power out. Even with unplowed streets. Even on Christmas Day.

But there was Damien. Or rather, there wasn't Damien. She didn't know where he was, or if he was in trouble. And she couldn't run away without him, couldn't hide when he might be in danger or hurt.

It couldn't be the way it had been with her husband, she wouldn't lose anyone else while she sat by and watched. Particularly not because she imagined herself to be helpless. This wasn't like the last time. She was whole and mobile. There were things she could do, if she didn't give in to terror.

Brice scolded herself fiercely for even thinking about taking the coward's way out and finding Damien's vault. Fear was the worst enemy a person could have. She knew that firsthand. Her husband's death had felt like the end of her. But it hadn't been. She had survived to live day to day, moment to moment. When one painful breath ran out, she drew another. And then another. Grief and fear had tried to crush her then, but they hadn't succeeded. She hadn't been destroyed by crippling emotion then. She wouldn't be destroyed by it now. Neither would Damien.

But she was at her last retreat, unless there was some obvious way down from the rooftop. If Dippel followed her now, if she was cornered, she would have no choice except to shoot him.

Assuming that would do anything useful. It might not, if what the journal said was true—and she now more than half believed it was.

Brice shook her head in denial on this thought, unwilling to believe this last horrible thing could be real. Dippel had to be killable.

Muttering prayers to unspecified deities, she crept toward the French doors where she had seen Damien perching on that first night. She prayed they were unlocked, because she didn't think she had the nerve to climb back down the steep stairs and search the desk for the key.

I have traversed the seat of war in the Peninsula; I have been in some of the most oppressed provinces of Turkey; but never, under the most despotic of infidel governments, have I beheld such squalid wretchedness as I have seen since my return to the heart of this Christian country.

—*Letter from Byron to Lord Holland before addressing Parliament*

I have no doubt that my son is a great man. I simply pray that he may be a happy and prudent one as well.

—*Letter from Byron's mother to her attorney*

I am like a tiger. If I miss my first spring, I go growling back to my jungle.

—*From Byron's letters, November 18, 1820*

GET UP TO 5 FREE BOOKS!

Sign up for one of our book clubs today, and we'll send you
FREE* BOOKS
just for trying it out...**with no obligation to buy, ever!**

HISTORICAL ROMANCE BOOK CLUB

Travel from the Scottish Highlands to the American West, the decadent ballrooms of Regency England to Viking ships. Your shipments will include authors such as CONNIE MASON, CASSIE EDWARDS, LYNSAY SANDS, LEIGH GREENWOOD, and many, many more.

LOVE SPELL BOOK CLUB

Bring a little magic into your life with the romances of Love Spell—fun contemporaries, paranormals, time-travels, futuristics, and more. Your shipments will include authors such as KATIE MACALISTER, SUSAN GRANT, NINA BANGS, SANDRA HILL, and more.

As a book club member you also receive the following special benefits:

- **30% OFF** all orders through our website & telecenter!
  (Plus, you still get 1 book FREE for every 5 books you buy!)
- **Exclusive access to** special discounts!
- **Convenient** home delivery **and 10 days to return any books you don't want to keep.**

There is no minimum number of books to buy, and you may cancel membership at any time. See back to sign up!

*Please include $2.00 for shipping and handling.

YES! ☐

Sign me up for the **Historical Romance Book Club** and send my THREE FREE BOOKS! If I choose to stay in the club, I will pay only $13.50* each month, a savings of $6.47!

YES! ☐

Sign me up for the **Love Spell Book Club** and send my TWO FREE BOOKS! If I choose to stay in the club, I will pay only $8.50* each month, a savings of $5.48!

NAME: _____

ADDRESS: _____

_____

TELEPHONE: _____

E-MAIL: _____

☐ **I WANT TO PAY BY CREDIT CARD.**

☐ VISA   ☐ MasterCard.   ☐ DISCOVER

ACCOUNT #: _____

EXPIRATION DATE: _____

SIGNATURE: _____

Send this card along with $2.00 shipping & handling for each club you wish to join, to:

**Romance Book Clubs
20 Academy Street
Norwalk, CT 06850-4032**

Or fax (must include credit card information!) to: 610.995.9274.
You can also sign up online at www.dorchesterpub.com.

*Plus $2.00 for shipping. Offer open to residents of the U.S. and Canada only.
Canadian residents please call 1.800.481.9191 for pricing information.

If under 18, a parent or guardian must sign. Terms, prices and conditions subject to change. Subscription subject
to acceptance. Dorchester Publishing reserves the right to reject any order or cancel any subscription.

JOIN NOW!

Chapter Twelve

Brice paused on the stairs, hands clenching the iron rail. Dippel had come back while she was halfway to the upper tier of the library. And now there was a second creature in the apartment below.

It was hard not to sweat and wheeze when she could actually feel her pulse in her throat trying to gag her with fear.

Don't look up! Don't look up! There's nobody here but us books and shadows.

Lightning flared, lighting up her aerie, and thunder crashed right behind it. The iron staircase seemed to shiver beneath her. Was it afraid of Dippel too? Could metal be scared?

More likely it was the storm. Lightning could well be hitting the roof now, sending its hot fingers into the building's iron bones.

And into her, while she perched on the stairs, or a fire

escape? The thought just added terror to terror. Brice had to fight hard not to close her eyes and whimper.

The monstrous soldier who had appeared and was seemingly taking orders from Dippel wasn't wearing jackboots, but Brice felt he should have been. Perhaps it was his gait. He walked stiffly, almost as if his knees were fused. His long, misshapen face also twitched erratically above his lip, as though some living thing were heaving under the skin, some parasite that wanted out. It was also apparent from her vantage point that Dippel's therapy hadn't cured the creature's baldness.

Dippel was growing agitated. He said something loud in German and waved his larger arm about. The limb looked hideous on his body. Had he stolen it off some champion arm-wrestler? Or a gorilla?

The second creature belched a reply. Spittle and some things that Brice imagined were maggots spewed from its mouth and onto Dippel. The doctor didn't seem to notice, or else he didn't care.

That was a sort of plus, Brice thought hysterically. If she vomited on the doctor, maybe he wouldn't be angry.

As useful as it would have been to hear their conversation, Brice could no longer bear being close to the monsters and that unpleasant odor of rot and chemicals that surrounded them. This wasn't her venue, not the place where she could shine. She was not a person given to gladiatorial risk—acts of physical and insane courage, even in the single-minded pursuit of escape. All she wanted was to get away without confrontation.

And to find Damien.

And to not be seen. That most of all. But she had to get away from the monsters—*right now*. Before she threw up.

Brice took a slow breath, then continued her slow upward retreat to the roof, being more careful than ever to make no sound. Her eyes never left the two creatures on the floor as she backed up the twisting stairs.

There came a crack and then a loud whine followed by a second sharp crack that alarmed the ears. Splinters of shattered stone splattered Damien in a sharp, short hail.

He dove behind Karen's desk, cursing himself for not being more cautious. The upper tiers of the library were the perfect place for an ambush, and he should have thought of this. Now the silence was broken and the slim hope of remaining unnoticed gone.

He hadn't heard these sounds for a long while, but one never really forgot the sick thrill of being under fire, of standing at the border that separated life from extinction while some hostile person tried to hurry you over the edge at the point of a gun.

Interesting to note—there was a clear, almost operatic echo that followed the first crack. That sound, combined with the direction of the stones, told him where his attacker was shooting from in the long gallery that encircled the library dome.

The second bit of data was analyzed even as he rolled for deeper cover: The shooter was using a rifle. A long one. Probably a Remington. A handgun would have sounded more like a bark. The clap had been much louder. This fellow wasn't larking about with a pellet gun or a lady's purse pistol. But then, he'd already known that.

A second bullet went into the floor near his foot, this time muffled. The shot came quickly, but not quickly enough to catch him. Damien looked at the bloom of copper in the carpet and thought, *It looks pretty nestled in the rug. Far prettier there than lodged in my body.* He knew this from past experience. He'd been shot before. Several times, in fact. Neither he nor the bullets were improved by the experience.

The Remington was an odd choice of gun, though. Old-fashioned. Not that he wasn't thankful the creature didn't have an Uzi.

Damien reflexively checked his own gun. Usually, a pistol was no match for a rifle when handled by an average marksman, but he was not an average shot. And his target was making no effort to stand behind cover. The hulking creature just stood there in the open, blazing away as if he were invulnerable.

And maybe he was.

A third point—and the best as far as Damien was concerned: The attacker wasn't a good shot and had been wasting ammunition on these unsuccessful attacks. Soon he would need to reload. That would be Damien's moment of opportunity.

Even if the creature was a crack shot, Damien would still take him on. Because it wasn't Damien's day to die. He and Brice had things to do, places to see, people to find. He was going to live for a long time to come—they both were. Other people might be questioning themselves about now, wondering if Fate had caught up with them, wondering if it was time to let go and go gently into that dark night. But not Damien. Life had always been his choice, his goal—his destiny even. Let others give up, he never would. He loved almost everything about the human condition, the whole fabulous floor show that was humanity—the good, the bad, the average, the sublime.

So, damn you all.

Damien took a deep breath and then another, preparing for this last battle by night. He did not hurry. He did not let himself rage.

Soon his eyes were readjusted to the dark. The pre-battle pep talk was over. The creature had run out of bullets. There was no flag to salute, no stirring speech to make, no loved ones to kiss. It was time to go.

Damien rolled from behind the desk and onto his feet, aiming and then firing in one smooth motion.

The eyes. They were the best target.

He looked up, aimed for the twin spots of yellowish white that peered down from the railing, and pulled the trigger.

Dippel and the creature were finally gone. She could open the door.

Brice forced the door open against the drifted snow and wind, then made herself step into the cold, stormy night that frightened her almost as much as Dippel.

We'll die out here, whimpered the part of her that feared the storm.

We'll die if we stay inside, answered the part that feared Dippel more.

A sheet of loosely woven ice crystals immediately peeled off the roof and rose up like a ghost, reaching for her with cold arms. Brice flinched back, stumbling on one of the ridges of frozen water that rose like a dune every eighteen inches or so. She avoided its clutch by stepping back into the comparatively warm doorway, and was relieved when it came apart and fell back to the ground with a soft shattering sound.

It was just snow. Nothing more.

Hands trembling, she closed the door quietly and began searching for the fire escape—which had to be there. It was mandatory on all residential buildings, wasn't it? She clung to the wall for balance as she threaded the strange frozen dunes that looked like ripples on a pond. Brice ducked down whenever she came to a window, crawling on her hands and knees over the brittle frost; she didn't want her silhouette to block out the light and give her position away to anyone who might be looking up.

She shivered violently as she moved. Lightning was lighting up the horizon, and the wind cut like an ice knife, tearing through her clothes and into her skin. It seemed Mother Nature was in league with the doctor and making a serious attempt to kill her.

A plane passed overhead, its tiny windows alight, silhouetting a small army of heads. Brice had the mad impulse to rush out into the open, waving her arms and screaming. But she would never be seen by the plane. It wasn't likely that anyone would notice the small block of darkness where Ruthven Tower lay, let alone a pale woman waving in the snow atop it. And even if they did, they wouldn't understand her message or be able to reach her before the monsters did.

It was hard to watch the plane go, though.

Damien stepped over the toppled body and picked up the Remington. It had been a long fall, and the creature had landed on its feet. The leg bones had shattered into yellow kindling and matchsticks. The creature's form on the way down had been imperfect, but it had really aced the landing. Damien had to give it a 9.5 for the flip dismount.

The bloody lump moved.

Damien stepped closer. The damned thing should be dead—its head was almost gone, along with the bottom twenty inches of its legs—but the body was still twitching, the hands trying to grasp at something.

The rifle barrel of the Remington lying some three feet away glinted in the moonlight. He wasn't fond of rifles. Perhaps it was his nineteenth-century sensibilities, but rifles seemed brutishly aggressive and inelegant. However, this wasn't the sort of night when you refused Fate's offerings. Not if you wanted to live.

The rifle was useless without ammunition, though. Damien knelt and started searching the patchwork corpse for extra bullets. He noted, as he shoved the shirt aside to reach the pants pockets—pants from a tuxedo, unless he missed his guess—that some of the corpse's wounds were barely fused together. It was apparently a recent creation of Dippel's, perhaps made when the doctor realized he would need help in taking out the poet who had turned warrior.

Damien worked quickly in his search, avoiding the creature's grasping hands and with one ear turned toward the door. He didn't want to be surprised a second time. He might not be as lucky in escaping the next ambush.

Damn—he had to get to Brice. He'd seen her slip outside, a small shadow slinking around the glass dome that crowned the building like the top of a wedding cake. It was the best place for her to be, with bullets flying below, but she wouldn't last long out in the cold. Especially not if anyone else had followed her while he was occupied with this creature.

Brice moved slowly. She had no choice. As though aware of her presence, the storm had suddenly reawakened and shifted around to follow her. The first thin flakes of the new assault, driven by the northeast wind, were running hard and almost parallel to the rooftop. The bitter air stream and stinging snow left her nearly blind as she finished her circuit on the east side of the building. The bottom terrace had had no fire escape.

Knowing it was probably futile, she had still climbed

up the iron ladder to the next tier that ringed the dome. Staggering from the minimal shelter of iron support to iron support, she relied upon the diminishing feeling in her ungloved hands and booted feet to tell her if she was straying from the edge of the steep-pitched dome that crowned the library.

The moonlight that came and went with the furious, rolling clouds was both a blessing and a curse. It lit her way so that she did not trip over the frozen furrows of ice. It also lit her way so that others might see and follow. Looking back frequently, Brice kept the steep-sided glass slope beneath her left hand and shuffled forward.

She wondered: If she had to, could she manage to climb up the thing? Could her attackers? And was there anything up there except more of the sharp iron pickets that decorated every metal seam that joined the dome's glass panels? Also, would it hold her weight or would she fall through, cut to ribbons before her body shattered on the marble floor some hundred feet below?

A hundred feet?

Yes, it was about that. Many stories, in any event. Not something she would be likely to survive.

Brice turned the corner, escaping the worst of the wind. She was careful near the chimney stacks that disrupted the roof's frozen floor. She counted five, all but one cold and smokeless. She wished that the one belching smoke were larger, so she could hide in its warm shadow. She also wished passionately that the roof had more than a thigh-high wall around it. The catwalk was more ornamental than functional and narrow enough to give even a surefooted feline a moment's pause. Especially in the dark and covered with ice.

"Just keep moving," she whispered.

She was more than three-quarters of the way around

the building now and had found no sign of escape. She wondered if all else failed, could she burrow into the snow near the king gargoyle's feet and perhaps have her little igloo be mistaken for a set of very large toes?

There was noise in the elevator shaft, and yet another creature at the base of the stairs. Damien hesitated for a moment, weighing what was best to do. Gunshots would be loud, perhaps summoning others—not an advisable thing to do. Sighing, he slipped his pistol into the waistband of his pants.

He crept up silently on the creature and then went in fast, coming up behind the patchwork man in a rush of uncoiling muscles. Just as he had been trained to do, he hit the median nerve to paralyze the arm that held the gun. Damien used a lot of force, more than he would have on a normal man. It should have caused enough pain to leave the creature vomiting, but the assassin didn't react. At all.

Not waiting to see if the creature eventually dropped the gun it carried, Damien brought his hands down hard, snapping both collar bones.

Still no reaction. He had half expected this, but confronting the actual fact of a soldier who did not respond to pain like a normal human being was alarming. The very unnaturalness of it raised the small hairs at his nape.

What the hell had Dippel created?

Annoyed and further alarmed when the creature began to turn and lift its gun, Damien jumped back, pulling out his pistol.

A part of him was amused to note that his subconscious was actually indignant at this creature's reactions. Why weren't they afraid of him? When you came at a man out of the dark, there should be something in your foe's eyes.

If not surprise, then anxiety, fear or calculation. But these creatures never reacted. Their facial muscles, even their pupils, remained fixed. Their blink reflexes didn't work normally either.

"Well, hell," he said. "So we do it the hard way."

Not waiting for the thing to complete its turn, Damien brought his gun up and put the first round through its temple. The second and third shots went through the eyes.

The thing was blind then and had no brain left, but it still didn't drop its gun. Disbelieving, Damien lowered his own weapon a few inches and systematically emptied the clip into the creature's knees and hips. Then he moved back up to the neck, attempting decapitation.

The pistol was finally empty. Near silence and the smell of gunpowder filled the room.

Damien noted with detached interest that near-decapitation caused total blood loss from the head in a matter of seconds, and it didn't matter if it was done with an ax or a gun. The body bled out rather more slowly once the heart stopped, but still the creature should have stopped moving almost immediately. The shuffling feet were unnerving—like a chicken that kept running after it was dead.

What was it trying to do without its head?

Slightly intimidated, Damien turned and left quickly, listening for sounds of pursuit. And they were there, close by. Another wave of zombie soldiers had exited the elevator. He'd have to take another route to the roof, leading them away from his planned path, or he risked guiding them up the stairs and to Brice.

Some legends said that zombies would die if their creator did. That would be handy. If he could kill Dippel, maybe all these walking dead would go away. He'd have to find the doctor, though, and shove the bastard into the great beyond. It was too much to hope that Dippel would suddenly succumb to guilt over what he was doing and obligingly swallow hemlock or jump off the building.

In fact, the doctor would most likely be hiding behind his creatures, playing general and waiting to see what the shots were all about.

Damien had to find Brice and get her out of here before Dippel got to her. She must not see the doctor. She would be repulsed, and might wonder about her lover and what he could become over time.

Once she was safe, he would come back and deal with the others, Damien promised himself. These soldiers were strong and programmed to kill, but they weren't particularly smart or fast. But Dippel was. Or he had once been. Very, very fast. Very, very smart. Very, very stubborn. And more than a little bit insane, even when Damien first met him. It wasn't a happy combination in an enemy that one knew would have to be killed.

Shots. From the staircase in the library.

That was good and that was bad. It was good if it was Damien, or if it was the guards shooting at bad guys and killing them. It was bad if it was Damien and guards shooting at bad guys and *not* killing them. Or if the bad guys were shooting at Damien.

What should she do? Go back inside and see who was winning?

And get your head blown off? Get out of sight, stupid. Wait. And don't leave easy tracks for the monsters to follow if they come out here.

The only shelter large enough to hide in was provided

by the gargoyles. And there was only one way to get to them and not leave prints in the snow.

"Damn."

The wind was moaning an eerie obbligato that raised the small hairs on the back of Brice's neck. It helped take her mind off the feeling of suffocation that was growing in her chest as the warm air was slowly bled from her lungs and was replaced with ice.

Though she didn't like it, she took her own advice about leaving obvious tracks in the snow. Brice climbed up the iron trellis and then carefully stepped from ornamental girder to ornamental girder. Finally reaching the west side of the building, she grabbed a thick iron chain that was anchored between the building and the gargoyle's studded collar. She wrapped her legs around it and made like a human caterpillar, inching out to where more gargoyles stood guard. There would be shelter of sorts there, and she would be hidden from the windows. Maybe no one would guess she was there.

Dangling upside-down was hard, but she could stare at the distant moon instead of the distant sidewalks below. It helped slightly with her growing vertigo.

Her destination was the center gargoyle, a veritable leviathan of metal among the decorative monsters. She reached it easily enough and it was certainly huge, with a lot of iron protrusions to grab on to. Yet somehow the space between hip and scaly knee didn't look large enough when one was making an eight-foot drop from a swaying chain.

More shots. More wind. Another flash of lightning. Brice tried not to flinch.

Neck craned downward as she checked her position one last time, and feeling especially heavy with the load

212

of cold fear in her belly, she let go with her legs and extended her body as far as it would go. Though less than three feet stood between her and the monstrous shelter, it seemed a distance of yards—even miles.

Hands screaming with pain and going numb, she finally let go. Brice landed with a teeth-rattling jar, missing her intended handhold on the creature's chest plate, but managed not to scream or fall off.

Mission accomplished.

Sobbing once, she curled up in the gargoyle's lap and peered under its scaly arm back at the door she had come through—when? How long had she been outside? She was having trouble judging the passage of time.

The wind moaned. Brice got colder.

There hadn't been any shots for a while. And she was cold, so very, very cold. Could she get up now?

Her brain began a babbling litany. *Where was Damien? He'd said he was coming right back. He was a crack shot. And maybe he had guards to help him. Everything was fine. Fine! But where was he?*

Hearing a stealthy rustle behind her, she whipped around in the opposite direction and peered down at the ledge.

It was a mistake.

The view of the street below was terrifying and, unfortunately, vertigo-inducing. One peep over the side had bile clawing up from her stomach and trying to escape her mouth. Heights didn't usually bother her, but knowing that those tiny lights in the distance were actually automobiles served to remind her of how small and fragile, and how high up, she was. There should have been streetlights to fill out the lighting, but darkness had flooded that part of the city. She was sure Damien was right. This wasn't something brought about by a careless power operator somewhere; Dippel had planned his attack carefully.

Moaning softly, Brice retreated as far from the edge as she could, clinging tighter to the leering gargoyle, not minding his teeth pressed to her breast so long as he kept her safe from the ground and the eerie westering moon, which said mockingly as it peeked through the clouds that she was still on the wrong side of sunrise, in the place where evil held sway.

The lightning also marched closer and closer, though Brice kept her eyes and ears closed to it. She didn't want to think about having to leave the gargoyle yet. Or trying to negotiate an iron fire escape—supposing she could find one—with lightning striking around her.

"Please," she whispered. "Please help me now."

"My pleasure, but stop suckling that beast and give me your hand," Damien whispered back impatiently, as though her being on the roof wasn't at least partly his fault and his appearance wasn't a miracle.

Brice's eyes popped open. Her mouth did too.

She could see from the disturbed snow that Damien had walked out along the low wall that circled the roof, apparently unbothered by the narrowness of the path or the distance from the ground. He stood, bent slightly and was holding a hand out to her. He added; "Unless fear has truly lent you wings and you want to try flying out of here—then by all means, stay there until you are ready."

"You're really here," she gasped, relief making her dangerously weak. She reached out with half-frozen fingers that looked blue in the light of the moon. "Y-y-you're really here. I didn't see you come out the door. After those gunshots I was so afraid!"

"I used a window and came up the side of the building. It seemed prudent after all that shooting."

"I-I-I still can't b-believe you're really here," she said again, brain and body partly frozen into stupidity along with its semi-rigidity.

"We won't be here long if you don't stop messing about. Another lightning storm is headed right for us. This place is going to turn into the world's biggest electric chair, and I won't be in any shape to help you if I get hit." Unable to stop herself, Brice looked at Damien's lap. He laughed shortly. "Yes, the beast rises. It's a sure sign that the pyrotechnics are about to begin. Unfortunately, that isn't the only thing that happens to me when I get near the stuff."

Brice swallowed and finally took his hand. As ever, it was warm to the touch.

Her tongue and brain finally unstuck themselves.

"H-h-how many of them are there? More than t-two? And where are the guards? Have they gone for h-h-help?" she asked as he led her along the ledge. Brice looked at Damien and not the street below. Yet, even with this fierce concentration, she could feel the bile rising at the back of her throat. She figured that if she survived the night, she would probably have a new phobia to live with. She didn't understand how Damien managed. He made the trek along the narrow rail as if he were doing nothing more dangerous than pushing a broom down a sidewalk. And he was doing it backwards.

"Three creatures are dead, at least two are living. And Dippel is somewhere nearby, you can bet on it."

"Th-the guards?" she asked again.

"The guards have been murdered—shot down in cold

blood." His voice was calm, but she sensed his barely controlled rage.

"I s-saw Dippel. I'm sure it was him," Brice said, then started to shiver so violently that she had to stop talking. Emotional sinews were feeling the strain of overuse as much and more than the ones connected to her bones. The cold wasn't helping her either. She paused a long moment to get her balance. "H-h-he's a monster, just like the others. Only w-worse."

"Yes," Damien agreed calmly, stopping at the corner of the roof. The wind eddied around them. "But then, he always was."

"Wh-where's the fire escape?" Brice asked, her teeth beginning to chatter hard enough to cause pain. "I t-t-tried but I couldn't find it."

"There isn't one on this floor. At least not a conventional one. We are going down this drainpipe. Don't worry, I've done it before. It's a piece of cake."

Her jaw would have dropped again, but it was clenched tight against the cold.

"You're j-joking."

"No."

"D-D-Damien," she said, her voice annoyingly helpless. "I can't."

Damien swore, executed a sharp pivot and took a step toward her. He pulled her close and then gave her a brief kiss. The heat of his body, pressed full-length against her, drove the worst of the cold away. Unfortunately, it had an immediate effect on his body too.

"My poor love." He released her abruptly and moved back to the corner. "No, this isn't a jest—if only it were. I'll go first. There are brackets every three feet. Use them as hand and footholds," he instructed, kneeling down and then sliding off the edge feet first. "And whatever you do, don't look down. It isn't far to the next floor, and I've already cracked a window open. Just stare straight ahead and it will all be over soon."

"I-I-I'm not really the hero type, you know," Brice told him in a small voice. "I don't like being d-daring. In fact, I'm a c-coward."

"Sometimes heroism is a choice. But sometimes it isn't." He looked into her eyes, feeding her strength with his mind as he had given her warmth with his body. "Either way, there are consequences to taking an active part in something. The good news is that they usually aren't as unpleasant as the kind that come with failure and cowardice."

It was one hell of a moment for a lecture. But he was right. She thought about how Mark had died and what it had been like to be trapped, truly helpless. The only thing holding her back was her own fear. Damien wouldn't ask her to do anything beyond her physical capabilities.

"I—I don't want to do this," Brice said, but she was already beginning to kneel. She did it very slowly. The wind was shoving at her, playful now that they were on the west side of the building, but it could get serious at any moment.

Damien's head disappeared, but his voice was clear enough. "No sane person would. But you'll do it anyway because it's better than waiting for Dippel to come out and get you."

She decided that he had a really good point. She turned as Damien had done and cautiously lowered her body over the side. His hand was there immediately, guiding her foot to the first brace on the drainpipe.

"H-h-he's evil—like a demon. They all are . . . b-b-bloated and unnatural. I didn't understand that. Not until

I saw the eyes. It was like looking into hell." Brice gasped as snow slid under her shirt and pressed against her belly and breasts.

"But only a lesser demon. Dippel is evil, but he isn't quite His Infernal Majesty. We can manage him. And the rest are basically just stupid zombies."

"Who h-h-have guns."

"For all the good it's done them. I've already killed three."

Brice was glad that one of them thought this would be easy. Personally, she was certain that it was all getting beyond her.

One step at a time. You can mange that much.

Brice squeezed her eyes tight and relied on Damien's warm hand to guide her to the proper footholds. It occurred to her that she literally placed her life in his hands.

Are we aware of our obligation to the mob? It is the mob that labors in our fields, and serves in our houses—that man the navy, and recruit the army . . . You may call them the mob, but do not forget the mob too often expresses the true sentiments of the people.
—*Letter from Lord Byron to Lord Holland, containing a draft of his speech to Parliament*

A man is given a choice between loving women and understanding them.
—*Ninon de Lenclos*

As the sword is the worst argument that can be used, it should be the last. In this instance, it has been the first.
—*Byron's speech to Parliament, February 27, 1812*

Chapter Thirteen

Damien went through the window first, checking carefully that the room he had chosen was in fact still empty. He would have been happier to continue on to the fifth floor via the drainpipe, but Brice was too cold to remain out in the weather. In fact, she was barely able to uncurl her fingers when he plucked her off the ledge and pulled her into the small, well-insulated office where he kept his computer and a rotary phone. He liked these machines and relied on them as much as anyone, but didn't want all the ugly hardware in what he thought of as his real office. There was also the little matter of sometimes messing up the clock on his computer when it was storming.

Brice's teeth were chattering loudly and her lips were pale blue. Damien put his rifle and handgun aside and then secured the window. After that, he set about warming her up. He rubbed her briskly from head to foot, getting the matted ice out of her hair and then taking off her boots, which were partially packed with snow. It took a few moments of massage before feeling returned to her feet, and when it did she tried bravely to stifle a moan.

"Sorry, love," he said again, but softly and with one ear turned toward the door. He carefully pulled the gun from her pocket. She watched him, unblinking and eyes filled with tears. Her irises glowed in the light of the smoke detector, the only part of her that looked warm. "The good news is that there isn't any sign of frostbite. You're just very cold."

"V-v-very, very cold," she agreed, barely able to get the words out as the shivering increased and her teeth chattered like castanets. "W-where are we?"

"My computer office."

Brice was able to make out a desk and a monitor. The floor was covered in some sort of rubber matting, and the desk and chair both had chains hanging from them. She knew that these were grounds, used to protect delicate equipment from the static electricity that could build up in carpets and clothing.

Other than that, the room was empty, austere even, and she found it extremely appealing. Not perhaps anything to excite an interior decorator, or to picture on Christmas cards, but it was warm, quiet, and free of monsters. That made it the most appealing room she could imagine.

Brice sneezed violently and then gasped with pain. She was so cold that it felt as if her skull were made of shattered glass and its stiletto tips were being driven out through her face and eyes. The only other sensation in her body was long, shooting pains that traversed her legs from ankles to thighs. Her muscles hadn't liked the rigors of the climb any more than the bitter cold. Suddenly it was all she could do just to stand.

"Let's go into the bathroom," Damien said, then picked her up when she didn't immediately respond. "There's a heat lamp in there. Poor love—it's cold enough to freeze the teats off a snow leopard."

Brice curled into his warmth, slipping her arms around his neck. Lifting her limbs required massive effort. She was so tired.

"Y-you're better than a-a-any heat lamp," she said groggily.

Damien couldn't help but smile, but it was an expression tinged with grimness. The storm was rising, and his wildness was too. A part of him wanted nothing more than to lay Brice on the floor and have his way with her, over and over again.

"I'm glad you prefer me to electronic appliances. Some of them leave a fellow feeling unmanned."

Brice actually chuckled. "I've n-n-never owned a vibrator," she confessed. "They sound too much like a swarm of bees. Hard to get in the mood with that image in my head."

Damien set her on her feet, but kept one arm around Brice's waist in case her legs buckled. He reached out with his right hand and flipped on the heat lamp, then locked the door behind him.

Nothing happened.

"No power. I forgot," she whispered in the dark and sagged against him in disappointment. He felt the shudders running through her body.

"I have candles, though. We can have light," he said. Damien ordered himself to start thinking straight and reached for the lighter and candles he kept near the sink.

There were a half dozen of them, and it took only a moment to set them ablaze.

"I daren't run you a bath. They might hear the water," he said, finally getting a look at her pale face and feeling fresh alarm. "But you need to get warm."

"Then help me," she said, turning her face up to him. "You can make me warm."

Damien looked into her eyes, trying to read what was there. All he could see was a weird combination of passion, affection and maybe shock. There was no anger, no horror, no hysterics.

He wanted her. His brain seemed stuck on this thought.

"Help me get these wet clothes off," Brice whispered, her voice also trembling. "My hands are still too numb. I can't manage the buttons."

"Of course." Damien cursed the storm, which not only affected his body but also his ability to think. If it got worse, he'd start having hallucinations, perhaps seeing ghosts of long-dead enemies. It had happened before.

Carefully he backed Brice against the counter beside the shower so that she would be braced if her legs felt weak. A few bottles overturned as she laid her unsteady hands flat on the granite.

Damien started to undress her. His body reacted as he knew it would. Such lack of control was embarrassing, but he decided that if she could ignore it, he could as well. Concentration on the task at hand—that was the key.

"I thought—a few times—that you might be dead," Brice told him. Her voice was hushed, perhaps by returning caution, perhaps by unpleasant emotion that tended to constrict the muscles of the throat. "But I didn't let myself believe it. Because I couldn't."

"Don't think about it," he said, kneeling so he could slide her pants off. Her entire body was alabaster white and as cold as the snow they had crawled through. He added more to himself than to her, "It serves no purpose to torture ourselves. I had a few bad moments worrying about you too. But we're obviously both fine, so we have to let it go." He paused. "We have to, or we won't be able to go on."

But was she fine? Damien had seen corpses with better color, and she was moving awkwardly. Like she didn't have complete control of her body yet.

"I couldn't *not* think about it," she answered. "The last man I lov—cared for—died while I looked on, helpless to stop what was happening." There was the resonance of old grief in her voice that he didn't want to hear. It stung to think he was responsible for reawakening her pain. "I never want to do that again."

"What happened?" he heard himself ask as he worked the wet clothes down her thighs. Damien didn't have any desire to own the pain he heard in her voice, didn't want it added to the library of tragedies that touched those he cared about, but he also needed to know what had happened that had put so much hurt in her soul. And if he could do anything to heal it.

Brice hesitated a moment as though considering whether she should go on, and for a second he thought maybe they would be spared the sharing of a painful memory.

But this wasn't a night for anyone to be spared. Brice began speaking.

"It was Christmas Eve. We'd been to a party at a

friend's house. Tabitha urged us to stay over because the roads were icy, but Mark had been careful about not drinking and he wanted to get home so that I could have my Christmas present in the morning. I had a bad feeling, but he insisted that we leave." She swallowed and then laid a hand in Damien's hair. Her hand shook.

"The roads should have been deserted that late on Christmas Eve, but we had another neighbor who had also been to a party, and he wasn't as careful about drinking and then driving on icy roads." She stopped, breathing hard.

"It's all right. I understand," Damien said, tossing her pants aside. Still kneeling, he laid his face against her bare stomach and wrapped his arms around her. He began stroking up and down her legs and back, trying to chase away the chills that had invaded her body and spirit.

"Our car ended up upside down in a stream, which was rising fast because of the storm." She swallowed again. "I was trapped under the dashboard, unable to get to my seat belt or Mark's. Both my legs and my pelvis were broken. My arms and head were pinned by tree roots. Movement was impossible. I was on the high side of the embankment, but Mark. . . . My only consolation was that he was unconscious when the water rose over his head. He didn't know what was happening. But I knew. The moon was quite bright that night. I saw it all. I sat in the cold and watched him die and there was nothing—*nothing*—I could do."

"Stop," Damien whispered against her skin, her terrible words piercing his heart. "Please stop. You've had enough pain. You don't need to think about this now."

She'd had enough. He'd had enough. But he knew that there could be more pain coming. They would not have an easy escape from Dippel. More people were going to die. Damien didn't say that, though. There was only so much that a person could endure, and Brice was nearing her limit.

"Yes, you're right," she finally answered, taking a deep breath and then another. "But you see why I didn't want it to happen again. Why I hated waiting, helpless. You can't leave me again, Damien. I have to know where you are and that you're all right. I need to know what I can do to help—not just stand around and be helpless."

"I understand."

"I pray you do."

Her hands went from his hair to his shirt and began tugging at the collar. Thinking she wanted him to stand, Damien rose quickly. But she didn't stop pulling on his shirt, and he realized that she was doing her awkward best to undress him.

Body warmth. Of course. That was what she needed. It was the fastest way to get warm. He was glad one of them was thinking clearly. It would be bad if the storm craziness affected her too.

Damien began helping her with his shirt.

"I do understand what you are saying, love, and why you feel this way—truly I do. But, Brice," he began, suddenly wondering how to tell her that he was even odder than she suspected, less human, and that this difference was what was going to allow him to kill these creatures that threatened them. "Please believe me when I say that it's better that I do this alone. First off, Dippel may not even know about you. After all, he is only after me, and there hasn't been anyone in my life for a long, long time. Having you as a secret weapon is just good strategy. Secondly . . . well, let's say that you needn't worry so much about my health. I am not—I'm not that easy to kill. Yes, I can be hurt and even die if the wound is sufficiently grievous. But I've been shot six times in battle—and six times I've lived." He didn't mention the time he had been bayoneted.

He waited. The silence spun out uncomfortably.

"It's because of the lightning?" she asked, clearly not wanting to. His shirt was tossed away. She reached for his waist. "It did something else to you?"

"Yes. I heal very quickly."

"And you're very strong. I noticed that when you pulled open the elevator."

"And I'm very strong," he agreed levelly. "And very fast." *And very angry*.

"My German isn't especially fluent, and I may have made some mistakes in translation, but you are saying that you're like those . . . soldiers Dippel wrote about?" Her voice held no expression. Neither did her white face.

"Not exactly. They are unusual. I'm . . ." He tried to think of some way to describe himself that wouldn't seem unbearably horrible.

"Zombies, you called them. Did you mean it?" she asked. Her gaze never wavered.

"Yes—at least that's as good a word as I can come up with. They started off as dead things, and Dippel pieced them together, attaching dead limbs to living hearts and organs. Their brains are fried, their wills hijacked, their bodies not especially quick but very determined to carry out whatever mission they are given." They weren't quick, not by his standards. They would seem plenty fast to Brice, though. It was another thing he chose not to say. "It isn't magic or voodoo that animates them, but the result is the same. The dead are up and walking around."

"You're talking about the real Frankenstein monsters. You're saying that everything in Dippel's journal was true. He really raised the dead."

"Yes. It seems his experiments succeeded. He's finally managed to make his nearly undying soldier." Damien looked full into her eyes, waiting to see if she understood the implications, and if the understanding repulsed her.

Brice finally nodded. "I see," she said, and looked away quickly, as though suddenly unable to bear the sight of him. Her next words surprised him.

"Aren't you going to finish undressing? I know what you're thinking, but this doesn't change anything. I still want you, you know. I probably always will."

Her eyes were deep pools. He wanted to jump into them and dive to the very bottom where her deepest thoughts lay. And even if he could do that, Damien knew it wouldn't be enough.

Her declaration seemed to open some floodgate of emotion inside Damien, and Brice found herself pulled from the narrow counter and held tight against the entire length of his body. Between them, steam began to rise. She could feel his heat penetrating her organs and limbs, driving out the horrible cold.

"Consider this carefully. It's a little early for us to be thinking about happy-ever-afters," he said, and abruptly his voice was low and rough. Outside, thunder roared, shaking the building.

Brice ran her hands over Damien's arms and then down his back. The gold mesh of scars was beginning to rise.

"Erectile tissue," she murmured, smiling slightly.

Damien made a low sound that might have been a

laugh. It might equally have been a moan. He lowered his mouth to her neck and bit down, once.

Brice shuddered, but no longer with cold. The primitive caress sent the last of the old chill fleeing.

"I haven't thought about ever-after for a long time," she finally said. She turned her head and buried her face in his hair. Her hands, much more dexterous now, began searching for the zipper of his pants. "I'm not asking you to promise me one now."

"But you *should* ask," he said. "You have every right to expect one."

"You mean I'm due because I'm a good person and I've suffered a loss," she said gently, shaking her head. "But we both know it doesn't work that way."

"I do know. And I don't like it. If I could, I would change it all. I would keep all this pain from you."

Brice looked up then and the expression on Damien's face made her want to cry out. She had never seen such naked need. She stopped wrestling with the wet fabric of his pants and brought both arms around his neck. She leaned up on her toes and set her mouth to his.

The kiss stole from her the ability to speak, to think, and for a moment to breathe. His body was hard, burning to the touch, and she knew that he was exercising extreme restraint in not taking her right there on the counter.

Not that she would have minded.

"We aren't truly safe here, and less so in the bedroom," he said, his voice rough when he finally lifted his head from hers.

"We don't need a bedroom."

"But this floor, the counter, even the shower—all are unpolished granite. It would abrade your skin, bruise you."

"Not if we act with care," Brice answered, and seeing the crystal decanter that held some sort of oil, she pulled out the stopper and then poured the oil in an arc on the wide shower floor. The smell of sandalwood filled the air.

"That's real sandalwood oil, isn't it? Sorry," she said. "That will be some expensive lubricant."

This time Damien did laugh. He stepped away from his pants and toward the shower, tugging her after him. His eyes were hot. "Extravagance has never bothered me."

They sank down onto the floor. It was cold, but Brice didn't notice. There was no sill to the shower, and the floor sloped downhill toward a drain. Brice reached out quickly, intercepting the stream of oil that was trying to escape. With slippery hands she reached for Damien.

Her fingers hummed with pleasure as she kneaded the muscles of Damien's arms and chest. Her whole body thrilled when he wet his hands and slid them down her back and over her buttocks, then around her thighs. He left hot, bright trails of oil behind that glowed gold in the candle's flickering light.

"How you fascinate me," he said. A small shudder passed down his body. "You look at me with those wide eyes and I can see your desire as plainly as the moon or sun. And you don't hide it—not from yourself. Not from me. You're half afraid of me, of what I am. Yet I know that when I touch you, the fires will rise in you and you will burn along with me. Do you know how rare that is—how long I have waited for this?"

Brice nodded her head and then immediately shook it. "You fascinate me too," she said a bit helplessly, unable to find a way to explain the fierce longing and attraction he had always caused in her. "You have always fascinated me. Your words reached across centuries and touched me, brought me back from grief, made me want to live again. Whatever those rational, timid parts of me want, how could I do anything but go into the fire with you when you ask this of me?"

His hands framed her face as he looked into her eyes and then her soul, searching for the reality.

"It's the truth," she told him.

"I thought that I had nothing left to learn about passion or compassion," he answered. "But I was wrong. I've learned about both things tonight."

Damien's black eyes shone like a night full of stars as he brought his mouth to hers. Brice reached eagerly for the embers that blazed to life between them.

The warmth of her mouth called to him, and, unable to be calm any longer, Damien laid her out on the floor. A part of him worried about bruising her on the stone, but just as she predicted, their bodies moved smoothly over the oil. Damien loved the contrast of cold, hard granite and soft, warm Brice on his overheated skin.

He touched her again, loving the curve of her hip as it swooped from waist to thigh. He lay down beside her, getting close—as close as he could and not yet be inside her. He touched all of her, lovely face and soft breasts, lithe legs and delicate hands, and all of it thrilled him.

And she touched back, no shyness or hesitation slowing her as she explored his body.

Thunder again sounded, the late announcement of the lightning's continuing approach, but he didn't need to hear it to know the storm was rising. Tempests of pleasure ripped through him, making his muscles quake and his heart stutter as hurricanes of desire laid him low.

Moved by a kind of hunger he'd never felt before,

Damien returned to Brice's lips. His hands shifted on her body, reaching into the cleft between her thighs where the heat was strongest, where he most wanted to be. And her response was instinctive. The male animal asked and she responded, opening to him, leaving herself undefended because she trusted that the wildness in him would not hurt her.

Color had returned to her body while they kissed, and she wore a pink flush over all her skin. Lips and tips of her breasts were again dark with the blush of passion.

Intrigued, Damien touched one nipple and watched as sensation burst in her body, telling him of the sensitivity of her skin. Her back arched, and he watched as the blush traveled outward, marking her fair complexion with a deeper blush.

A part of him said that Brice was a miracle he shouldn't believe in, that there was no passion that could reach deeper than old pain. The rest of him knew she was a once-in-a-lifetime chance at emotional rebirth that he couldn't refuse.

His hands slid under her and her buttocks filled his hands—warm, smooth, as fine as softest kidskin. He flexed his fingers once, enjoying the resiliency of her muscles, and he pulled her over him, rolling carefully so her knees would be spared. She slid into place—almost into place, and looked down at him with her passion-darkened eyes.

This was safer, he told himself. Let her be in control. He was more than a little crazy now; the charge growing inside him was buzzing in his brain.

"I want you," she said. "Don't hold back. There's no need."

He wanted her too—hands, mouth, body and in no

particular order. Groaning, he rolled back over, putting her under him. He wanted to be on top, he wanted control, he wanted . . . *everything*. He'd just be careful while he took it. Surely he had that much control left.

Sheened in sweat, skin a mass of crisscrossed scars, breathing too hard, he knelt over her. He lowered himself to one breast, taking it into his mouth, teasing it with lip and tongue until the taste of sandalwood gagged him.

Brice, who had been busy biting the muscled forearm propped by her head, also spat.

"Maybe I don't like sandalwood after all," she said, wrinkling her face.

Damien found himself smiling, in spite of the bitter taste that coated his mouth.

"Yet I will always recall this scent fondly when I remember this night." He inched his way upward, letting his arousal settle between them. Heat radiated up from her now, telling him that she, too, burned with need.

"And we will remember it? You truly believe we'll have tomorrows to recall this in?"

"Oh, yes. This isn't our night to die." His voice was full of conviction and so strong that it banished her doubts.

"Good. I want there to be more tomorrows. Many, many of them."

Brice rocked against him, a siren calling to her—what? Mate? Prey? At that moment, he didn't care. Accepting her invitation, he slowly slid inside her, inch by excruciating inch, enjoying the torture of delayed gratification. Then he retreated again, teasing them both. But soon he moved less slowly. The passionate heat and fragmented commands were too powerful to ignore—and he and Brice both wanted. *Needed.*

The fire went wild. Their responses became involuntary, as inevitable as the beating of their hearts. Electricity arced between them, covering their bodies in a sheet of white fire that should have meant death but instead was all about life.

Their eyes were wide open, and neither hesitated once in giving themselves to the storm.

Like measles, love is most dangerous when it comes late in life.

—*Byron*

It's strange that modesty is the rule for women when what they admire most in men is boldness.

—*Ninon de Lenclos*

When someone blunders, we say that he makes a misstep. Is it then not clear that all the ills of mankind, all the tragic misfortunes that fill our history books, all the political blunders, all the failures of the great leaders have arisen merely from a lack of skill in dancing?

—*Molière*

I never wrote anything worth mentioning till I was in love.

—*Byron* (Conversations, *1824*)

Chapter Fourteen

They did the best they could to clean up with towels. Most of the oil came off, but Brice feared that they both smelled like a bordello.

"We need to dress and leave immediately. This was complete insanity. These stupid storms make my I.Q. plummet," Damien muttered in self-disgust.

"How soon they forget," Brice muttered back. "Ten minutes ago I was a goddess. Now I'm back to being luggage."

She looked over at her wet clothes and shuddered at the thought of putting them on again.

"I haven't forgotten," Damien answered, taking hold of her hair and tipping her head back for a quick kiss. "And I'm not complaining. That was the loveliest bit of insanity I've ever experienced. But unless we are actually prepared to die for our love, we really need to leave."

"No one's bugged us yet." That was a non sequitur and

237

she knew it, but Brice wasn't ready for round two of Lord Byron vs. Frankenstein's monsters.

"The door to the office is subtle and blends with the paneling, and the insulation that keeps out magnetic waves also dampens sound, but it isn't exactly a hidden, soundproof, bullet-proof room. They will eventually find it." Damien pulled a dark blue robe of alpaca wool off the back of the door and handed it to her. "It's not like the vault—where you would be safe."

Brice sniffed. "You lock yourself in the vault with me and you've got a deal."

"Don't be ridiculous." Damien frowned at the robe as she held it up against her. "You'll have to roll up the sleeves. But it will be warm, and not too much in the way. You'll have to wear your own boots, though. My slippers won't fit."

"Thanks."

Feeling suddenly at a loss as reality rushed back around them, Brice shook out the robe and slipped it on slowly, paying unneeded attention to the belt as she tied it with elaborate care. "So, where exactly do we go now?"

"I fear you won't like this much," Damien began.

"You aren't proposing to leave me again, are you?" she asked quickly, rolling up her sleeves, this time in a most purposeful manner. "I don't want to get stuck in any vault—I don't care how well hidden it is. What if there's another fire?"

"I understand your concern. And I fear that I *am* suggesting something like that—but hear me out. There is an executive bathroom in the lawyers' offices on the fifth floor. It can only be opened with a key, which you would have. The door is heavy, and the room is lined with marble and is as safe as a bunker. You can wait there while I go down to the generators and get the power turned on."

238

"No. I am going with you—and I don't want to hear any arguments. Damien, I mean it! Short of tying me up, you can't make me stay there."

Damien looked at her with narrowed eyes, and she knew for a moment he was actually considering the option of doing just that.

"You wouldn't dare," she said, shaking her head as she backed up a step.

"No, I suppose not. I can't leave you in a position where you are unable to defend yourself." He sounded regretful as he pulled on his shirt. It was damp but would dry quickly on his overheated body, so Brice didn't waste time feeling sorry for him. "Okay, here's the drill. You can come with me—as long as you can manage elevator shafts and dark stairwells. At the first sign of trouble, I am ditching you in the nearest place of shelter and going after these bastards. I have to take them out when I find them; and I don't want them to know about you, so, no, you can't help by playing Doc Holliday to my Jesse James." Brice opened her mouth to argue, but he over-rode whatever she might have said. "That's the deal, Brice. It's this or the executive bathroom. I can take a bullet, as long as it isn't to the head. You can't. And I can deal with these creatures—they aren't that hard to kill—but not if I also look after you."

"Okay," she said, not liking the options but choosing the one that seemed less evil. She reached for her pistol and stowed it in the robe's large pocket. It made the garment hang crookedly, but she didn't care.

The silence of the building was eerie. In a high-rise this size there should have been constant background noise from elevators, heaters and fans. And people—voices talking, heeled shoes walking, toilets flushing. But all was dead quiet except for the soft swishing of the bathrobe Brice wore.

The only other exception to the abnormal silence was when they passed through the stairwell on the sixth floor where Cyber QT, a personalized self-help software company, was located. There, the various and sundry motivational screen-savers were still active, flashing and chirping and generally being obnoxious. Brice wondered how long the backup batteries on the computers would hold out. The very best of them wouldn't last more than ten hours. Three was more common.

Though Brice would just as soon have given it a miss, she and Damien made a brief stop there while he looked for weapons. They stopped everywhere to look for weapons. Or, more accurately, for ammunition. Unfortunately, all that immediately offered itself was a small flashlight, which he pocketed.

While Damien hunted for bullets, Brice stole candy off of desks, munching on anything she could find because her hunger had come roaring back. *Nothing like a near-death experience to give a girl an appetite. Or maybe it was playing Slip-N-Slide with Damien*, she thought in an inappropriate spurt of humor.

"I'm glad you can still smile," Damien remarked, looking up from the desk he was ransacking.

"I could frown, but would that help anything? Besides, frowning makes bad lines on the face," she added lightly. The comment earned a quick grin from Damien.

Brice wandered off and soon found the employees' lounge where she helped herself to a can of orange juice and then reached for another. The cans and bottles in the silent refrigerator were still cool, and she realized that she was feeling dehydrated.

Damien joined her for a short drink, but was ill at ease in the windowed room and soon pulled her out.

They saw no one and heard nothing on that floor. Brice was feeling hopeful that Dippel had given up and left, but Damien seemed positive that he was still somewhere in the building.

Their luck held for three more floors. They encountered no one in the stairwells, and the batteries in the smoke detectors continued to work, providing them with light so that they could conserve the batteries in their small flashlight. The occasional sharp chirp from the alarms overhead was at first unnerving, but Brice was growing accustomed to the electronic *cheep*ing and was soon able to mostly ignore it.

They left the stairwell again on the third floor, taking an immediate left and going down a long, unlit corridor, which would have been scary and too claustrophobic without the feeble beam from the flashlight. By consensus they walked silently, side by side until they reached another door. Damien pressed his ear against the panel and listened for a long moment before he pushed the latch and eased it open with the tip of his plundered rifle.

Brice followed him down another hall, their steps again muffled by more of the black rubber matting like that in Damien's office. All through their trek down dark stairwells and unlit corridors, he had remained calm and efficient—almost like a cat stalking its prey. Brice's nerves were still on edge, but Damien looked about as panicked as a sack of potatoes. She found that immensely, though probably unreasonably, reassuring.

"This is it."

They stopped in front of a long gray box that had

high-voltage warning stickers on it. Damien opened the metal door carefully and then began to swear in Greek.

"They've been here too?" Brice asked, feeling suddenly deflated.

"Yes, and with a mallet, from the looks of things. Damn it."

"It's really that bad?"

"It's pure Humpty-Dumpty." Damien stepped back and shone their weak light inside. There were broken dials and gauges, and tangles of torn loose wires that glinted in the feeble illumination. Even the most electrically ignorant person could see that the case for repair was hopeless.

"And I don't suppose there is backup to the backup maybe down in the basement?" Brice asked, clutching at straws.

"You 'don't suppose' correctly." He paused. "Unless . . . that computer company on the sixth floor has giant UPS's on their computers."

"Network-sized backup battery systems?" Brice asked. "I suppose they might."

"Yes. But I'm not sure they're useful even if they're there. They'd have to be cabled together, which I haven't a clue how to do, and then wired into the main electrical system. They wouldn't last long anyway if they had to supply power to the whole building. We'd have to figure out how to send power to selected floors. I don't suppose that you—"

"You 'don't suppose' correctly," she said, smiling without humor as she parroted his words back at him.

"Well, then." Damien turned to look at Brice. His serious expression warned her of what was coming.

"Don't say it," she begged. "It is *such* a bad idea. Don't

you ever watch horror movies? People split up and they end up dead."

"I'm afraid we are out of options." Damien began counting off the obstacles on his fingers. "Without power, we can't use the regular phones."

"Regular phones?"

"I have a rotary phone in my office for those occasions when I absolutely must use one. It's possible, if I can get to the basement that perhaps I can get the phone lines back up—if the bastards have just thrown a switch instead of turning our boy with the mallet loose down there."

"Then I could come with you—"

"No. The only way down is the service elevator shaft. It's worse than the regular one. Very tight, and the ladder is older and half rusted through. It isn't safe. Sorry." Damien didn't sound very sorry.

Brice made a frustrated sound and damned her claustrophobia.

"Why can't we just leave?" she asked him. "We'll take the stairs down, get out and call your detectives or something."

"Because, if Dippel was smart, he tripped the building's alarm system before taking out that backup generator. That causes a bank-vault-like lockdown on the lobby floor. That also means I can't disengage the locks on those doors until the power is up, so we are trapped inside. Breaking the glass isn't an option either, since it's shatter-proof—didn't want looters breaking in and hurting anyone if there was a riot, you know." Damien didn't smile at this irony of safety reversal. "He will also have posted at least one guard in the lobby. The only other way out is down the side of the building, and the fire

escape ends on the second floor—supposing that he has
left that unguarded. You'd have to do the rest of it climbing down a drainpipe, on your own, and the storm is
worse now. Much worse." The skin at his throat and
wrists was still marked by the jagged lightning marks
which proclaimed the state of the weather.

Brice looked into Damien's dark eyes. Underneath all
the wildness of the storm there were equal parts of anger
and revulsion. He hated what he was doing.

"It doesn't matter. I'm not leaving you to face this
alone," she said quietly. "And you aren't going to let this
go until they're all dead, are you? Which means a lot
more killing, and then explaining a bunch of bodies to
the police."

"I can't let it go," he said simply, regretfully. "He's
already killed five times—that I know of. And I suspect
he has murdered even more. I don't want to spend my
entire life—*our* entire lives—looking over our shoulders
for Dippel or his creatures. He has to be gotten rid of.
They all have to be destroyed. Now. While we have the
chance."

Our lives. Our shoulders. Yes, she was involved too.

As a set of general guidelines for her life, Brice found
the whole let's-kill-them-all thing an unacceptable philosophy to live by. She had always had mixed feeling
about the death penalty and favored gun control. But on
this particular night, she was willing to embrace Dippel's
annihilation as her goal. She would worry about finding
another loftier—and hopefully more pacifistic—ambi-
tion if she lived to see another day.

Resolved, if not particularly happy, Brice nodded jerk-
ily and then straightened. She pushed back the sleeves of
her borrowed robe. Thinking about Dippel persecuting

Damien for all eternity made her angry, and that helped her to keep the other, undermining emotions away.

"I agree. So what can I do to help? Besides cower in a bathroom."

"You can cower in the lawyers' bathroom with a portable PC," Damien said immediately. "I've just recalled that the offices on the fifth floor have wireless Internet. You can use that while the portable's battery holds out. We'll borrow one from Cyber QT. Someone is bound to have forgotten to lock theirs down before they left for the holiday."

He didn't suggest climbing all the way back up to his apartment to get her own portable, and neither did she.

Brice blinked.

"And do what with a PC?"

"Find out how to contact the police or fire department on-line—or the utility company. E-mail. Or maybe there is something for the hearing impaired. Anyhow, we need a fall-back plan if something goes wrong. I don't want you stuck in here over Christmas." Brice stared at him, wanting to protest his utterance of the unthinkable in case the perverse gods were listening. *Something going wrong* meant she needed a way out if he got killed.

"Don't look like that, love," he said gently, brushing a finger over her cheek. His eyes were serious, but not worried. "Nothing is going to go wrong—I already promised, didn't I? This is just for luck. You know that if you go to a lot of bother, you'll never need anything. It's Murphy's Corollary for Crises."

She wanted desperately to argue, but she didn't. As much as she hated the idea of Damien assuming the role of executioner and facing these creatures alone—and knew she would have a difficult time closing a dark door on the horrors of this night—Damien was correct. Heaven help them both! In spite of the danger, Dippel and his monsters had to be hunted down and destroyed. And she and Damien had to do it without outside help, if that was at all possible. Even if no one in authority ever asked difficult questions about the physical state of the corpses already scattered about—and the coroner would have to have lost all sense of sight and smell to miss how different these bodies were—they would surely want to know who had shot them.

Of course, that did rather beg the question of what they were going to do with all the bodies when they were finally exterminated, but Brice wasn't going to ask about that plan. One horrible thing at a time was all she could manage.

"Okay, if it's to be done, best it be done quickly," she said, misquoting Shakespeare. "The sooner it's over, the better for both of us. Let's go steal a laptop, and then you can show me this fancy bathroom."

"Thank you, love," Damien said softly.

"Don't thank me. I still think it's wrong to split up and it's bloody unfair that you should have to face the monsters alone."

He nodded. "There's an old Chinese proverb. It asks: Who must do the difficult thing? The answer is: He who can."

Brice exhaled slowly and then nodded assent.

If people will stop at the first tense of *"aimer"* they must not be surprised if one finishes the conjugation with somebody else.

    —*Byron (from a letter dated January 13, 1814)*

Sorrow is knowledge, those who know the most must mourn the deepest, for the tree of knowledge is not the tree of life.

        —*Byron*

We die only once, and for such a long time.

        —*Molière*

Chapter Fifteen

Brice sat on the counter in the most sumptuous bathroom she'd ever seen and did her best to find a way to contact the NYPD on the portable computer. It had taken her and Damien a while to find one at Cyber QT that wasn't locked into a docking station and protected by a password.

Her cyber search wasn't going well. You could submit an e-mail and someone would eventually get back to you—they promised. But there was no mention of when. For some reason, it seemed that most people didn't choose to report all emergencies via e-mail. If they needed the police, they generally needed them *right now*. Likewise, the fire department seemed to feel that most people would prefer to phone in their emergencies. She could contact the utility company, but only if she had her account number and knew the name of the party she wished to e-mail.

Frustrated and unable to stop worrying about what Dippel might be doing, Brice decided that she needed to think about something else. Something engrossing. Naturally enough, she ruminated on her new and perhaps fragile relationship with Damien Ruthven—who had once been Lord Byron.

Lord Byron!

Only now he wasn't, because he had let a homicidal doctor perform some mad experiment on him, the result of which was that he was now peculiar. Not quite human. A person forever in disguise.

"You don't mean that. He's human," she whispered to herself, to the judgmental voice inside, hoping that she truly didn't think otherwise. Brice didn't usually use religious vocabulary to describe her feelings, but a few notions kept coming up in moments of terror that were uncomfortably close to the spiritual dogma she had long ago rejected. It bothered her. She didn't like discovering that, in an emergency, she retreated to these shady places in the landscape of her psyche, ugly quagmires of old religious training where one might get stuck and even drown.

Judge not, lest ye be judged?

Exactly.

What would she have done if she were sitting—or, more accurately, lying—at the edge of her own mortality while her brain besieged itself with violent seizures? On the one hand, there was almost certain death. On the other, a chance at life—albeit one so different that it defied all known laws relating to human lifespan. What would she have done?

If she had had the power, wouldn't she have used it the night her husband died? If she could have saved Mark, wouldn't she have done the same thing, whatever the long-term effect?

And Damien hadn't known what the outcome would be. He only thought he was curing his epilepsy.

Okay. Maybe that was true the first time. But what about the times after that?

Brice rubbed her forehead.

What? He should surrender and let epilepsy claim him now?

Look at it another way. Weren't scientists the world over experimenting with similar things? With their work in medicine, weren't they all seeking to prolong life? To cure disease? To end suffering from illness? How was what Damien did any different than Brice herself taking antibiotics or vitamins or having had her appendix out when she was twelve?

And, bottom line, could she really wish that Damien wasn't here? That they had never met?

"No! God, no!" She was just afraid and lashing out.

Brice shifted restlessly, pulling her robe tighter. The extra ammunition Damien had pressed upon her tinkled against her borrowed gun.

There was no denying that Dippel was a perversion, an absolute monster, an absolute abomination in the eyes of nature and probably in the eyes of any divinity. True. But was that his fault? Sometimes experiments went awry, didn't they? He could just be a victim.

And what did all this mean in regard to Damien? That was the key question here, wasn't it? Would Damien eventually become a monster? Would his continued existence pervert him like it had seemed to pervert Dippel?

Brice thought for a while, but decided she was at a dead end. She couldn't know if Dippel had always been a little off, and that was what had led him to this line of work; or if, just as likely, it was the work that had finally twisted him.

Of course, even this wasn't the very bottom line. What was bothering her was what Damien had suggested—that she might also be able to make the change. She could, perhaps, extend her life. Be with him for centuries.

Brice glanced over at the mirrors that surrounded her. One look was enough. Even in the computer's dim light, she could see that the skin beneath her eyes was painted with bruises. She looked tired. And old. At least, older than she ever had. How would she feel when these changes were permanent? When her hair grayed and her skin became lined? When she grew weary, and he remained young and healthy and vibrant? Would he be repulsed by her? Would he leave her rather than stay and see her ravaged by the diseases of old age? He had already sustained so many losses—could she ask him to endure another?

And yet, what would their life be like if she did make the change? Could any relationship sustain itself for centuries? What would happen if she did this thing— and then she and Damien eventually grew apart? Or what if she did this and felt changed inside? Unclean. Evil.

A part of Brice, a part she didn't want to deal with just then, recognized that whatever she decided, she had already left her old existence behind. She might return to her cozy little house with its warped door, but her life— that safe little hollow of blissful ignorance—was over. The ocean of human experience was deeper than she'd ever thought. And monsters swam there. She'd never be able to pretend otherwise again.

And to think that she'd once spent her time worrying about the IRS and global warming!

Unhappy, and more than a bit confused, Brice looked down at the portable PC she had "borrowed" and started typing in a made-up account number for the utility company.

Just in case.

The barometer was falling again; he could feel it clouding his brain. The next wave of this unnatural, endless storm was about to hit.

Damien hated war; he always had. But at one time he had felt that war was the only answer in certain situations. Of course, sometimes it still was the only answer, but he loathed it now more than ever. Even, or perhaps especially, if his foe was the man who had extended his life.

It helped somewhat to think of this as a game—a deadly game, but one which could be won with intuition, experience, ruthlessness and a bit of luck. He didn't let himself think about the fact that he was tired of holocausts, that a man shouldn't be asked to see or participate in more than one in a lifetime. What happened now was a conflict he couldn't avoid.

This war was also different for another reason. It was personal. He wasn't here out of idealism, fighting an unknown enemy for some higher principle. He was here because his life—and Brice's—were being threatened by someone in his past.

Damien had never gone to war for gain—personal or political. Always it had been to help people. Unfortunately, too often the *help* that came in military form left the very people you were trying to assist sitting in smoldering ruins. Such *help* meant death and destruction and lost as many lives as it saved. So, for Damien, deciding on a way to help the needy grew increasingly more difficult. Technology had only upped the ante. It was why he had moved into spying, rather than actual fighting. But even then, he could not escape the knowledge that there were consequences to his actions that affected innocent people. He didn't drop bombs, but he told others where they should be placed. He didn't invade villages, but he told generals where to send the dogs of war.

And sometimes innocent people got hurt because they were in the wrong place at the wrong time.

Like Brice.

"Damn you," he whispered—and he was speaking not just to Dippel, but to all the tyrants who had sought greatness with a sword.

Damnation. Did he believe in eternal punishment? He believed in hell. War had finally taught him to accept that there was such a thing. It wasn't the hell of the theologians who had educated him as a child. Their claims of spiritual damnation had never seemed as terrifying as earthly bombs, mustard gas and the napalm he had seen. But he now believed that hell existed, and what was most fearsome was that it would last a very long time.

A smoke detector flashed annoyingly, throwing Damien's shadow against a sterile white door. It made him recall the cafeteria on that floor, and so Damien jogged to the right.

He didn't like the Memuria cafeteria. The place was aesthetically offensive. It was a stark white room filled with brushed-aluminum tables and plastic chairs, and had one long wall of vending machines whose humming gave him a headache. These things didn't interest him. But the attached kitchen, and its potential collection of knives and cleavers, did.

Probably, everything would be locked up, but he was certain he could get in. He had to. He was low on ammunition, and with his new experiences that showed his foes were tough to make *dead* dead—he could just hope to make them dead enough to be sidelined—he couldn't afford to pass up any potential equipment.

Damien pulled on handle after handle on cupboards and drawers, even tearing one off. Nothing—every cabinet was locked tight and no one had thoughtfully left keys or a pry bar lying about. The only knives were plastic ones nestled in a tray next to equally useless spoons and forks.

He did find two metal forks in the sink. Not much use as weapons, but he pocketed them anyway. The door to the old telephone exchange might well be locked, but as long as no one had replaced the antiquated lock, he would be able to bend the forks' tines into useful tools for picking it. Mac would approve.

Mac. There was the war again. He couldn't escape his memories tonight.

Yet Damien smiled a little as he headed for the stairwell. He hadn't thought about Mac in ages. It was Mac—Colonel James McCallum—who had seen to Damien's unorthodox training in the last war. Colonel McCallum had been a man ahead of his time. He was one of the first to realize that spying on other nations could not remain the hobby of gentlemen, and that while gentlemanly honor was a lovely and noble thing, the skills of thieves, pickpockets and assassins had their place in this new quiet kind of warfare.

The two of them—the colonel and Adrian Ruthven, as Damien had then been known—had spent many long nights sitting at the scarred wooden table inside the colonel's tent, the apparently older man guiding Damien through a course in lock picking and eventually a more advanced one in safecracking. Every failure had brought out a fresh wad of pipe tobacco that was stuffed into Mac's old briarwood pipe, every success a shot of single-malt whisky from his family distillery.

It was shameful how often these skills had been of use to Damien even after he left the army.

"Thank you, Mac," he whispered, laying an ear against the stairwell door. "You may, yet again, save my life."

No sounds came from the other side, but something smelled wrong. There was a certain sharp odor . . .

Damien lay down and looked under the door. In the blinking red light of the stairwell smoke detector, he could see a faint shadow as fine as a thread hovering over the floor at the top of the stairs. A less suspicious person might have dismissed it as a stray cobweb.

"Dippel, you nasty, nasty creature," he said softly. "Where did you learn such tricks?"

Damien rose to his knees and eased the door open. He looked at the line of filament that was tied to the pin wedged in the stairs' ornate railing. It was a simple thing, this common fragmentary grenade, but it would have done the job if he had wandered into it.

"A bit out of your normal style, Doctor. You'll regret this," he whispered, for it must have been Dippel who rigged the trap. The zombies didn't seem intelligent enough, and Damien had found no sign of any other humans left in the building.

The nice thing about this abandoned gift was that it didn't care who its master was. Nor did it care when and where it exploded. It would work equally well for everyone, and would do just as good a job dropped on a zombie as it would on a poet in a stairwell.

Damien worked quickly and carefully, freeing his deadly discovery. His hands were steady but he was quick to drop the thing into a pocket. He found the metal device repulsive, and he wasn't sure if there was any danger from the heat of his hands making it unstable.

"'The benefit of training learned in desperate situations,'" he said, quoting Mac to the air. "'Nothing like impending death to supply a man with much-needed inspiration.'"

His words were light but his mood was not. Damien had his fury under control, but he was still very angry—enraged at the death Dippel had wrought on innocent men in Damien's employ, infuriated by the fear he had seen in Brice's lovely eyes when he found her huddled on the roof, preferring to freeze to death rather than face the monsters inside. He was also very angry at having Damien Ruthven's life upset years ahead of schedule—especially now that he had found Brice and wanted time to explain himself to her so his existence wouldn't seem so unnatural.

He hadn't said anything to Brice, but it could be that Damien Ruthven would have to disappear. It was a contingency he always planned for. He had gotten good at slipping away from tight situations, leaving no finger- or footprints behind.

But Brice had never faced a situation like this. He had watched her carefully while he described what his life was like, and he could see that she'd been appalled. Damien liked to think that she would go with him and eventually learn to be happy. But a part of him feared that she would never agree.

* * *

Brice wrinkled her nose and set the laptop aside. The bathroom looked fabulous, but the cleaning crew really needed to visit more regularly. It smelled as if something had died in one of the stalls and—

"Oh, shit!" She jumped off the counter and reached for her gun. A part of her couldn't believe that she managed to locate and draw it without shooting herself.

There came a familiar wheezing, the sort of whistling sound that can happen when two pieces of pipe get misaligned and a breeze passes over them.

No, no, no, she prayed. *Go the other way!* But the whistling grew louder. It stopped right outside the bathroom door. The stink had grown even stronger.

It can't get in. It was a thick, heavy door, and she had the key. She and Damien had checked. The door was locked. And it was built of solid oak panels, the hardware made of heavy brass. It would take an elephant to break it down. And anyway, the zombie couldn't know she was here.

There came a scrape and a creak, and then, impossibly, the scream of splitting wood.

The whistling grew louder. The creature was in the room. With her. On the other side of the bank of stalls!

Brice's mouth was dry with terror as her stalker rounded the bank and shambled toward her, but she didn't panic, not even when its long, doglike tongue flicked out and passed quickly over its scaly mouth and jowls.

It's not really human, she thought, aiming her pistol. *Not human at all. You can do this.*

Still, she hesitated for a moment. Her handgun could deliver a heart-stopping dose of lead—but would that be effective? If Dippel's journal was truthful, stopping the heart didn't mean stopping his creature. Not right away. As sick as the idea made her, Brice followed Damien's harsh advice and brought the pistol up until it was level with the thing's uneven head. She didn't look into its eyes, not wanting to see if there was anyone at home there. She took a last deep breath and then, without any of the standard police stop-or-I'll-shoot warnings, she pulled the trigger.

When the first bullet had no effect except to open up a small hole in the creature's left forehead, she lowered her aim just slightly and shot again. And again.

Soon the head was ruined, but the creature kept walking toward her. She moved her aim down about forty degrees and pulled the trigger until all the bullets were gone. The creature finally toppled over about five feet away from her.

"Holy hell." Brice sagged against the counter. The stench of gunpowder filled her nose, for a moment overriding the creature's stink. Her ears rang and her legs felt weak.

She understood now what they meant by time standing still in an emergency. It couldn't have taken her a minute—half a minute—to have shot the creature with everything in her gun. Yet those seconds just past had seemed like hours.

It was swell that the body had eventually fallen—after she'd switched from the ruined head to shooting the legs. The thing had not, however, stopped twitching and flexing its hands. It still wasn't dead.

"What are you?" she whispered.

She started forward slowly, unable to look away. Her mouth may have been dry before, but now it was flooded with saliva, proclaiming her nausea just in case she hadn't already noticed her upset stomach. Between the gunshots and this thing's noisy exhalations—it was slightly quieter with the vocal cords gone, but still too loud—escape was proving a noisy, smelly process. It seemed that this creature wasn't going to bleed to death quietly like a decent zombie should.

"Shut up," Brice begged it, trying to listen for sounds of other monsters who might have heard the gunfire and been drawn to the area. All she could hear was the wheezing and the hum of insects—blowflies. They were already gathering. They had probably already been here, riding the walking corpse.

The thought was too much. Brice gagged. She turned toward the sink and let her stomach have its way.

Eventually the spasm subsided. Hands shaking, Brice stood up and reloaded her pistol with the last of the spare bullets Damien had given her. The strange pistol carried only eight.

Only eight! That should have been adequate to any occasion she would ever face. It was hardly fair to fault the designers for not anticipating the situation she was currently in. Still, she wished she had something with more ammo and more power—an Uzi maybe.

Brice stared with intense concentration, slotting each bullet carefully, waiting for the zombie to die; willing it to give up the struggle and stop moving.

But the creature didn't comply. It was still twitching, still trying to move when she had the gun reloaded. She thought about shooting it some more, but suspected it wouldn't do any more good than the first magazine of bullets had done. She could shoot it into a dozen pieces and it would still move. And the noise might attract the wrong kind of attention—assuming she had escaped that so far.

"Damien," she whispered, looking about quickly. The word was a prayer. "Please hurry."

The body twitched violently at the sound of her voice and tried to sit up. Brice stepped back. It twitched again.

It is trying to get to me! Still!

Feeling panicky, Brice backed out of the bathroom through the broken door. The panel was split, cracked down the middle, and the wood scraped at her legs and tried to pull her robe away where the rough edge snagged.

Somehow the creature sensed where she was and spun what was left of its head toward her. A hand groped in her direction, and the body seemed intent on rolling onto its hands and what remained of its knees.

Should she shoot it some more?

No, she might need her eight bullets for someone—some*thing*—else.

But she had to stop it! She needed to get to Damien, and she couldn't go up those dark stairs alone if she knew the thing would come crawling after her. It might attract other creatures as well—others that weren't really dead. She could end up with a whole parade of zombies following her through the dark.

A padded chair stopped her backward progress. Clipped in the back of the knees, she sat abruptly, and rolled into a nearby desk with a small crash. Swiveling around quickly, she opened the nearest desk drawer, looking for another weapon or rope, a flashlight, anything—but just as Damien had discovered on their previous visit, there was nothing to be had. Just scissors, pens, papers, lipstick, a set of false nails, some kind of super nail glue . . .

Nail adhesive. Three tubes of it. Brice reached for the

package of white tubes. *Waterproof, peel-proof, stick it and it stays, the world's best nail glue,* it said.

"Will it work?" She hoped it lived up to its billing. There wasn't any rope, and she needed to make sure that this thing didn't get up and follow her.

She laughed once, a sound rough and devoid of any amusement. She stopped immediately, frightened by the hysterical sound.

Pulling open the package, Brice turned her chair back toward the twitching corpse, wondering what part of it she should glue to the floor. It was on its side, and only the ruined feet were still moving. Okay, hands and head seemed best. The nose was mostly intact and would make a good anchor. And for good measure, she'd glue the damaged right eyelid shut if anything was left of it.

A part of her felt sick at what she was doing. It was the smell—what a horrible stench, and getting worse all the time—but also at the idea of desecrating the dead.

Only, it wasn't exactly dead. It was *undead*. Another legend had come to life for her. Wasn't she a lucky girl? She'd remember this moment forever. There was nothing like shooting a zombie to leave a lasting impression on a stressed-out brain.

"Hell, I could end up in tabloids." Her hands shook as she pulled off the cap of the nail glue tube, then inserted the sharp end into the tip, breaking the seal. A pungent, chemical smell drifted up to her nose. Brice welcomed it—anything was better than the smell of the monster.

"Just do it." But she still hesitated, revulsion and fear making her reluctant and slow.

And there was something else too. It was that religious quagmire opening up in front of her again. It was all in her head, but it kept her stranded as surely as real quicksand would have done. She had to find a way to negotiate it.

Brice exhaled slowly. *Fine.* She could do this. She had become a master at using logic and rationalization.

To begin with, she had to believe that this creature— or rather, conglomeration of creatures—should be dead. In fact, whatever its movements, that it was already dead in every way that counted.

Therefore, she hadn't murdered it. She'd shot it, but that wasn't murder. She had really done it a favor, hastening it to a return to its natural state. She was not marked like Cain. And what she was doing now was not being done to a live person. This wasn't a puppy or a baby or anything else alive. It was a dead monster. Gluing it to the floor wasn't desecration, it was self-defense. Just as shooting the thing had been.

"I had to. I have to," she said softly, making her voice firm and convincing.

Her childhood beliefs said that God was supposed to be merciful and all-forgiving. This monster wouldn't be blamed for what Dippel had done to it. There should be a place for him—all of them—in heaven once the soul was forced away. Surely it would depart soon.

Was she sure about that?

Mostly.

But if there weren't any accommodations there, or in hell, then she had to make sure that this thing didn't come back to the earthly plane and follow her with its hideous, twitching body.

The quagmire slowly subsided and Brice could again see her way. She stood up slowly and started for the bathroom, eyes fixed on the shuddering ruin squirming toward the threshold. It was growing excited, agitated by her presence.

"I can do this," she whispered, putting conviction in her voice. But before she had taken five steps toward the shattered door, something black and heavy fell over her head. Brice never even had time to scream.

One certainly has a soul; but how it came to allow itself to be enclosed in a body is more than I can imagine. I only know if mine gets out, I'll have a bit of a tussle before I let it get in again.

—*Byron*

As long as men believe in absurdities, they will continue to commit atrocities.

—*Voltaire*

Chapter Sixteen

Brice awoke slowly. Her first thought was that someone had been using her mouth as a lint trap on a dryer. Her second thought was that her situation was probably worse than that.

She didn't want to do it, but she forced open her dry eyes. It took them a moment to focus. When they did, she regretted her decision to rejoin the waking world.

"I am Johann Conrad Dippel," the monster said, enunciating each word carefully.

Brice tried to answer but couldn't.

The clock on the wall said it was 4:22—he'd been gone twenty minutes. Only twenty minutes, but the twitching corpse on the floor said he was likely too late. Dippel had probably gotten Brice.

They could now use the rotary phone to summon help. Had it been worth it?

Wanting to be certain that he had overlooked no

clue—*blood; her blood, don't you mean?*—Damien dropped to the floor and searched carefully. He found the casings from spent shells. Brice had obviously emptied her pistol into this creature to stop him. Shots to the head and to the knees, all well placed. That meant she hadn't been too panicked to defend herself.

It was also a reassuring sign that there was no fresh blood anywhere, only the brown clotted stuff that the zombies bled.

Damien sighed, feeling slightly relieved. Brice hadn't been hurt in the fight here—not enough to bleed. And the fact that she had been willing to defend herself said that she hadn't been lost to blind terror; it was just possible that she had managed to get away before Dippel found her.

Kneeling, Damien found a tube of nail glue under the twitching corpse's pantleg. He felt his heart contract as nascent hope died. Nail glue. An open tube. That was ingenious. Since it wasn't likely that Brice had been taking time out to repair a broken nail, it seemed a good guess that she'd been intent on gluing this zombie to the floor so it couldn't follow her.

But since she hadn't finished the job, it seemed likely that someone had interrupted her while she was working.

The list of candidates wasn't pleasant. Try as he might, Damien couldn't bring himself to believe that she'd found an overdedicated Santa Claus, an overlooked janitor, or a third security guard doing his rounds.

Damien stood slowly, noticing the veil of disturbed vapor that hovered near his skin. He marveled that his body could be hot enough to cause steam when he felt so cold inside.

He also realized that he needed the bathroom. How could his bladder intrude at such a moment?

But that was the body for you—always needing something. Of course, you had to give it what it needed if you were to ask extraordinary things of it. And he would be asking.

Damien stepped into the nearest stall. He was calm. He didn't hurry. But all around him, the cool air boiled as he made his plans.

"He must come. He wants you, and he was always foolishly brave." Dippel spoke from behind the desk. The doctor used English, but it was heavily accented with German. The distorted voice echoed around her. It radiated insanity as surely as the sun shed light—and as effortlessly.

But Brice did not feel warm. Something about Dippel—perhaps his vaguely chemical smell—made her feel deathly cold. His repeated chopping at her manuscript and other documents with a surgical saw didn't help her nerves either. It put him in a class with book burners. In her opinion, a man who would destroy books was capable of anything.

At least he hadn't touched Ninon's letters. Yet. But he was working his way toward them.

Brice began to rock her wrists back and forth, trying to loosen her bonds. It didn't seem to have any effect, but she'd seen enough movies to know that she had to keep trying.

"So much time wasted," the doctor muttered. "Always, always, there are people trying to stop me."

Brice looked across the room. There was another source of uneasiness. Dippel had built up the fire in the grate until it was dangerously large. She'd have to speak to Damien about this. Such a fire was hazardous in a high-rise. Why hadn't he converted to gas logs?

MELANIE JACKSON

She was trying not to think about the ox roast she had attended in England. There were no oxen or livestock of any kind in this skyscraper, yet the image persisted. It took effort to not start down the path of speculation about what else could be roasted in the flames. A library? A man? A woman? All of the above? She hoped her nervousness wasn't flickering in her eyes. Showing fear would probably be unwise.

"I think I have spiders in my brain," Dippel said suddenly. "I can feel them . . . crawling. They may be eating it. I feel so empty sometimes. It's the hippocampus, I'm sure. It shows rapid deterioration in some subjects—possibly because they were altered after death. But perhaps because the process cannot be continued forever."

Since he had gagged her, Brice assumed that she wasn't expected to answer this alarming observation. She wouldn't have known what to say anyway. If his brain was filled with spiders, her brain felt like cottage cheese. This was a step beyond the Mad Hatter's tea party. Panic and unreason were nigh. She'd been making some heavy withdrawals from the banked funds of rationality during the last twenty-four hours, and that wasn't an account with overdraft protection. If she crossed the line, would she end up insane too?

Suddenly she remembered the old saw about how for writers there were no bad experiences, it was all just material for the next book.

Oh, God! Let me live to write this story!

Dippel spoke. "I had so many rehearsals—Byron among them—before I was able to perfect my technique for creating these wonderful foot soldiers. They are almost perfect now, don't you think? Just their brains have failed to improve. If only I had more time . . . Bah! I cannot regret now. At least they should be sterile. Not that any of my soldiers has ever evidenced any interest in reproduction. Not like my living subjects." He turned and glared, but not at her. *Through* her. He began to pace. His voice was anguished as he went on.

"Your eyes accuse me. But understand that this isn't what I want. I have to destroy my life's work. It's a huge sacrifice, but I understand now that there'll be no place for me in heaven while my blasphemies yet live. I shall never know salvation. It's in the Epistle to the Romans—sanctification through repentance. It's the only way. I must return myself to grace before my brain is gone."

He stared at her intently before again turning away. "My foot soldiers don't matter. They don't know how they were created, don't know how to renew themselves. They'll die soon enough—they're rotting where they stand, since I have stopped transfusing them and letting them feed. But my special ones—they must be killed by a certain method. It's the only way. The only way. I've tried to be kind, but they've all fought me! They've made me be cruel and ruthless." His mouth worked. The jaws creaked, a sound like rubber-soled shoes on a highly polished floor. Then the doctor said: "Judas."

He turned to face her again. This time Dippel's face was covered in clotted tears that looked more like slime than saline. He leaned in close, like a lover, his lips only inches from her cheek. Brice didn't want to provoke him, but she couldn't help recoiling. She wouldn't want a kiss from Death, and even less did she want one from this man, if that was what he planned.

She briefly tried to feel compassion for the creature, but it was impossible when she saw the huge scalpel in his hand. He meant that for someone, and the list of possibilities was short. It was either her or Damien. His heart may not have been made in hell, but it had been fired there sometime in the last centuries. He was insane and he was evil—and irresponsible. There was no point in wasting compassion on him. It would only get in the way of anything she might have to do.

Because she *would* do something if she got the chance. Her feelings about the death penalty may have always been ambivalent, but she suddenly found the answer in this situation was very clear. There were no moral quagmires. Dippel, unlike his monsters, was definitely born human. But he had exiled himself from the realm of civilized men by committing vile deeds. And he planned another murder—maybe more than one. That meant he had to be stopped, and by any means possible. He had to die before Damien did. If Brice had to be the one to kill him, so be it. It would be a righteous killing.

Thunder boomed, making both Dippel and Brice jump. But the blizzard blowing outside was no match for the one forming within her. Brice embraced her stormy rage, hoping the power would make her strong and unafraid.

Another creature entered the room, its smell preceding it. Brice stared, fixated. She thought she had seen the worst of Dippel's creations, but this abomination surpassed her worst nightmares. The creature looked like a wax doll—an honest-to-goodness corpse from a wax museum horror flick. But that couldn't be. It was walking around, moving, bending, more flexible than the other

272

one had been—and more alert. No, it had once been human. Maybe many humans.

Perhaps it was the scar that made his waxy face seem inflexible. Or perhaps it was just that the creature had been away from normal people for so long that it had forgotten how to use facial expressions. But—Brice wondered sickly—if she scratched its face, would it actually bleed, or would she just plow furrows in dead skin?

The monster grunted something, its lips barely moving. But they moved enough for her to see what was inside them as it bent over her. The jaws had been wired together at one time, and there were maggots. Dippel had apparently been in so great a hurry that he hadn't bothered to remove the undertaker's sutures from the creature's mouth. He'd simply clipped them and left them there.

When Dippel finished speaking, the creature took a deep breath, snuffling Brice's robe like a hunting dog gathering a scent. She tried not to notice the maggots that fell in her lap. The alert yellow eyes studied her for a moment, and then the monster stood up. Its movements were fast, precise. Not like the other one. This creature was . . . not fresher, but newer. And there was intelligence in its eyes.

What had Dippel done, raided the local morgue? The cemetery? Brice wondered hysterically. That made sense— what else could he have done? Flown his European monsters first-class into JFK, or hidden them in trunks and hoped Customs didn't notice anything odd?

Brice swallowed as best she could, trying not to breathe any of the air the creature brought with it. If she threw up, she might well choke on her own vomit.

Dippel seemed to want her alive for now, but his ability to pay attention to reality seemed erratic at best. He might not notice her choking.

Maybe it was those spiders in his brain, she thought. And then she wished she hadn't. After seeing those maggots, the explanation seemed entirely too likely.

The more sins you confess, the more books you will sell.
—*Ninon de Lenclos*

The lapse of ages changes all things—time, language, the earth, the bounds of the sea, the stars of the sky, and every thing "about, around, and underneath" man, except man himself.

—*Byron*

To hold a pen is to be at war.

—*Voltaire*

Chapter Seventeen

Damien stepped outside the executive bathroom and looked around carefully. No one was there that he could see. He supposed someone might be hiding in one of the office cubicles, but that wasn't these zombies' style. They had no cunning. Still, he listened intently. He scented the air. No hint of sandalwood. Nothing. Brice really was gone, not just hiding somewhere. Nevertheless, he walked cautiously among the bolted-together panels that made up the peons' offices, peering over those low enough to offer a view of the working-class prisons.

He disliked this place. Damien didn't understand why management thought underlings needed to be treated like veal, to be confined in identical pens while they worked. Such an environment would make his brain numb. Surely it would do the same to any thinking man or woman.

Of course, right now numb sounded pretty good. Anything was better than imagining what might be happening to Brice.

Damien had known fear before—anger, even despair. But this was worse. It was a witch's brew of terror and rage, with empathy and guilt added for spice. He was two centuries old, and had lived hard enough for any dozen men, and if you had asked him a week ago, he'd have said that he'd seen and done and experienced everything at least once. This was one hell of a time to discover that he was wrong. That there in fact did exist a new kind of awful emotion that could be attached to love.

Time was ticking down; he knew it, but Damien didn't consult any of the clocks mounted on the walls. He wouldn't consult with anything other than his gun and perhaps his hand grenade until he found Brice and killed Dippel.

Dippel. The man was an exception to so many rules. That bastard was going to be killed dead, dead, dead—reduced to molecules so small that there was no chance of him ever resurrecting. It would be Damien's favor to humanity.

Flash, flash, went the small red light. Hurry! Hurry!

Damien's inner rage wanted him to rush about, smashing things, yelling, to find Brice immediately. But he didn't give way to emotion. He was her only hope of escape—he couldn't afford to be hurt or killed before rescuing her. He had to be smart.

Instead of haste, Damien used logic. It was difficult, with the storm and his anger urging him to action, but he persevered, using pain to focus himself when his thoughts veered onto unproductive paths. It was doing neither the plaster nor his knuckles any good, but he found punching the walls oddly satisfying.

Damien knew that she wasn't on any of the floors

below him. He'd checked them all from basement to level five. He hadn't seen anyone, or discovered any booby traps since disarming the hand grenade in the stairwell. That meant they were retreating upward.

To his apartment?

Yes, that made sense. Dippel always had been into symbolism. He would want to kill Damien on his home ground.

"They tried to burn me, you know," Dippel said softly. "It was an epiphanic moment really, the first time I understood about purification by fire."

The doctor stood and began pacing. His different-sized arms swung unevenly. Occasionally, the doctor tried to make eye contact with her, but Brice had a difficult time taking her eyes off the scalpel still clutched in his right hand. Nothing had ever appeared more threatening.

"They chained me and my helpers to the wall and piled up the faggots. But it was April, and the wood was green. The Dominicans would have known better than to use it, but those peasants! They'd never cooked anyone before. They didn't even have the kindness to garrote my people before burning them." Dippel's voice was full of contempt. "The fire was slow to start and stayed sullen, even when they added straw. Eventually they got it to light, but it didn't burn hot enough, and there wasn't enough smoke to put my people out of their misery. They just singed and smoldered."

Brice shuddered, but Dippel didn't notice. He was caught up in his memories.

"I didn't die, of course, and after a while the superstitious fools got afraid and ran away. Eventually I got free—I had to. The screaming was making me crazy. The smell was maddening too—like roasting pork, but I knew it was my own legs."

Dippel looked at the fireplace. He went over and threw the last of the wood on the pyre.

Pyre?

"At first, I did nothing. The castle was ruined, my labs destroyed, and I thought I would heal. But the cellular regeneration wasn't happening quickly enough. The fire had done permanent damage to my tissues. I finally realized that I couldn't wait anymore. I had to have new legs and another hand before those fools found their courage and regrouped." Dippel resumed pacing. "I was fortunate. They'd hung Schmidt upside-down before they burned him. His eyeballs had burst and his ears were gone, but the legs were almost untouched."

Poor, poor Schmidt. Brice closed her eyes and tried to make Dippel's voice go away.

"I didn't kill him—no one can say that. The mob did it! That sin can't be laid at my door. I just ended his suffering, let his soul move on to heaven." He added pettishly, "They weren't *his* legs anyway. I gave them to him in the first place, and he wouldn't need them in heaven. God would make him whole."

Brice felt sick, hearing her own rationalizations for killing coming out of the mouth of this monster. And there were other reasons to feel ill. It was all too easy to picture the mob scene he recounted, with the flames in Damien's fireplace roaring, highlighting Dippel's many scars.

His arms were especially mismatched, one scarred and one not, and she wondered if one of them might also have belonged to the unfortunate Schmidt who went to heaven without his legs.

Though it didn't seem possible that the horror of their

conversation could in any way increase, Dippel's next words fell like a physical blow, knocking the wind from her lungs. Brice had half expected to hear this from the moment she saw the blaze, but listening to him voice his intentions out loud was more than she could stand.

"I wonder if this fire is hot enough. Byron is strong, you know. He won't want to burn. But, of course, he must. Suffering is the only way to be redeemed. I understand that now." Dippel's voice was one of fanatical earnestness. "I was wrong to try to escape that fire. I should have let it end there."

Brice's eyes opened again.

Evil. Dippel was Evil with a big E—Satan's paw, the devil's spawn. She didn't want to start thinking in religious terms again, but it was impossible not to. This wasn't just madness. Insanity may have cracked open his mind and let the Evil in, but his psychopathy was just a small part of what prompted his actions now.

And Evil had just played its trump card on Brice: fear. Fear of watching another loved one die while she looked on helpless to stop what was happening.

"You look so frightened. Don't worry, my dear. I am a compassionate man. I shall offer you the kindness that mob failed to offer me. I'm quite good at these things, you know. I'm a doctor. And I won't let my soldiers have you. Not 'til you're dead." Dippel patted her shoulder as he paced by. He still had the scalpel in his right hand.

The moment his back was turned, Brice resumed pulling on her bonds. She felt her skin break open and blood start to flow. She kept on tugging, not caring if she sawed clean through her flesh and bones. If Dippel could do it, so could she. She *had* to get away. She *had* to warn Damien! Anything—*anything!*—was better than waiting for Dippel to enact his horrible plan.

* * *

Damien found another zombie in the stairwell between the sixth and seventh floors. He smelled the creature before he saw the outline of its head, peering down into the darkness and snuffling for its prey. Damien took a bead on it, but he didn't shoot. A single bullet wouldn't put it down, and would only alert the creature to his whereabouts.

Confronting it headlong while climbing upstairs would be a mistake too. He'd be at a terrible disadvantage. Fortunately, there were other options.

Damien waited until the giant head withdrew; then he put down his rifle and grabbed the railing, mounting it gingerly. Water vapor in the air was beginning to condense and the pipes were slippery. Once he was sure of his balance, Damien began to climb.

He moved silently, controlling his breathing, being careful not to make squeaking noises as he grasped and let go of the painted iron pipes. The last bit of the deadly jungle gym required a stretch—a potentially dangerous one since, if he slipped, he'd fall all the way to the lobby. But the maneuver allowed him to get behind his quarry.

Though Damien made no noise, the creature sensed him and turned swiftly as Damien vaulted over the rail. The zombie was fast, but there was no time for it to aim its rifle. Damien lashed out with his foot, shoving the thing backward down the stairs.

It grunted upon the impact of the sole of his shoe, but then its right hand flashed out and grasped Damien's ankle with what felt like a steel claw. The left hand held fast to its gun even though it might have been able to right itself by grabbing the rail.

Their gazes locked. The thing had evil eyes, hot eyes that seemed to glow even after the red smoke-detector light flashed off. There was also an intelligence there that hadn't existed in the other creatures.

But that awareness was where any connection to humanity ended. It had no hair and the skin looked scaly, almost reptilian. Even the underlying bone structure of the head was wrong, though that wasn't the first thing Damien noticed. Its face was distorted by a long, curving scar that pulled its lips back from its teeth.

Alarmed and repulsed by the feel of its talons gripping his ankle, Damien dropped to the ground, changing the thing's center of gravity and pulling it off balance. As the creature jerked forward, Damien kicked out with his other foot, connecting with its midriff and knocking the monster away. It crashed down the steps.

Damien rolled quickly to the edge of the landing and watched it fall. The movement looked odd in the slow pulse of the red smoke-detector light. And the thing grunted as it fell, giving audible punctuation as each step forced a small bit of air from its lungs.

It finally reached the bottom of the flight of stairs, and there let out an enraged howl that shook the air of the stairwell. Damien shuddered at the sound. What the hell was this thing? The monstrosity was faster than the others, stronger too. Damien was suddenly willing to bet that this was the creature who'd laid the trap for him.

And apparently, all he'd accomplished by shoving it down the stairs was pissing it off. The damn thing was making enough noise to alert everyone in a ten-block radius.

Damien checked his pistol. Three bullets, and there were two in the rifle, plus whatever the creature had in its own gun. He was willing to bet that wouldn't be enough.

"Bloody hell." Damien ran down the stairs until he was at the next landing. There he stopped, sighted on the zombie—no, *ghoul*. The word popped into his head. That's what it was: a graveyard haunt. The old legends said that ghouls were faster than zombies, smarter too because they survived by eating raw human flesh.

Damien stepped closer. The beast was still clinging to its gun, though the rifle had gotten jammed in the stair railing during the fall. Damien was repulsed, but though he wanted to put his last shots into the creature's growling mouth, he aimed at the clawed fist trying to free the gun.

The rifle dropped along with the creature's hand, but the ghoul snarled up at Damien with its long, sharp teeth. Free of its weapon, it leapt to its feet.

Yeah, this creature was a lot faster than the others. It was also sporting some nonhuman tooth braces. Or were those . . . wire? Whichever, Dippel had outdone himself.

With unbelievable speed, the creature bounded halfway up the stairs, taking the dozen steps in a single leap. It was on Damien a half second later, nails of its right hand clawing at Damien's face and jaws snapping as it tried to lock on his throat with its filthy teeth.

Damien rolled backward, pulling his knees into his chest and getting his feet planted against the creature. Again he threw the ghoul off, shoving as hard as he could into the soft part of its body.

There was a horrible cracking noise when Damien's boot punched a hole in the creature's chest, knocking some organs loose. A gush of dark sludge cascaded down Damien's leg. It burned like acid.

"Bloody hell!" Damien kicked out again, aiming for the head.

The thing shrieked with rage and down it went, toppling end over end down another flight of stairs.

This time, Damien didn't wait for it to regain its feet. He jumped after it, landing on the creature's chest and finishing the destruction of its ribs. The blow knocked the air out of its lungs, and while that stopped the creature from screaming, it didn't slow it any. The monster apparently didn't need air to live.

Damien fought the creature off, avoiding its awful jaws while he wrestled the grenade out of his pocket. Claws tore through his clothing and then into the skin of his legs, shredding it into thick ribbons. Then teeth found his arm, midway between wrist and elbow. Damien jerked away, leaving a bit of his flesh and a lot of his shirt behind.

Ignoring the pain, Damien pulled the pin and stuffed the grenade deep into the creature's chest cavity. He pushed the thing into some soft tissue where it stuck. Then he head-butted the creature—catching some teeth on his forehead—and rolled away, letting himself tumble down the stairs until he smacked against the railing of the next landing. Falling down a flight of stairs hurt only marginally less than being bitten, but at least he would be safe from the blast.

A small explosion rocked the stairwell, followed by a soft rain and the stench of barbecue.

Winded, bruised, bleeding from both arms, his night vision ruined and his ears ringing, Damien gave himself a moment to recover before climbing back up to see what he'd wrought with the nasty little bomb the creature had intended to use on him. He climbed slowly and stopped at the landing, unwilling to step in the gore that oozed down the stairs like black honey.

Flash, flash. The smoke detector's light blinked tirelessly on and off, its warning color making everything more vivid and garish.

Things were a mess. The walls, the stairs, the ceiling all were dripping with dark brown clots. And, as Damien had predicted, the grenade had effectively reduced the body to bits. He couldn't even tell what the creature had been anymore; it might have been any large animal—a deer, a cow, a pony.

The explosion had also opened up a hole in the wall that abutted the elevator shaft. The emergency ladder was hanging crookedly, some of its rungs bent. As far as Damien could tell, the cables that guided the elevator were undamaged, but he wasn't willing to risk his life testing the observation.

"Bloody hell," Damien said again, and then listened intently to see if anyone was coming to investigate.

Nothing stirred. Which probably meant that only Dippel was left. Dippel, who was too busy tormenting Brice to come exploring.

But then again, maybe not. There could be more ghouls laying other traps, getting ready to ambush Damien as he climbed upward toward Brice.

One thing was certain: Using the stairs to reach his apartment was no longer an option. He'd leave blood-spattered footprints everywhere. The service elevator was out too. Little though he fancied it, Damien decided that it was time to move back outside and take his chances with the drainpipe.

The storm was worse now; he could feel it in his muscle and bone. But that was a partial benefit. He'd be alone out there. And no one would expect him to come that way. Only an insane person would try it.

Damien wasn't aware of it, but he was grinning ferociously, part of him amused by the idea that he was insane.

Mad dogs and Englishmen.

Moving slowly, Damien pulled off his shirt and tore it into pieces. He began bandaging his arms. They were two-toned with blood—his own and the now-dead creature's. He worked carefully, scraping them clean. This wasn't a time for slippery hands.

In every author, let us distinguish the man from his work.
—*Voltaire*

Garden tools—£1. 8s. 6d.
Forest seed—£4. 5s.
Income Tax—£47. 9s. 7d.
(some expenses are unavoidable)
        —*From the accounting ledgers of Lord Byron's mother*

Constancy . . . that small change of love, which people exact so rigidly, receive in such counterfeit coin, and repay in baser metal.
        —*Byron (letter to Thomas Moore, November 17, 1816)*

Chapter Eighteen

Damien scrambled over the icy parapet that lined the roof and immediately took in the tableau being acted out in the library. The world slowed abruptly, time again shifting into some other place.

He saw Dippel reach for Brice, the terrified look on her face as she stared at the scalpel in his hand. Screaming, Damien rushed toward the door.

Time slowed even further as he moved through the air, and Damien had long moments in which to notice the many changes that the last two centuries had brought to the good doctor. Dippel had been taking some home-brewed steroids and had gotten himself burned at some time or another. And maybe he'd been doing a little parts-replacement. His left arm was considerably larger than it used to be. Damien couldn't imagine why the man hadn't replaced both limbs while he was at it; then he realized that Dippel was right-handed and would have needed that hand and arm to perform the operation.

The thought of such a surgery turned his stomach, and it confirmed Damien's belief that Dippel was truly both mad and evil.

Looking through the glass, Damien could plainly see the doctor's eyes. They were dark like his own—and yet not. Dippel's gaze was insane; it held wounds, his pupils black pits that had bled darkness into the whites of his eyes and drowned them. They were now twin holes where madness and malevolence hemorrhaged. The doctor's claim to humanity, assuming he had ever had one, was now so weak as to be nonexistent. He was as great a monster as any of his creations.

Damien threw himself against the door, surprised when it sprang open easily.

Brice heard the crash of the French doors hitting the walls and felt the icy draft of the storm a moment before Dippel swung around behind her, nearly overturning her chair.

"You came," he said, his voice ecstatic. Then: "Now good-bye, my dear."

Dippel took his dull scalpel and slashed Brice's throat. She saw it coming from the corner of her eye. Only her tangled hair saved her from an immediately fatal cut, but the line of fire that burned across her neck and the spill of hot blood down her chest told her that she was probably in trouble.

At the sight of Brice's blood, Damien's own monster broke free. He screamed as he saw the scalpel move across Brice's throat and he was on his foe in an instant.

The heel of his hand caught Dippel squarely beneath the chin, snapping the man's head back and breaking his neck like a stalk of ripe celery. He bore the doctor's body over, riding it to the ground where he tried to bury it in the floor.

A stunned Dippel slashed at Damien, but he couldn't see with his head turned at such an unnatural angle, and Damien ignored the shallow cuts that were inflicted.

"Time to die," Damien snarled. He drew back his arm for a second strike, aiming for the sternum with fingers cocked upward and held stiff like the blade of an ax.

He felt the tip of the doctor's breastbone break off as he drove the heel of his hand upward into the man's heart. The ribs cracked, flesh tore, and Damien's hand disappeared inside. He grabbed the heart, forcing his fingers through pulsing muscle and then tore it loose. Blood geysered over both men. With a roar, Damien flung the heart into the fire.

When Dippel still didn't release his blade, Damien took out his pistol and, laying it against the doctor's wrist, pulled the trigger, blowing off the hand that had cut Brice's throat. He rose quickly, kicking the scalpel away. Then he stood up and emptied the gun into Dippel's ear.

It took eleven shots, but Dippel's body finally stopped moving.

Only then did Damien turn to Brice.

Lightning flashed, illuminating the room with painful brightness. She didn't look good. Dippel's blade hadn't been especially sharp, and her hair had helped deflect some of the cut. Still, the wound at the right side of her neck went deep and there was too much blood.

Shocked and not knowing what else to do, Damien took up the doctor's bloody blade, carefully removed her gag and cut her other bonds. The ropes were saturated with blood too and buried in her swollen flesh. Brice had all but amputated her hands in trying to get away.

Damien watched in horror as she raised her swollen and bloodied fingers to her neck. The delicate digits pressed firmly, but they couldn't hold back the blood leaking from her throat. She was dying.

Really, she was dead.

Looking into her eyes, he could see the knowledge there. She understood what was happening.

"No," he breathed. "God, no."

"You got the phone working? But there's no time for an ambulance, is there?" Brice whispered as he knelt beside her. Her face was white with pain, her voice only a soft murmur.

"No, we don't need an ambulance." He pulled off what was left of his shirt and started to stanch the blood, but it was hopeless. He wanted to scream at God. He wanted to kill Dippel all over again. Mostly, he wanted to turn back time—just sixty seconds. That was all he would need to put things right, to get there just a minute sooner.

But as Damien had said before, for all his amazing gifts, he couldn't do that one thing. Time ran only one way, and that was away from them.

Damien forced himself to look into Brice's dilated eyes, to confront the horror there so she wouldn't be alone. He wanted to ask her to let him try to save her. He knew about her feelings of moral ambiguity regarding prolonged life such as he had; that part of her had spent too many years in Sunday school to ever accept what he offered. Though she had never uttered a word of reproof at his tale, part of her probably saw what he had done as subverting God's will, making him as evil as Dippel. That part of her would probably feel eternally guilty if she accepted his offer and survived.

So don't make the offer, a voice in his head whispered. *Don't make her choose.*

"Got any spare bullets? I'm such a coward about pain." Brice's voice, already weak, was fading. Damien touched her face with gentle fingers and she wondered if he felt what she did—that her skin was dreadfully cold but the unwilling tears that fell from her eyes stayed scalding.

"No," he lied. It was probably obvious that she was bleeding quickly, dying. She could feel it happening. There wouldn't be any need for bullets and a mercy killing.

"Damn it," she whispered in a flash of anger. "We were supposed to have more time."

"Yes." He brushed her tears away, but more fell. They came from his eyes now too, and burned like fire where they touched her.

She treasured them anyway, because they were tears for her.

"Don't cry," she rasped stupidly, watching the steam rise from his body. "I'm the one who's dying."

"I know. And I can't bear it." Damien looked up. His eyes were blacker than she had ever seen them, more filled with purpose, more filled with rage. He calmly reached around her torn throat and put pressure behind her ears. "Forgive me. I do this out of love."

"What are you doing to me?" Brice asked. She wondered wildly if he was trying to strangle her, trying to put her out of her misery as Dippel had promised to do.

"Don't worry about anything now. It drives up your blood pressure, and you must remain calm. Just trust me."

"Damien?" she thought she asked. His shadow seemed to grow. It became huge, like nightfall, and covered everything until the world was in darkness.

"Let me take the pain away," he said. "Trust me."

"I do," she whispered, surrendering to the cold. If she had to die, in Damien's arms was the best place for it.

Brice slid quietly into unconsciousness.

"You can't have her," Damien called fiercely as the next strike of lightning pierced the glass and seared his eyes. Ghosts—his old friends and enemies—were gathering around Brice, their gazes avid. They had appeared the moment she lost consciousness. Or perhaps it had been at the moment when he'd completely lost his mind. "She's not going with you—not today. I won't let this happen. There's still time."

Damien went to the desk and opened a second secret panel. He pulled out two syringes and two ampoules containing a mix of adrenaline and amphetamines, which he shoved in his pocket with a bloodied hand. He was still bleeding, but he ignored his wounds.

He went back to the unconscious Brice and scooped her up in his arms, not feeling the pain of his many cuts and bites. He wasn't feeling anything anymore. Damien ran for the roof, taking no notice of the gash in his side though the blood was flowing freely now.

Brice began to reawaken but was too weak or too confused to cry out in pain.

The taint of wood smoke followed them from the room. It was bitter on his tongue. Still, Damien inhaled it. It meant he was alive—that he could yet save Brice.

It remained as cold as the innermost circle of hell outside, and vapor rose from her wound like a miniature ghost the moment they reached the crisp air. The sight frightened Damien, reminding him that her spirit was also slipping away, bleeding off with every rivulet of blood that trickled into the snow.

He laid her carefully in the lap of the largest gargoyle and then tore her bathrobe away. There was little difference between the color of her flesh and the snow in which she rested.

He began unhooking frozen chains from the gargoyle's neck and draping them around her wrists and ankles and waist where he locked them in place. He plucked a spiked medallion from the beast's breast, broke it in half and laid one side over Brice's heart. The other he shoved beneath her. He pressed firmly, driving the small prongs into her body. There was no time for any topical anesthetic. No time to apply a barrier between the metal and her skin.

The lightning was close now. *One-one-thousand. Two-one-thousand.*

He loaded a dose of adrenaline and amphetamine into the first syringe. He had to guess on the amount. She couldn't weigh much more than a hundred and ten pounds.

Oh, God! He could kill her—even if the lightning brought her back. The twin blows of electrocution and an overdose of the revival drugs on top of blood loss could be too much. And there would be horrible pain without an anesthetic. That could send her into shock. If only he could spare her that cruel fire burning her skin!

Petroleum jelly might work, but he had none and there was no time to search the building.

The ghosts danced around Damien and the gargoyle, bobbing about in the wind, veiling and unveiling Brice's body as though they were trying to shield her from his actions.

A shield.

"Maybe *I* can spare her."

Knowing it was a risk because it would stop his heart, too, he quickly loaded a second syringe with a larger dose and stripped off his clothes. Carefully he laid himself down over her body, grasping the chains and taking most of his weight on his forearms so he wouldn't crush her. Perhaps he would be burned instead of her. He prayed it would be so. The lightning would pass through both of them, but perhaps she would not be scarred, would not know the horrible pain of rebirth firsthand, would not feel the metal searing her flesh as it conducted the electricity into her heart.

"Hang on, love," he murmured. She was cold— so cold—and he could barely feel her breathing. Only her blood continued to move, and it had slowed to a trickle.

"Hurry. It's what you've been waiting for all these days," he commanded the night and the dark clouds that rode the sky. And then, to Brice: "Don't die. At least, don't die yet. Wait for the fire. Wait for me."

He turned his head eastward, watched and waited. The precious adrenaline was near, the two syringes cushioned in the snow, the dose for him closest at hand. He'd have to get to it immediately because his heart would be stopped and his eyesight gone. Brice's too. They would be blind and there would only be seconds in which to work before they froze and brain damage began to occur.

"I cannot believe that this has happened," he said, addressing Divinity. "How cruel are you? You bring me love and then bring her death? And you wonder why I have hated you all these years—refused to worship at your bloody shrine? Where is the mercy they all say you have? Is it real? I pray so. You may have none for me, but this woman has done nothing to deserve this fate. Take it back!"

There was no answer from heaven, no vision of angels. He was not being given divine dispensation for this act.

In that instant, Damien had a moment of affinity with Dippel's other creatures—his evil brothers that he had killed this night. He understood them now. Damien had a mission set in motion by Dippel, and he, too, would have to keep moving even after he was dead.

The lightning came.

One-one—

Thunder on the inside. And it seemed that all the light in the world—even the cold moon hiding in the clouds—roared aloud and then stabbed through his skin. It entered every fiber of Damien's body, spreading its cruel fire. It was the fire of a neutron bomb. But it didn't burn; rather, it melted. It filled his head with merciless white noise, a noise not understood by the ears but was rather a vibration that altered tissues, disturbed the molecules of the body and drove them into violent rearrangement. Then the flock of black birds, or perhaps bats, swooped in and buffeted his brain, confusing him and making it so he could no longer tell what was happening to his body, though he knew that death was closing in quickly.

He prayed that Brice didn't feel it. He knew she was being electrocuted. Her body had bowed, lifting him off the metal monster where they lay. But she didn't make a single sound.

It lasted forever, pain and light trying to pull his soul from his body.

"Noooooo!" Damien screamed as his agony reached its zenith.

And then it was over. Lightning danced over the iron monster and died out slowly, a last climax of eerie, incandescent light. And then Damien's world went dark. He was blind.

He was dead. Again.

But he had expected this. It happened every time. He would not be afraid—and he would not fail.

Damien reached down into the snow and felt for the adrenaline. It took a moment to locate the syringe with his clumsy fingers.

He touched his burned chest. There was no heartbeat. Feeling between the ribs, he found the correct spot and jammed the needle home.

Pain! Terrible pain as the adrenaline hit! But his heart was well trained and began to beat again almost immediately. The windmill of thought started back up in his brain, its sharp blades rotating through his head, slicing the veil that shrouded his thoughts. Clarity returned.

Gasping as his lungs recalled how to function, he felt for the second syringe. He ran his fingers along the large needle. Slowly his vision returned.

His first sight was Brice. Her mouth and eyes were open, her face a picture of frozen agony. But the wound in her neck had closed. It was, in fact, barely visible.

"Forgive me," Damien whispered, shoving the medallion between her breasts aside. She, too, was burned, but the small spike wounds closed almost instantly. "I never meant to cause you pain. I never meant for this to happen. And if God is offended by what I do, His anger will be with me."

He reached for her chest with clumsy fingers that seemed to have forgotten where their joints were located. Her heart was still—still and dead—and her face was absolutely colorless. But he could feel the spot where he needed to inject. It was marked with a small golden scar that glowed eerily even though the lightning had gone.

Reassured by this sign of potential life, and not allowing himself to reconsider his actions, Damien drove the needle into her heart.

"Start," he pleaded, pulling the empty syringe away. "Live! God—You let her live! Don't You punish her because You're angry with me!"

For a long moment, nothing happened. Then Brice's eyes and mouth moved, and she shuddered and started retching, trying to gulp in air with lungs that had forgotten how to do their job, trying to roll off the gargoyle and escape the cold and pain.

He grabbed her so that she wouldn't fall off the roof and pulled her away from the narrow parapet that was slick with ice. The snow clung to her bare skin.

All at once, Damien could feel the cold eating at his body and knew that she would soon feel it too. They had to get back inside before their organs froze. For a short time, they would be vulnerable to the elements.

Trembling, he picked up her still spasming body and staggered into the library. He didn't want her to regain awareness and see Dippel's body, to awaken in the place where she had been killed. But they both had to get warm. Immediately. And inside was the only available fire.

If I am a poet, I owe it to the air of Greece.
    —*Byron (translated from the Greek on Byron's Stone)*

If my son were of age—and the lady properly disengaged—it is still the last of all connections that I would wish to take place.
    —*Letter from Byron's mother to her attorney before his marriage*

Chapter Nineteen

Brice's eyes opened onto a world of dazzling fire, but she was not afraid because Damien sat between her and the flames and there was gentle music in the air.

"We have power back," he said, smiling. "The good guys won."

Brice nodded stiffly. Her neck hurt. "He meant that to be your crematorium," she said after a moment, her voice a harsh whisper.

"I know. I'm not sure why, but his intent was fairly clear. Here—you must be thirsty." Damien helped Brice sit up, using his body as a prop and a pillow. He offered her some brandy cut heavily with water.

"Are they all gone now?" she asked, certain they were because Damien was so calm. The worst of the storm must also have passed over them because his scars were barely noticeable.

"Yes. At least . . . well, they may not be completely dead yet, but they aren't going anywhere."

"I tried to glue one to the floor," Brice told him, swallowing some more of the weak brandy. It seemed to be helping. The tightness in her throat eased, and she was beginning to feel comfortably warm. It was the first time in hours that the chill hadn't gripped her bones.

"I saw that. It was ingenious." Damien's voice was gentle, as were his hands as he stroked slowly down her arms.

"Well, I tried conventional methods and they weren't working. Strange to think that in a building this size I couldn't find a single canister of mace or pepper spray." She turned her face into Damien's neck and inhaled. He was sweaty and smelled of cordite, but she drank in the scent because it was his.

A small eruption of sparks went up the chimney. Looking toward the fireplace, Brice finally noticed her nudity, and then Damien's. She asked without much interest: "Where's my robe?"

"Outside. With my clothes," he answered. Then, diffidently: "Do you remember what happened?"

Brice touched her chest, tracing its new scar. Her hands were more or less clean, but there were traces of blood under her fingernails that he had missed when he wiped her clean.

"I . . . no. I know what happened—what you did—but all I really recall is being attacked by a murder of crows." She looked toward the windows where the gargoyles perched. "Then, when I thought I couldn't stand it, they turned into doves and everything went white."

"An exaltation of doves," Damien said. "That's what they call such flocks."

"An exaltation," she murmured. "That sounds beautiful."

Brice wasn't certain that the crows and doves had been real, but she hoped they had headed south and weren't trying to weather the storm. Enough death had come to New York that night; she didn't want to see any more.

Damien watched his beloved gaze into the night, wondering what she was thinking, and also wondering when he would be called to account for what he had done.

As he had carried her inside, he'd thought about what he'd ended—both for Dippel and for Brice. His retaliation against his nemesis had been swift, brutal and merciless. He had become a feral animal that knew no compassion for the thing he killed. And he wasn't the least bit sorry. Dippel had tried to kill Brice—had, in fact, succeeded. That Damien had later managed to bring her back was irrelevant. Her life as she knew it was over, taken from her without consent. Dippel deserved to die with fear of hell bright in his mind.

Damien looked at the impossible treasure in his arms. A wild zigzag of scar tissue bisected her body, unlike his own which was covered in fresh golden marks that still faintly glowed.

Brice turned to face him.

"Am I . . . will I live forever now?" she asked. Her voice held neither wonder nor fear.

"Not unless you want to. There will come a time when you will have to choose whether to go back into the lightning or face death."

"When?"

"I don't know. I made it almost fifty years before I was called the first time. You will know the moment, though. That wound in your throat will begin to ache and eventually bleed." The words were hard to say.

"It's bad? When it comes back?"

Damien nodded. Suddenly his eyes felt filled with acid. They flooded with bitter tears as he recalled the slow return of his epilepsy. It had seemed terrible. Things would be even worse for Brice.

"I see." She touched her chest, tracing her scar. Would she think it hideous? A mark of shame?

"Damn it." Damien blinked, hard. He hated weeping. He would not do it!

He also hated that he had reason to fear for Brice. More than anything, he wanted to spare her the pain she had endured and would endure again. But that was impossible. He abhorred this fact—this condition—of their existence, but that was the deal, the terms of survival. Damien kept his voice steady and calm as he spoke to her. He would not lie about this, nor would he weep in her presence. He had no right to burden her further.

Brice's hand reached for her neck. The wound was closed, the scar barely noticeable. For now.

"I wouldn't have chosen this," Brice said softly.

Damien stopped breathing.

Then she smiled faintly and looked up into his eyes. "But I wasn't ready to die tonight either—so thank you. Thank you for giving me back my life."

Damien exhaled slowly and buried his face in her hair. *Forgiveness*, he thought. *So this is what a state of grace feels like.*

The stereo began playing Neil Diamond's "The Story of My Life," and Brice, listening to the lyrics for the first time, felt an odd stirring of emotion. Her eyes were misty with tears. The pain the song summoned was sharp and sweet. When was the last hour she had felt—or even believed in—a love like that?

She knew the answer, but didn't look at it too closely. It belonged to another life, the life she'd had before she met this stranger whom she now knew better than anyone on earth.

Damien, looking at the salty diamonds on the ends of Brice's lashes, thought she wore tears well, but he couldn't bear to see them. There had been so much pain already. He stroked them away.

"Hush, love," he said. And he took her in his arms and pulled her to her feet. By the light of the fire, they danced.

"I know that using the name Byron isn't wise," she whispered a few minutes later. "And Damien is a fine name, of course, but do you think in your next incarnation that you could be George? I'd be more at home with that. You might be too."

Brice was her logical self again. Damien smiled.

"That can probably be arranged." He kissed her hair, still reveling in his blessings, wondering if this meant that he would have to be less angry at God now.

Probably.

"You can choose another name for me too. When the time comes," she volunteered. "I'm not fussy. Just don't call me Gertrude. Or Mavis. I had an Aunt Mavis and absolutely loathed her."

"You know, I must tip my hat in admiration," Damien said. Awe and a bit of laughter filled him.

"It's nothing," Brice assured him. "I've always wanted a pseudonym."

"No, not that. You were hit with what amounts to a natural impossibility—something that should have bent your brain into knots and landed you in a sanatorium—and you not only grasped the facts immediately, you also waltzed them twice around the floor before vanquishing your fear."

"I shot those monsters too," Brice bragged. She swallowed and cuddled closer, resting her cheek against his bare chest. "I'm glad I did it. Glad I *could* do it, so you didn't have to. But I didn't like it at all."

"Yes, I know. But you did what you had to. You climbed a skyscraper in a snowstorm, braved the dark on your own, killed a zombie, faced a supernatural madman—and are still smiling. You are without any doubt the most valiant person I know. And I shall be grateful from now until my dying day that I have known you."

Brice smiled. "Hopefully, that day is a long, long way off. Where's Dippel now?" she asked after a moment. Her question was practical but her body was still relaxed against Damien's. She was finally warm, and any other urgency was slow to show itself. Brice wondered if that was because the storm had not yet retreated, or if it was a side effect of all that had happened. After all, once you'd faced violent death, everything else was bound to seem less important.

"Outside. But let's not worry about him for a few more minutes. We need to bathe and get dressed." Damien didn't add that it would probably be less distressing if the zombies quit moving before they saw them again.

"We're going to have to get rid of the bodies, you know. There's no explaining them," Brice remarked, as though reading his mind.

"I know. Don't worry. I have a plan," he assured her. Then Damien lifted her into the air and spun her about.

Brice laughed softly. "Of course you do."

"I've never known as much horror, fear and pain as I have this night," Damien told her.

"I know," Brice answered as she was set back on her feet. "Me either."

"But you know what I feel now," Damien said, standing

still and looking deeply into her dark eyes. It was almost a question. There was a half smile on his lips. "It isn't just the end-of-the-storm high."

"Happiness," Brice said. Her smile was wholehearted. And it wasn't the storm that affected her either.

"Yes." Damien pulled her close and kissed her.

Can you commit a whole county to their own prisons? Will you erect a gibbet in every field and hang up men like scarecrows?
—*Lord Byron's speech to Parliament in defense of the poor, February 27, 1812*

The enemy is without, and distress within. It is too late to cavil on doctrinal points, when we must unite in defense of things more important.
—*Lord Byron's speech in defense of freedom of religion to Parliament, April 21, 1812*

Chapter Twenty

"We must be practical," Brice said as Damien blotted her hair dry with a towel. It was a relief to finally be rid of the last of the sandalwood oil. Though she had enjoyed the smell, she would now always associate it with the second-worst night of her life.

Or perhaps she was looking at this the wrong way around. She and Damien were still alive. Maybe this was the best night of her life.

"Of course." There was enough of a smile in Damien's voice that Brice felt compelled to push the towel away and make eye contact.

"Be serious. We have a real mess here."

"Of course," he said again. This time the smile was obvious.

"Do you have a digital camera?" Brice asked. She wasn't sure what was prompting his grin. She had been filling in Damien on Dippel's last minutes, telling him everything she could remember of their conversations—

about the mob that had stormed his castle, about his belief that the only way he could achieve salvation was if all his creations were destroyed. None of it was amusing.

She had noticed that Damien wasn't as forthcoming about how he'd spent his time away from her, but Brice didn't press for immediate answers. The zombies were all dead, and he had been the one to kill them.

"I don't own a camera, but Karen does. She keeps it in her desk. However, it might be unwise to take photos of this," he said, knowing what she was thinking. "It isn't precisely the thing to send out with the Christmas cards or put in the photo album. And it could be used as evidence against us if it were ever found by the authorities."

"But it would also be proof of . . . of this craziness. If we ever start to doubt what happened. Or need to prove it to someone else." Brice leaned toward the mirror and looked at her reflection. Her eyes were now as dark as Damien's, and she looked as if she had spent a week tanning on a beach in Hawaii. There was also the scar in the middle of her chest that matched Damien's.

"Do you really think *we'll* ever need proof?" Damien asked. "I don't know about you, but for me, this qualifies as something I'll never forget."

Forget? She might want to. Brice thought about Dippel as she had last seen him. Damien had dragged his corpse out onto the roof and left it to the elements. With its clothes torn aside, it was easy to see that the body was a conglomeration of mismatched limbs. A black tongue had poked out between rows of rotten teeth. The body also smelled heavily of chemicals. It could only barely pass for human, but *barely* was still enough to cause trouble with the police.

"I don't think we can leave him out in the snow. Even if we roll him down onto the sidewalk, there is no way he will pass for a homeless person caught in the blizzard. I mean, he's missing his heart." Brice's voice was calm. Hysteria might come eventually, but it wasn't there yet. "That probably goes for the others as well."

"I've thought about this," Damien answered. "There's an old furnace in the basement. Cremation would be the safest thing anyway—I wouldn't want these creatures somehow getting into the food chain."

Brice looked at her lover. He was calmly buttoning his shirt. They might have been talking about what to have for breakfast instead of destroying zombie bodies before scavengers like pigeons or rats or squirrels ate them and . . . and what? Became poisoned? Became zombie pigeons?

"Will it . . ." She paused a moment to gather her nerve to ask the next question. "Will it be hot enough to do the job?"

"Enough. It seems highly unlikely that these creatures will have recent dental records, even if the teeth survive."

"We don't know that for sure, though." Brice pulled a sweater on over her head. She picked up her pistol. Damien did the same.

"No, but the ones I killed didn't have any obvious dental work—no dentures or fillings."

"Good. I wouldn't want to have to rake through the ashes collecting bits and pieces."

Damien smiled a little and handed Brice her boots. *Damn!* She really did not understand what amused him.

Thinking about another way they'd get caught: "There must be some sort of scrubbers on the ventilation system, but there may still be some odor. Those bodies smell hideous. Burning them . . . no one will mistake that for roasting goose," Brice remarked severely. She was proud of herself for thinking of this. Usually her mind was quite flexible and quick, but she still felt as if her brain had grown a layer of rust that she would need to scrape away before resuming normal life—whatever normal life might be now.

She had thought a bit about what it would mean if she had to give up her present existence. It had been cloistered and she had no dependents—not even house plants. She did have a few friends, the odd distant cousin, but when she weighed them against a lifetime with Damien, her path was clear.

"Yes, the police may come calling—looking for a methamphetamine lab probably. But they won't find anything in the way of drug paraphernalia in this building. And it may not occur to them to check the old furnace. They will likely assume it was disconnected years ago."

"But we'll have to get the place cleaned up by the time they get here—just in case they do look."

Damien nodded, then frowned. He started toward the bedroom window.

"What is it?" Brice asked as Damien reached for the latch. She hurried to his side. "What the devil . . . ?"

Could she really hear someone singing "God rest ye merry, gentlemen?" Brice peered down into the city. At the margins of the darkened block there stood a contingent of the Salvation Army. The cavalry had finally come with the sunrise, but they were too late, and much too far away. And promising salvation or not, this army was ill-equipped to handle the kind of evil that had visited New York last night.

Brice jumped at the sound of a horn in a distant street. Firecrackers followed. She knew what they were, but the sound still made her cringe. A few hours before, she had desperately wanted to escape into the world. Now it was too close.

"Easy, it's just the Christmas throng," Damien said, and Brice wondered if she was going to be nervous for very long. If she would always be somewhat wary of strangers now. Her experience certainly hadn't improved her feeling about the Yuletide season.

Damien hugged her briefly and then closed the window against the winter. It wasn't bothering her the way it had, because her body temperature had shot up and she seemed able to ward off the cold, but psychologically Brice still found the snow intimidating.

"Next year's holidays will be better," he promised.

"They certainly couldn't be worse."

"Hm—best not tempt Fate with statements like that."

Brice sighed. "She's a real bitch sometimes."

"Often even," he agreed. Absently he added, "It's a loss, you know. Surgeons the world over could help their patients if they knew how to reattach limbs or graft donor digits." He led the way back to the library.

"Maybe. But I don't think the public is ready for this kind of cadaver-donation program. Think how freaky it would be to find yourself confronting a stranger wearing your grandpa's arm. Or head. Anyway, you saw what happened to Dippel. There could be other psychopaths out there who would abuse the power. Think what would happen if his journal was posted on the Internet."

"The mind boggles," Damien admitted. "We may have to destroy it."

"Destroy it or lock it up somewhere really safe. And speaking of mind-boggling . . ." Brice looked at the mess around them and sighed. Her shredded manuscript was replaceable, and the one Damien had been reading for review surely wasn't the only copy in existence. "I'm glad your place is mostly granite and marble. It will be easier to clean up."

"Yes. By the way, have you seen Dippel's hand? It should be around here someplace," Damien said. "I'm afraid I rather lost track of it while I was taking the body outside."

Brice swallowed hard. And just when she'd thought things couldn't get any weirder. "Have you looked under the desk? We really have to get the *bodies* cleared away."

They stared down at the zombie. If anything, it looked worse without its head. "Are you sure you want to help with this?" Damien asked doubtfully.

"No, but I think I'd better. We don't know how much time we have to get this done. The next shift of security guards might show up at any time."

"I hope this tarp doesn't leak," Damien complained, grasping the zombie by arm and leg and heaving it onto the green oilcloth. He quickly folded the flaps over the corpse. "Hand me the string."

Brice gave him the ball of twine and the scissors she'd been holding. She helped hold the flaps down, trying to ignore that the corpse was still occasionally twitching. Her stomach held firm until Damien was done, but then she bolted for the bathroom.

She didn't linger long, and when she returned, she found Damien at the window.

"I wonder if we could drop him down to the sidewalk and then bring him in through the lobby."

Brice joined him. They carefully scanned the windows of the adjacent buildings. So far they all remained dark. No eager beavers bucking for promotion had come in for the holiday.

"It's a long drop. Do you think the tarp will hold?" Brice asked, her voice hesitant. She really, really didn't want to have to shovel the body up again, along with a lot of bloody snow.

"The snowbank would cushion the fall," Damien said.

"It will leave tracks when we drag it," she argued. "Maybe bloody ones."

"I suppose you're right. And speaking of bloody tracks, I think we better avoid the main elevators as much as possible. We'll take the service elevator instead—after I test it. It goes directly to the basement," Damien added, stooping down. He stood rapidly, heaving the smelly bundle over his shoulder. He walked toward the elevators.

Brice wondered if she was stronger than she used to be, but decided she didn't want to test her new muscles by lifting corpses.

"Why go that way? You said we should avoid the main elevators," she pointed out as Damien headed in that direction. "The stairs are closer. Just one floor and we'll be right by the service elevator."

"Trust me. You don't want to take the stairs. We'll use the service elevator after this floor. I really need to test it." After a pause, he explained, "There was a slight explosion in the stairwell."

Brice glanced over at the fire door. She couldn't be sure, but it looked as if maybe something was leaking underneath. Gore?

"Okay. I believe you." Brice followed Damien. Her nose wrinkled. "Geez—he stinks!"

"I'm aware of that. I'd grab some room freshener, but I don't think it would help."

"Are they all this bad?" Brice asked, doing her best to not sound like she was complaining.

"Pretty much. Listen, you don't need to help with this.

Why don't you find the janitor's closet and get a mop and pail?"

"Oh, sure—leave the cleanup to the woman," Brice joked. But she was happy enough to turn away. Watching the bundle on Damien's back twitch and wriggle was getting to what was left of her nerves.

Two hours later, Brice and Damien stood before their impromptu crematorium, reeking of disinfectant cleansers. They'd been feeding it zombie bodies for the last hour. As impossible as it would have seemed, Brice had lost much of her horror at what they were doing. The only difficult thing for her now was picking up the tarps while they were still moving, because that brought to mind her persistent childhood terror of the witch from *Hansel and Gretel* trying to stuff children in the oven.

"Are things clean enough upstairs, do you think?" she asked. It was now after noon, but they couldn't tell it, standing in the windowless basement. She was mainly concerned about the mess in the stairwell, which she had insisted on helping to clean up. She'd never seen anything like that in her life, and prayed she never would again.

"If no one starts looking for bullet holes outside the security office, we should be fine."

They had decided not to destroy the guards' bodies, partly because it would have been cruel for the families of the missing men. And partly because a missing-persons investigation would bring more attention than a plain old double homicide and theft.

Brice and Damien had argued for a bit about whether the guards should be thought to have walked in on a drug deal gone wrong, or to have interrupted a robbery. Robbery was chosen—it was easy to take stuff and hide it; providing bits of illegal drugs for the police to find would have been harder.

"And if they do start looking?" Brice asked, thinking of the hole blown in the wall where Damien had used the grenade. "That would make things difficult for you. Are you . . . prepared?"

"You mustn't worry. All appearances aside, I'm as much an ant as a grasshopper. I have been meticulous about arranging an emergency escape for the day the unthinkable happened. If the truth is discovered here, I have the means to disappear." Damien paused, then added, "I can arrange for Brice Ashton to disappear too. If that's what you want."

"I would have to?" she asked, already knowing the answer.

"If it comes down to a large investigation, I fear so. Too many people know you're here. And if you didn't come with me, I could probably never come near you again."

A thin thread of smoke escaped the furnace door and coiled toward the ceiling. The fire inside spread a blood-red glow across the marble floor, which was lightly spattered with droplets of the zombies' clotted blood. The droplets glittered brighter than any ruby ever cut and polished. The view was almost beautiful, but all Brice felt was disgust and a small degree of hope that the gasoline-soaked monster would burn thoroughly.

She sighed aloud and reached again for the mop. They were almost out of cleaner.

"Will I be able to finish my book on Ninon?" Brice asked.

"Yes. But not for this publisher." He meant that they'd

have to fake Brice's death, and publishing a book from beyond the grave might be tricky. L. Ron Hubbard had managed it, but things were different for him.

Damien continued, "It might have to be under another name and for another publishing house, but you would be able to bring out that biography eventually."

Brice sighed. "I'd really hate breaking my contract. I like my editor. Let's hope it doesn't come to that."

"Yes." Damien studied her. This time he didn't smile. "Right now I am thinking that it would be best if we were away from here while the investigation is going on. They might believe that we didn't hear any shooting since it happened several floors below us, but we were bound to notice that the power was out. We would be well advised to have some alibi that places us outside the city, in case anyone asks."

"We have to take Ninon's letters with us," Brice said swiftly. That made Damien laugh, though he sobered almost instantly.

"We'll take everything of value—just in case."

"What? All the paintings and art?" Brice asked, startled and dismayed.

"No," Damien answered. "I wasn't speaking of things with monetary value. Though I suppose the thieves could have robbed me, too, if you have any favorites."

"Oh." Brice nodded approvingly. "That might work. Though you'd have to report stuff stolen and deal with the police then."

"Maybe. Or Karen can do it. That would be more in character for Damien Ruthven. Ninon's letters shouldn't be a problem, though. No one knows I have them. And they may hold important clues," Damien said, finally slamming the furnace's iron door shut. He had to use a hammer. The whole machine was glowing hot. The high-rise was going to be very warm for a while. They'd have to hope that it cooled off before anyone investigated and found that the old, non-environmentally-approved furnace had been used. After all, what they were doing was not just frowned upon socially, it was also illegal.

Damien didn't dwell on it, but their whole constructed alibi was a house of cards, that relied heavily on the police and insurance investigators being very careless. Brice would soon realize that.

"Clues? Of course they hold clues!" Brice said enthusiastically. "There may be facts about Ninon's life outside Paris that no one is aware of. There could be—"

"No, that isn't what I meant," Damien interrupted. "I mean clues to her present whereabouts."

"What?" Brice stared at him. She repeated: "What?"

"I truly believe that Ninon is still alive," he answered. "And at one time she told her friend, the philosopher Saint-Evremond, that she was thinking of emigrating to the Americas—to one of the plantation islands. It would be the perfect place for her to go after her death. Especially if she wanted to escape the son of her dark man."

"Alive? Really?" Brice knew she sounded stupid, but she was having trouble taking in the idea. She shouldn't be surprised. Damien had hinted at this before. Then she understood the rest of what he'd said. "Saint Germain! She said that in her letters. *And I have a son who shall be called Saint Germaine.*' You think he's alive too!"

"Perhaps. Certainly it is worth investigating. Not that it will be an easy task to find either of them," Damien warned. "I've already tried a few times. The lady is very wary, very good at covering her tracks. But this time I have something that I didn't before."

"What?" Brice asked.

"A bloodhound," Damien answered, smiling. "If anyone can find her, it's you. As a researcher, you have no peer."

"Maybe," Brice answered, forgetting to be modest. Her mind was already racing, trying to recall who among Ninon's friends had ever traveled to the Americas.

Damien watched her, his smile sad. He hoped her passion for the hunt and a chance to meet Ninon would be compensation enough when they had to leave their identities and lives behind.

It is singular how soon we lose the impression of what ceases to be constantly before us; a year impairs; a luster obliterates. There is little distinct left without an effort of memory.

—From Lord Byron's journal at Ravenna

Chapter Twenty-one

"The snow finally has slowed. It's time to fetch my car."

"Your car?" she asked, surprised.

"It's garaged nearby."

"And it can get through this snow? The streets still haven't been plowed, you know."

"My car can get through anything. It's been modified—it has high-traction tires, a fortified body and bulletproof glass. But I think we'll walk to it instead of driving through this. It's best not to leave tire tracks near the building. Of course, it will take a couple of trips to move all the stuff. We'll look a bit odd staggering along with our bags of stolen loot, but, hopefully, if anyone sees us, the bags will be mistaken for Christmas presents."

"Are we taking the guns?" Brice asked.

"Can you doubt it? Though we'll have to stop somewhere for ammunition," Damien answered.

Brice had found her pistol outside the bathroom's broken door and now kept it close at hand. She noticed Damien did the same.

"Where are we going? Have you decided?" she asked, pulling her hair back from her face.

"Your place," Damien answered. "We decided yesterday afternoon that we wanted to spend a romantic Christmas there."

"I see, a romantic Christmas Day. Well, I suppose that's just possible." Brice thought about her house. It was cozy, though no one would think it a love nest.

"Remind me to call Karen once we're on the road and casually mention that we did in fact leave for your place yesterday afternoon. I'll ask her to come by the building and get some papers for me tomorrow." Brice looked startled by his words. "Don't worry. The guards' bodies will have been discovered by then, and the place totally cleaned up. She won't be the first on the scene."

"The police will question her," Brice said slowly, beginning to piece together his plan.

"Yes, along with everyone else. And they will eventually discover that we've been at your place since the afternoon of the twenty-fourth and couldn't know anything about this."

"You're using Karen as a shield," she chided.

"Yes," he admitted regretfully. "Not the most gentlemanly of actions."

"They might question our story anyway."

"No, I don't think so," Damien said confidently. "They won't. Why should they? Philanthropist Damien Ruthven—who shall be offering a huge reward for any information about this crime—might be eccentric enough to dash off and spend Christmas with his new love, but he wouldn't have anything to do with criminal activity. Assuming anything else out of place is discovered." He waved a hand indicating his apartment and how normal it again appeared. "It really is the best alternative."

Brice, catching a glimpse of herself in the window, had to agree. Their twin sets of matching dark eyes—and their presently unseen golden scars—looked very suspicious to her. There was also the fact that she was an absolutely terrible liar.

She would also feel naked without a gun close at hand. Firearms could be explained away at home, where shooting vermin was quietly encouraged, but in New York? She wondered if Damien had a permit.

No, facing the police wasn't an option. Yet it seemed there were a dozen or two holes in this plan. The largest of which was in the wall next to the service elevator.

"Your driver is loyal?" she asked, trying to think of flaws they would be able to correct.

"Yes. I saved his life, pulled him out of a hellhole in Nicaragua. He's very grateful. However, I think that this time we will dispense with his services. He's away with his family. I'll call him later and tell him I took the car. He won't ask questions. Fortunately, there are no attendants at the garage and no security cameras. I chose it for that reason." After a moment Damien asked, "And on your end? Is there anyone—a housekeeper or gardener, someone who could contradict our story?"

"No. I always spend the holidays alone. And the house is somewhat isolated." She thought for a minute. "There is the matter of my unused plane ticket. Won't it look odd if I don't use it?"

"I never fly," Damien said. "It's one of my well-known idiosyncrasies. No one will think it odd—or at least not unusual—that I insisted we drive. You can cash it in later."

Brice exhaled slowly. "So, we have a plan."

"Yes. Or at least the general outline of one. We can flesh it out as we go."

"Do you like fishing?" Brice asked him suddenly. "We have excellent fishing at home."

Damien permitted himself a small smile. "Yes, I still like fishing. If we have the time and the weather permits, perhaps we will indulge."

Brice took a short stroll around the room—or at least that's what she told herself she did. *Strolling* sounded much better than *pacing*.

"I should be worried about this. I mean *really* worried. But I'm not. Why is that? Has standing hip-deep in zombies while I commit a dozen felonies made me lose my mind? Can one become sociopathic overnight, do you think?"

Damien shook his head. "No, of course not. But I don't think that anything will ever be able to truly frighten you again. It's one of those consequences of bravery that I was talking about before. And it's a good one—as long as it doesn't make you foolhardy. Life is to be *lived*."

Dark eyes met dark eyes. Brice smiled a little.

"There is plenty of reason to suppose me a fool. Look at the last two days—and now I am running off with a stranger."

"Am I any less foolish?" he asked, also smiling a little. There was something ancient and knowledgeable in the curve of those lips. This was a dangerous man—but not dangerous to Brice, she didn't think.

She shivered. It was mostly in a good way.

"Have I not experienced the same two days?" Damien asked when she didn't answer him. "Anyway, I don't think you can say that I am a stranger. After all, you know me very, very well."

"No," Brice argued, shaking her head. "I knew who you *were*. The future is still a big question mark. For both of us."

"An adventure," he corrected.

"An adventure," she agreed.

"Are you ready for it?" Damien asked, extending his hand.

Brice nodded slowly and reached for Damien. "Yes, I believe that I am." Their hands laced. She said quietly, "I've always loved you, you know—at least for my entire reading life."

"And I've waited all my life—all my *lives*—for you. You're what will complete my heart and maybe my soul. How Heaven will laugh at this, but your being here now is enough to make me believe in a merciful God."

Her smile was more radiant than the moon.

"We're going to have a wonderful life," he told her.

"I believe you."

The golden opportunity
Is never offered twice; seize then the hour
When Fortune smiles and Duty points the way.

—*Byron*

The event on which this new fiction of Mary Shelley's is founded has been supposed by some of the physiological writers of Germany to be an impossible occurrence. How wrong they are.

—*From the journal of Johann Conrad Dippel*

Chapter Twenty-two

December 27, 2005

If it wasn't one damned thing, it was another, Karl thought to himself as he rode down in the service elevator. First, there were those damn cops all over the place. And where there weren't cops, there were friggin' second-string reporters in a feeding frenzy, looking for the story that would make them big-time. Worst of all, there were gawkers everywhere. Hell! A man couldn't hardly find a quiet place to spark up. He'd finally had to pretend to Mr. Ruthven's secretary that there was something wrong with the drainpipe and go up on the roof. It was barely worth it. He'd got his smoke but damn near froze his ass off in the snow.

Then, when he'd finally got around to hitting his locker, he'd found out someone had messed with his tools—even the paintbrushes! Hell, it was that damned Rodney, he'd bet. The guy had been liberating supplies again. That was the only way to explain why all the floor cleaner was gone. It'd serve the bastard right if he went out to the cops and told them. A little stay downtown would teach that lazy-ass thief.

"Shit." Karl thought about spitting but didn't. Not many people rode this elevator, but if he hawked one out here, someone would notice. Security was actually watching their cameras now.

And it wasn't like Rodney would be along to clean it up. That sucker was on some hour-long coffee break down at the Memuria cafeteria. There was some hottie down there—April, he thought her name was—and Rodney was trying to make time with her. Which was fine for Rodney, but it left Karl doing all the work.

And now he was supposed to get up to the sixth floor and catch some rat a lady had seen behind the radiator in the women's bathroom. That wasn't in his job description. What the hell did they think he was—animal-fuckin'-control?

Karl stopped outside the women's restroom and knocked loudly. He'd learned to do that—and to keep knocking for a good long while. Ladies acted like he was some kind of pervert just because he went in and saw their feet under the door. What? Like they didn't pee like everyone else?

After a good long pound, Karl decided it was safe to go in. He put out the WET FLOOR sign and then wheeled his cart inside. He shut the door behind him. It might be funny to chase the rat out into the offices—maybe it would run up some stuck-up woman's dress. But there would probably be hell to pay if that happened, and Karl didn't want to lose another job.

He heard a soft scrabbling and shivered. A rat, sure enough. And he hated the friggin' things. He didn't like to admit it, but he was scared of 'em. They were nasty-ass animals, always trying to get in the lockers and eat his lunch.

Karl knelt reluctantly and peered under the radiator. Something was there, sure enough. He couldn't exactly tell what he was looking at, but something was definitely there, way in the back where the light didn't reach. It was pale and kind of fleshy looking. Maybe all the rat's hair had fallen out. Wouldn't that suck—especially in winter? Being a rat and being bald?

Then the smell hit him.

"Shit!" Karl reeled backward. The damned thing smelled bad enough to knock a starving buzzard off a garbage truck.

He fished out a broom. He'd try chasing the rat out and catching it with a bucket. That would be less messy than beating it to death, and he'd probably get in trouble for killing the thing. He could just imagine: Somebody would claim it was a rare kind of smelly bathroom rat, and that he'd killed some endangered species.

"Come on out, you smelly, bald sonuvabitch," Karl said in what he imagined to be a gentle voice. He poked the broom handle at the creature a couple of times. The third time, the broom stopped abruptly and then jerked hard enough to nearly be torn from his hand. "What the hell?"

The damn rat had grabbed the handle!

Shocked and a bit frightened, though he couldn't say exactly why, Karl snatched at his broom with both hands. He jerked the thing out, dragging the creature with it.

"Oh, shit!" Karl flung the broom against the wall, and the rat hit the window with a rubbery splat. Karl only caught a glimpse before it scuttled for a hole in the wall under the sink, but what he saw. . . . For sure his eyesight was going and he'd smoked a little too much weed—but that rat had looked like a hand. One torn off just above the wrist.

Karl stood for a moment, trembling and trying to convince himself of what he had seen.

It had looked like a hand—a damned ugly one with long fingernails and a ragged stump that ended about a third of the way up the arm. But that couldn't be. It just couldn't. The lady had seen a rat, hadn't she? It must have just been a bald rat who'd gotten its tail cut off. Maybe lost it in a trap.

Do you care? If it's a rat, it's a friggin' mutant. You don't want to be touchin' it. What if your hair falls out too? Or something more important?

Karl wanted to run. He wanted to take off like every friggin' bull in Pamplona was after his ass. Hell, he wanted to run faster than that—rats scared him senseless. And this thing?

"Shit." Karl finally pulled out his radio. He didn't like looking like a pussy, but he wasn't dealing with this shit alone.

"Rodney—you there? Rodney? Answer me, damn it!" Karl didn't like the way his voice sounded, all squeaky and afraid, not his usual tone at all.

Apparently, Rodney thought the same thing because he actually answered. "What's up, Karl?" His voice was thick, like he was chewing on something.

"I think we got us a rat problem here on six. You better call someone and then come on up."

There was a pause.

"Call someone?" The gears did another slow turn. "Like an exterminator?"

"No, I mean call the f—" Karl recalled others might be

listening in and changed his mind about using his favorite profanity. "The flippin' Pied Piper."

"Who?" Rodney sounded puzzled.

Karl took a deep breath and prayed for patience. He thumbed the button on his radio again. "Yes, call the exterminator. Right now. And then get up here. I need some help."

"Okay, unbunch your panties, man."

Karl wiped his face dry, then clipped the radio back on his belt. "They ain't payin' me enough to deal with this shit," he grunted.

He went over to the cart and got out his largest mop, jammed it against the hole the rat had used and then drove the handle into the opposite wall, hard enough to dent the plaster near the electric dryer. It was an imperfect fit, but it would have to do.

He shuddered and wiped his face again. It was a weird-looking hole. Rats must have chewed through from the hallway, though it looked a lot like the digging had come from this side of the wall. That was where all the shredded sheetrock and lathe had landed, at any rate.

Well, it wasn't in his job description, but Karl decided he wouldn't mind going down to the basement and getting a board and some nails to shut up this hole. He'd do it right away. Whatever the heck it was on the other side of the wall, he'd just as soon it stayed there until the exterminator arrived.

Cain: Then leave me.
Adam: Never, though thy God left thee.

—*Byron*

A man who knows everything and also never dies.
—*Voltaire on the Comte de Saint Germain*

That which is striking and beautiful is not always good,
but that which is good is always beautiful.
—*From a letter by Ninon de Lenclos*

Epilogue

The woman with red-gold hair and black eyes pushed the late-arriving Christmas cards aside and read the cable again. Her lips twitched at the *"C'est un vrai cinglé, ce type"* that concluded the brief report. Her informant was wrong, of course, though she understood his mistake. The great poet wasn't a nutcase; he was just involved in some unusual projects that required somewhat suspicious behavior.

Which was fortunate for her, because it seemed that he had taken care of the Dippel dilemma with commendable thoroughness. There remained just one other difficulty for the good doctor's few remaining projects—but she didn't know if it was the proper time to openly challenge Le Comte de Saint Germain about his intentions.

"Will there ever be a time?" she asked Aleister, who politely cracked an eye at her meditative enquiry. The cat yawned, showing his dainty but very sharp teeth, which was his way of shrugging.

Je ne le crois pas, his pea-green eyes said as he stared down from the mantel.

She sighed heavily, suggesting to the cat that she also thought not. "But what then do I do? What course is best for me to follow?"

Aleister sniffed once at the frangipani-scented air. He had no suggestions to make. That was regrettable, but then, really, it was not his problem. He had just eaten a large plate of fresh steamed shrimp, and it was time to drop back into a deep, contemplative state that closely resembled a nap but was actually where he thought about important cat things and listened to the sea where his next meal swam.

Being a perceptive creature—almost a feline, he felt—his mistress took the subtle hint and politely left him to his work.

The woman walked silently across the room, not disturbing the grass mats on the floor. Carefully she struck a match and lit one of the many candles on her old-fashioned writing table. The small flame was barely enough for a normal person to see by, but she didn't bother to light any of the others. There was no need; she saw everything she wanted. There wasn't a great deal to see. There was no computer on the desk, and no phone.

To write or not to write?

Several times in the nineteenth century, she had come close to contacting the poet. Then he had disappeared from Greece, not to be found again until the late twentieth century. It was tempting to look him up now because she could use an ally. She was quite aware of his continuing interest in her. But was it the right time?

No, she would wait. It wasn't likely that anyone was following her yet, but it was within the realm of the possible that her position had again been discovered and she would have to move. She wouldn't risk leading the Dark Man to Byron and his new consort. It was possible that Saint Germain didn't yet know the poet lived. If so, she would not be responsible for bringing more evil into Byron's life.

Sighing again, the woman who had once been Ninon de Lenclos folded the cable into fourths and then fed it to the candle's greedy flame.

When the last bit of ash was crushed out and swept into the wastebasket, she turned back to the cat and smiled fondly at his delicate snores. She loved to watch him slumber. It was the thing she missed most from her old life, being able to sleep.

Still, there were other compensations.

"*Trés bien,*" she said softly to the floral scented air that wafted in the window.

She leaned over and blew out the candle. As her silk blouse fell forward, any passing person might have observed the small golden scars over her heart. But there was no one passing by on this side of the island; that was why she liked it.

Author Note

I'm ashamed to admit it, but this story contains at least three historical inaccuracies needed for the sake of the plot. In spite of this, the *character* of the characters is—I believe—completely truthful to what they were in life, and what they would be if they had lived into this century.

The first inaccuracy is the suggestion that there was only one portrait done of Ninon de Lenclos. There were two done in her lifetime that I know of, though the second was a rather inferior effort—almost a caricature. The other portraits I've seen are all copies of these first and were undertaken after her death, but there are possibly others in existence.

The second inaccuracy is in letting readers think that she held sex classes in the *rue des Tournelles*. She gave private lessons and shared her philosophy of love with chosen partners, but she didn't have group orgies with a chalkboard and manuals. Thirdly, in spite of Brice Ashton's complaints, many of Ninon's letters and her *La Coquette Vengée* still exist in library archives and in the

hands of scholars. It isn't historians who have overlooked her; it is the general public—particularly in
America—who have not made an effort to know this
woman. Which is a shame, because she was an amazing
person, liberationist, feminist and philosopher. She considered emigrating to the Americas, and I am sorry that
she did not, because we might know her better today if
she had made our hemisphere her own.

As for Lord Byron, he is still the stuff of which real-
life heroes are made. Ignore the propaganda you were
taught in school. Byron was the equivalent of a movie
star in his day. His biographies were nearly all concoct-
ed by well-intentioned friends or worse-intentioned foes,
and are about as reliable as what we read in the tabloids
today. He was also government enemy #1. Because he
traveled widely and reported on what he saw, Byron
forced people to confront the war in which England had
been embroiled for twenty years and what that war actually meant. He also advocated allowing Catholics the
freedom to practice their religion without sanctions.
And—*gasp*—he believed in educating women when
they wished to learn.

However, the final straw was something that will be
difficult for those of our time to understand. Byron
admitted to, and wrote about, human sexuality. He was
the British voice of libido. This was still an era of
Puritanical hypocrisy and he grievously offended much
of the population with his frank poems and other writing.

The reference list at the end of this book gives the titles
of works which more accurately portray the poet.
Certainly he was flawed, but starting in his early youth,
though handicapped by a lame foot, he demonstrated
great physical bravery, often intervening on behalf of
weaker children or animals. He retained this physical
courage all his life, and as an adult added philosophical
and political bravery to his list of assets. He was an
advocate for the common man, and died helping others

win their freedom. His death was a tragedy, and the burning of his memoirs by Hobhouse and Murray was a literary crime.

The heroine, Brice Ashton, is not me. She sounds like me and shares many of my opinions, but I have made my peace regarding certain things with which she still struggles. And she is far wiser and braver than I am. Luckier too: I would dearly love to find a copy of *La Coquette Vengée*.

As for Johann Conrad Dippel...he did exist and is probably the basis for Mary Shelley's Dr. Frankenstein. He was an eighteenth-century grave-robber; however, I doubt he ever practiced grafting dead limbs onto his own body. That is my own horrific invention, as is his journal. According to history, he was born after Ninon's death and long gone before Byron was of an age to consult him about curing his epilepsy. But isn't it fun to pretend otherwise? Besides, he could have had a like-minded father and an equally twisted son to carry on the gruesome dynasty.

I mentioned two other women in this book and will be kind and spare the curious among you a hunt for an encyclopedia. Semiramis was Queen of Assyria who built the hanging gardens of Babylon, and in her spare time she conquered Egypt, Ethiopia and much of Asia. The other woman is Diane de Poitiers, a fifteenth-century beauty who was the mistress of Henry II of France and virtual ruler of that country for many years. These two, along with Ninon, Cleopatra and Helen of Troy, were supposed to have sold their souls for eternal beauty.

Of course, Diane de Poitiers claimed her greatest beauty aid was washing her face every day with clean well water. I believe her. Washing with anything would have been a great novelty at the time, and would have prevented many disfiguring ailments and diseases. Ninon followed that practice as well, at the command of the *"Dark Man"* who appeared on her eighteenth birthday and offered her lifelong beauty if she would sign his red book. Fortunately for Ninon, he was not actually the Devil, but rather a Jewish doctor who understood the power of the mind to heal a patient. His potions were placebos, which worked because people *believed*. Combining faith with cleanliness, his patients tended to live longer than the poor wretches who recoursed to the standard treatments of bleedings and leeches.

Lastly, my stories never get written in a vacuum. As always, there are people I need to thank for helping this book along. First and foremost in line for a share of gratitude is Harry Squires, who helped me with the gathering of reference material, and performed general cheerleading when I had moments of doubt about being so arrogant as to place undocumented opinions in Byron's twenty-first-century mouth. Next on the list is my husband, who has been very patient with my year-long raves of admiration about both Byron and Ninon de Lenclos (though, truthfully, I've raved about Ninon for a lot longer than that). Lesser men would have been jealous and probably bored, but my husband always manages to look attentive.

The third person who deserves a generous share of appreciation is my cousin, Richard, who reminded me that there are horror classics other than *Dracula*, and that *Frankenstein* was more closely associated with Lord Byron anyway.

Endless thanks go out to the author of the poem *Le Chevalier sans Paix*, which is printed in its entirety following this Author's Note. I needed a poem for Damien, and knew that I could never do him justice. It was an act of great generosity to let me borrow this work.

And lastly, I must thank my editor for being a brave soul. Some people might have shied away when they heard a working title of *Lord Byron vs. Frankenstein*. But he had faith that somehow I would carry it off.

As always, I love hearing from you and can be reached through my website at www.melaniejackson.com, or through snailmail at PO Box 574, Sonora, CA 95370-0574.

May you be warmed with sweet dreams of your own divine fires.

—*Melanie Jackson*

Le Chevalier Sans Paix

Invoke my memory and gift me peace:
that which I have sought, which thou art made
by seraphim straight and cherubim crook'd,
and wet thyself in my tears; thou art born
as I have released thee to thy valiance.
At home, nestled beneath my robes and quilt
I drift, without my liege, nor my honor,
ton chevalier sans le mot de ta coeur.
Awake! Arouse thyself as I could not
bear to breed bitterness and pain for naught,
and here we whiled past le lac de St. Clair:
a pretty pond, yet vaster than thy heart.
Presently, and pastly too, I had been found
bestridd'n by devils, weaker than my mind.
Et donné pas de nom a ma peine, Ami,
c'est toi, and christened thus I must leave thee,
shivering there, behind thine appointed.

Ignite me, O fire of isolation!
It hath not been long since I felt thine ice

and my soul's ticklish tears upon my cheek.
I have burned before, and stayed unscathed,
despite the draw of death: undenied
yet unrequited, and undermighted
to take so strong a keep as mine without
twelve-score men, and twenty-eight, for siege,
forsooth I shan't be beat without a fight.
Approaching now, armies of *l'avenir*:
avenging angels, a catalogue of crime,
mine own, and yet not mine alone.

Within this tower built of pride and pain,
in this keep on the bordering kingdom,
aye, I prepare alone for the coming siege.
The marble floor, crack'd with age,
doth suffice to grant rest to this tired old *kavalier*.
But dreams shall tireless flock to withered men
and ever show what brought their fall.
Awake, probing the gloom with sightless eyes,
I think of thee, *ami*, and thus succumb.

Ah! A memory imbibed – tasting of mist,
etherial wafts of wondrous dreams
and songs to thy immortality mine:
a gift given by my memory of late.
Eternal beauty, the soft solemn of thy lips,
the stormy cumuli collect beneath thy brows.
Lightning rolls thus to sea, pushed by winds no less
divine than that which moves
thy slender form and figure faint.
On course, it is a river I see—
washing clean the banks of that Ann's arbor.
The roots ravish the soil there
and rapids rape the shore,
carrying—nay, crevassing and abandoning—
the spoilt yet blessed earth which,
eager to be borne leaps lightly, swallowed by foam
and lusty waves, digesting thus the whole

and leaving mighty embankments
mellowed for the ages, worse for wear.
And yet the river bends on, babbling.
It is splashing away its rage,
while the oars of youth violate its ice
sheen surface and push through temples
to Neptune or naiads who sing and dance
naked 'neath the silent hills
of wat'ry swirl, capped by white,
softer than the mossy mounds; sought,
found by sailors for an anchor
which might save the vessel
tempest-tossed but for the stay of a line
parting the darkness
and tied to that which stands at the heart
of the ship—an open craft in stormy sea;
a rocking, roiling, rigorous pull.
Warm salty splashes from oars,
deeper and deeper they sink—trying,
praying desperately to banish the flames
which light the poles; the sails have torn free,
flapping about thy shoulders,
and yes! You are there my love—
your eyes are more violent than the storm.
Shaded, glass'd perhaps, but it is thee
and thou art greyer than this toil.
Now, thrice, the shrieks of boys erupt
and echo loudly 'cross this toiling tide.
A splash, and foam erupts, explodes!
The metal sheen—the shining hull
hast bared its sharp-edged belly
and swallowed: warm
water engulfing all, and salty;
yet not those salts which spice the sea
but the tang of youth which swells
and strays near the foundering forms
and 'neath the narrow straits.
Ripped by rocks; caressing, nuzzling nymphs

grip his legs and lick his lips
and he is breathing beneath:　resting deep.
A crackling like lightning and *voila*!
He is born anew to the sea,
sundered bonds and freedom offered.
He must swim, crawl through the eddies,
seeing the forms—shielded shapes
which neither bugs nor tailors
could discern themselves—forces of men
forces of God, thwarted thus and
thou art dry as I am drenched.
And eyes, grey and green, meet here
stopp'd not by shades nor shores
nor haughty pride and struggling here
I must not drown before my port.
This ship's new-built—its virgin sails
beg billows and breaks 'gainst gales
'fore sinking darkly to the deep.
I must find a parched plateau,
an isle, a cove, on which to dry
and light a fire with which to warm
these youthful yearnings that doth swarm
and sum this pair of eyes orbiting
thoughts too tired or timeless to think.
(I, a wraith, a waterlogged daemon, yes!
But dry within and kindling a flame
which smolders still, and has burned
bright in its day and in its place.)
The blue enclosing steel, the seating soft
in this, that horizon which I have flown.
Still I drip, still I drain
and see before me, above me, reflected
clouds again, shining somehow like grass
kiss'd by morning sun and spider silk
of night's clear dew which sheathes
the broken blades, as well as whole—
'tis thine eyes; they are thin, tight,
and yet they open the gates of God.

The best-laid plans, tailor made,
have placed me here—behind—
but thou hast sought me out.
I am here: Thou hast sought me and I am staid
behind sarcasm, words, lies, songs, stares—
the arsenal falls, distended and dysfunctional
for I am thine from henceforth and hereon.
Knight kiss'd, sailor subjected.   Princess poor
and landless hath yet won a champion
from life through death eternal.

This frigid eve, again art placed within
its rig'rous grip, and on this marble porch
they crouch, in silent secrecy, the torch
of the King and Queen's dominion yet bright,
flickering o'er their hunkered forms in night,
stridently proclaiming these thoughts bonds in sin.
He raises the gate; the light illumines
the door, the yard beyond, and steps across
with her: that treasure which must be returned
to this, a palace not far removed from
that grosse pointe where they had strolled 'til night full
beckoned them home to weary beds.
"It hath begun," he whispers to the moon,
which failing, falling from the sky's embrace
makes way for journey home in deep'ning dawn.
She turns, her slender fingers caress skin;
his lips have met her neck, and she whimpers,
caught first by novelty and next by heat:
liquid drizzled o'er the tender skin—gasp!—
gentled breath hummed with kisses lighting
on virgin flesh and stillborn sighs which live
and force flush, painful pure to cherry cheek,
pierced by evening's chilly archer,
shafts fletched by youth and loosed in innocence.
Nutted hair, straight to slope and shoulder sleek,
falls fair and fiery for that torch above,
and door shall ope soon enough: that vigil,

kept by Queen above.   Tonight must be all
for two but born, and who wait on ripe age
where time shall be their own.   She is stolen
behind barrier black, and gate closed, and
he must return to his own keep.
"O guarded citadel, you shall be mine,"
he vows, and turns him headlong home.

Time sighs, stretching. Its slender limbs lengthen
as a yawn, worn and weary, escapes from
wizened lips, and beneath its gaunt gaze,
inept for an instant, the eons ease
and a century dallies in a day.
Oh, what wondrous whims!   What sanguine sweetness
can overcome the angst of youth, giv'n
the rein to follow its fearless fancy!
Youth's sweet knight and princess pure find joy
in starless skies and each embrace is such
that misery is missed, its mastiffs eluded,
misdirected—thus they are prey no more
to terror, sadness, or to strife.   They are safe.
Her class is naught, for now, and know not that
they must fail by century's end.
Now, within the grip of knight's new graces,
rising and refined, they ride, a couplet
in a madrigal's mad refrain: bawdy.
Adventures wild. At the Hill of Freedom
they while in eves: elves feasting on the
merry meat of madness, yet rapturous
of all, despite the pats on backs of
friends of Yore. Klucks of disdain
hardly heard and overcome as well.
Fêtes, and feasts and *le renaissance*,
and here, to him, bestow'd her blade
to swing by side and shine for all: her steel
in his sheath, at his side, forevermore.
And on an eve, some three months hence,
hidden deep, dark beneath the palace keep,

that knight fell hard, and knelt for princess sweet.
In sobs they shared, shouldered a load,
which none have borne in better name
than theirs, and Tristan and Iseult could smile,
replete in that they—replaced, reborn—
might merge again, and joy and jubilance
reigned here, in dark and dirty dungeon.
The solemn smiles, the tortured tears,
simply symptoms of brighter bliss.
Queen and King above are watchful, but bow
their regal brows in silent submission,
beat'n by bond which conquer'd Cath'lic church
through human need and mortal mode.
Christus et Amor; Chrétien est Amoureuse.
The cue thus came for mighty union—
as faith founders, love stumbles scared;
'til gauntlet and glove grasp, grip tight the hand
of saving grace: the other.
In chivalric code, he is the mold:
honor, vigor, and loyalty here pledge
faithful force for love's new lass eternal.
But vigor's mighty arm grows weak with age,
and true, honor's thorough thought grows dim.
But loyalty: That great heart rules proudly 'til death
has silenced it within its vast cathedral.
For love's holy hymn, she is the harp,
evoking the melodies of a thousand songs,
but none named, all rapt'rous and still the soul.
But sweet strains, without an ear, grow stale,
so loyal lad who lends an ear gains all.
This new borne night, this newborn knight
has loved his liege and his liege learned love.

Months have pass'd, and bear weary witness
to tortured times and dimming dreams.
That flame which burned so brightly above
the porch of King and Queen, the torch afire
with passion's light burns low, and threats it gives

to plunge the night through deepest dusk
unheeded by the sentries posted here at home.
So seldom are guarded our hidden treasures,
so secure we see their secret's safety sure.
The princess? The knight? Where didst thou flee?
You sir! To urban 'scape where glory's made?
Princess? The same, and for your own renown?
What came of love and its rewards? And how?
Since your claim forsakes him not, where is thy love?
Ah. On thy sleeve, and nowhere else.
Both, look to thineselves, for thou hast lost
thy footing and thy defense in one slick step's descent!
Know not that thou art cursed before begun?
Princess, did not thy friend warn thee of this?
She, who told the tale of Priam's ruin;
she who Clytemnestra slew, since silent,
warned not this pair of lovers doomed?
Kavalier! Hast not thine own might and pow'r
taught thee sense? Dost thou seek glory too?
You will find it, buried deep in ennuyeux.
And hence they parted, company kept,
but somewhere, somehow, they disregarded
what once had made them one in two.
Spring hailed its mighty foe and Winter
fled once more to chilly clime whence had come.
Behind it, left: Hibernia's wake,
and visions of what happened here in haste.
She's courted now, and Sheep King's cry is such
that taken for a time she is by Greek glory.
Castoff knight, guilty of guarding greed,
leaves to find fortune in the art of gore.
Man the keep on the bordering kingdom!
Arm the farthest reaches of the fiefdom!
Now alone, he shrinks, scarred each sunset
by the loss of love and princess pure. Her blade,
sheathed for shame within his heart—
his melee since with footman's lance.
Wounded in battle at Belgrade Lakes,

in that damned mainland far removed,
he falls, faint—is nursed at Nottingham.
"Princess, please, your pilgrim's poor!
Canst thou not see me in my shame?
Arm me again with thy sharp steel
which soothed my strength and saved my soul!"
She whose holy word he won't abuse,
she, whose name he woos on waking,
comes unknownst to him, hidden from all sight.
As fleet as greyhound she travels light,
in sojourn sought to prove her promise.
Letters, soft as springtime's silky rain,
revive, relighten the borderlands.
And as regal dame steps down from carriage
their broken hearts repair souls' marriage.

The torch is lit anew!   It burns brightly
and sparks, smoking, as does a candle caught
by smoldering strike of sulf'rous match.
O revenants!   O gardeners of the gloom,
beware tonight!   This dusk must thou creep
and crawl, wallowing back to thine tombs,
for this twilight bears the torch of true faith!
Here an Adam, here an Eve,
have brought the fruit to their ashen mouths; bitten!
The slick soft core, tasted for the first time:
pulpy, sweet and redolent of summer-
time and stormy seascape, but too, Elysium.
Senses swell, overwhelmed, as thrumming
thunder wakes in cumulonimbus clouds
invading first the heavens, driving forth
the sun, which hurriedly flees behind the hills.
The warm winds and wet earth, which
decadent, fall on naked youths who play at
heathen heat in hurricane's rage.
Long, tossed tangles of hallowed hair,
willow branches, whipped wind whirls
as earth is shaken in divine delight.

And thus, the storm passes, its fury spent
in moments, like the melting of a 'berg
in molten blast of desert burning.
Here on this mainland, through this tempest,
the torch now burn'd bright, and burns anew.

Alas!   Could years pass as quick as that?
Couldst Time, angry at its impotence and
failure to break the bonds of men, re-seize
the sun, the summer storms, and hide them here
'neath Winter's wrath?   Aye, for the fawning age
of paradise passes, and celestial mourning
is here and naught shall ease for eons hence.
'Tis but a play of pretense past; presently,
aye, fought again within that mainland.
Again was played that dullest drama: knight
leaves home for buxom blond.
Aye, she was a fair dame, though not so fair
as one should wish.   For knights grow old
and tire of treaties, wish of war again to ride.
Alas, they forget they keep a homeland,
a hamlet safe, that none should harm.
But forth he rode in radiant armor,
forth he rode with shield shining...
encountered not one fearsome foe
for worthy war to wearily wage.
Like knights through ages, bored as such,
without a wound for lance to pierce,
he thus turned home, secure of that.
Alas, the fiefdom has been fought for:
a valiant lad who knelt and stay'd,
known loyal to the castle's cause.
"Come forth! Come forth and fight!" Knight's challenge
issues o'er the fields and farms of wheat.
But seeking to save the lives of lovers,
forth the princess angry came.
"You were he who left dominion;
you were he, left sword behind."

And thus she held aloft, luminous,
that which he'd harbored for years before.
Missed, forlorn, alone at his bedside—left
on that hurried morning months ago.
"It is thine," she says, she spaketh,
"But such is what remains for thee."
"But summer storms"—and so he hails her—
"Places peppered with our pain.   Shared so much,
had we forever, shall we give such ever end?"
She nods.

Anew is armed that far-off tower,
again the blades and battles blaze,
burning o'er the bordering kingdom.
There a tower, grey near gravesites
which litter its eastern edges, rises, ripp'd
stones built pointing towards the starscape.
Hidden betwixt its broken borders,
stirs the knight whose dream hath ceased.
At his side there sleeps a scabbard.
Though his head is bare of helmet,
and his chest is *sans le plastron*,
he is geared for that battle;
he is fitted for the fighting,
though he no longer loves the gore.
Knowledge now will make him master
like he was of men before.
This knight straps on his new-made cuirass,
solemn he lifts misshap'd shield.
The armies cometh, annihilation,
and yet he stands and stares at sky.
"'Tis I.   Know that I am unchangeable—
like the mountains I stand,
and will withstand the might of mortals, for I must.
I shall survive throughout the ages,
and I shall be when you return.
These armies are infants, beneath my might
strengthened by solitude and polish'd by pain.

In these travels, in these travails, I know—
I pray, I shall stay faithful, to thee, *ami*,
and thus to myself."

Il y a quelque chose plus grand que moi ou toi;
C'est nous.   Et j'usque-là, je peux batailler seulement.

REFERENCES

Nymphos and Other Maniacs by Irving Wallace

Lord Byron Discovered by Doris Langley Moore

Lord Byron: Accounts Rendered by Doris Langley Moore

The Technique of the Love Affair by Doris Langley Moore

Byron—The Last Journey by Harold Nicolson

John William Polidori by Franklin Bishop

Newstead Abbey by Philip Jones & Michael Riley

Portraits of Byron by Annette Peach

Byron—Selected Poetry and Letters by Edward E. Bostetter

The Immortal Ninon by Phyllis Tholin

Ninon de L'enclos and Her Century by Mary C. Powsell

An Underground Education by Richard Zacks

Little Brown Book of Anecdotes by Clifton Fadiman

The Worst Case Scenario Handbook (holidays) by Piven & Borgenicht

Pelican History of England, vol. 7, by J.H. Plumb

Christmas in New York by Daniel Pool

Charles Dickens's Fur Coat & Charlotte's Unanswered Letters by Daniel Pool

Familiar Quotations compiled by T.Y. Crowell

The Great Quotations compiled by George Seldes

Quotations compiled by Merriam Webster

Le Chevalier Sans Paix by C.E.K.